THE FIRST GWENEVERE

by

Claire Luana
&
J. Sundin

To the social advocates and
nature enthusiasts . . .

This swoony faerie tale is for you!

Glossary & Definitions

Adder Stone	(At-her stone) a stone from the Welsh *Mabinogion* that allows the beholder to see invisible magic. In Celtic beliefs at large, an adder stone (or magical snake egg) is created by the twining of serpent slime and saliva, especially on May Eve, so named after the European adder, and considered a highly esteemed talisman among Druids. But in reality, an adder stone is a naturally occurring glassy rock with a hole in it.
Afanc	(Ah-vank) a mythological lake/river monster of northwest Wales believed to have caused epic floods and held responsible for many small village deaths (also called an Addanc).
Aghanravel	(AH-gan-ra-vell) a fictional city in in the Glens of Antrim along Lough Neagh, province of Ulster, Northern Ireland. Home to the fictional Clann Allán.
Breton	(breh-tun) People from Brittany (a region in France) or who speak the Celtic language of Brittany (similar to Cornish).
Britannia	(breh-tan-knee-uh) A Roman province that incorporated all areas of the island of Britain south of Caledonia (what is mostly Scotland). This term is still used to this day.
Briton	(Bri-ten) the people who inhabited the island of Britain before the Anglo-Saxon invasion and who spoke Brittonic languages known today as Welsh, Cornish, and Breton. During the mid-

Briton (continued)	medieval period, they inhabited most of the west coastline of Britain, even up into parts of Scotland.
Caerleon	(Car-LEE-un) A city in Southern Wales. Known as the mighty Roman "City of the Legion" and where King Arthur is historically believed to have held court.
Clann / Clan	(Kl-an) A tribe of close-knit and/or interrelated people, spelled "clann" in Ireland and "clan" everywhere else.
Dál nAraidi	(Dahl-en-ah-ride-ee) a Cruithne kingdom, or possibly a confederation of Cruithne clanns in the medieval era, located in Northeastern Ireland around Lough Neagh.
Druid	(Drew-id) a person in ancient Celtic cultures who belonged to one of the highest-ranking professional classes. While some were religious leaders, many were also legal authorities, presided as judges, bards (aka lore keepers and historians), medical professionals, and political advisors. In neo-pagan circles, druids are considered nature magicians as well.
Fiann / Fianna	(FEE-an / FEE-an-uh) In Irish mythology, they were small war bands, typically semi-independent. In history, they were usually young warrior nobles / war bands who didn't own land of their own or hadn't yet come into their inheritance.
Fionnabhair	(FEE-oh-nuh-var) the Irish cognate of the Welsh name Gwenhwyfar or Gwenevere, meaning "white fay" or "white enchantress"
Fomorians (aka Fomhórach / Fomhóraigh)	(Foe-more-ee-ahn) They are known as the "people/tribes (children) of the goddess Domnu," a supernatural race and the enemies of the Túatha dé Danann, the first settlers of Ireland. Though many from both clanns intermarry. The Formorians are typically portrayed as orcish-like giants with water-monster features. Children born of Formorians and Túatha dé are

Fomorians	considered extremely beautiful.
Grail	(Gr-ALE) From the Old French "graal" which means crater, dish. Grail's were common serving dishes. The idea of a "cup" or "chalice" is from the 13th–14th century.
Gwen	(Gwin) Welsh for a young woman who is so profoundly beautiful, you'll die if you gaze upon her for too long. A sacred and holy form of beauty tied to being a sun or moon demi-goddess, or a goddess of light.
Gwenevere	(Gwin-iv-eer) the English spelling of Gwenhwyfar, Welsh name for "white fay" or "white enchantress"
In–Between	The shadow "foggy" world in Celtic mythology that lies between the mortal and Otherworld realms. The place of "mist."
Lough Insholin	(Lock Inch-uh-oh-lin) means "Lake of the O'Lynn Island," for the Ó Fhloinn family, or O'Lynn, who hailed originally from Londonderry, Ulster, and eventually took over most of Antrim.
Lough Neagh	(Lock Nay) A large lake in the province of Ulster, Northern Ireland.
Ogham	(Ome) the ancient 20-letter rune alphabet of Britain and Ireland, used primarily by druids. Also used as divination runes in neo-pagan magic.
Otherworld	(Uh-thur-werld) also known as Tír na nÓg in Irish mythology, it is the realm of the gods and the dead
Pendragon	(Pen-drah-gun) the title given to the King of Briton during and after Roman occupation through the medieval period, primarily held by a king in Wales. Also known as the Head Dragon.

Sídhe	(Shay) The faerie people of Irish mythology (Túatha dé Danann) who lived beneath the hills (gateway to the Otherworld).
The Morrígan	(More-ree-ghon) the Celtic goddess of war and fate, the Great Phantom (Fay) Queen, often interpreted as a triple sister goddess. Also known as the "Crow of Battle" or the "Carrion Crow" and can shapeshift into a crow. Some scholars believe Morgan la Fay / Morgana stemmed from The Morrígan.
Tintagel	(Tin-TAH-jell) City in North Cornwall, where Arthur was conceived.
Túatha dé Danann	(Too-ah day don-an) is translated as "people/tribes (children) of the goddess Danu" and were a supernatural race in Irish mythology who lived in the Otherworld, but who interacted with humans in the mortal realms. They are also known as the first settlers of Ireland. Often called "faeries" and "elves." Though Irish, the mythological figures appear throughout the Celtic/Gaelic world.
Twrch Trwyth	(Tork Troy-th) The Welsh re-telling of the mythological faerie boar of Ireland (Triath) as found in the Welsh romance prose *Culhwch and Olwen*, where King Arthur assists Cullwch in completing one of his impossible tasks by retrieving a magical razor and grooming kit from the bristles of a monstrous faerie boar for Olwen's father, a giant, who must shave his beard before his daughter's wedding.
Uí Tuírtri	(Oo-EE tour-tree) A clann of Northern Ireland, descending from one of the three Collas, primarily ruled by the O'Lynn chiefs.
Ulster	(Ohl-stir) Province in Northern Ireland

MORAY
ALBA
Caer Benic
Castellum Puellarum
CASTLE OF MAIDENS
STRATHCLYDE
Lough Isholin
ULSTER
Aghanravel
IRELAND
Dublin
ISLE OF MAN
Irish Sea
NORTHUMBRIA
GWYNEDD
Brunanburh
Betws-y-Coed
Chester
Maesbury Marsh
MERCIA
Talgarth
SEISYLLWG
EAST ANGLIA
Swansea
Caerleon
ARTHUR'S KEEP
Severn Sea
ESSEX
Tintagel
WESSEX
CORNWALL
King Arthur's
Britain
1 BUEITT
2 BRYCHEINIOG
3 GWENT
4 MORGANNWG
5 DYFED
6 ANTRIM
7 LONDONBERRY
8 LOUGH NEAGH

"Like many cruel and evil women,
Morgan le Fay knew men's weaknesses
and discounted their strengths. And she
knew also that most improbable actions
may be successful so long as they are
undertaken boldly and without hesitation,
for men believe beyond proof to the
contrary that blood is thicker than water
and that a beautiful woman cannot be evil."

John Steinbeck
The Acts of King Arthur and His Noble Knights

Prologue

Morgana

Ships lined the harbor in Dublin as far as the crow's dark, beady eye could see. The salty air brimmed with the scents of impending war. The crow cawed in delight and swooped low, skimming along the shimmering Irish Sea. Then a certain scent hit her—one she craved and knew anywhere. Weakness. Greed. *Him.* The man with a heart as shadowed as her own. Stupid mortal.

In a swirl of sea mist, the crow dipped to land on a makeshift dock and transformed into her female form. A fae queen.

Morgana's lips curled into a wicked smile at O'Lynn's widened eyes as he took in her sudden appearance. "Expecting someone else?" she asked casually while stepping toward the Irish king.

"I never look at crows the same now." He blew out a slow breath and then shuffled his feet to a sturdier posture. "Especially carrion crows."

Her smile grew wider for several quick beats of

the mortal's heart before she switched her focus to the ships and warriors. Men and women moved past them on the dock, oak chests and barrels filled with weapons and food in tow. Farther down the harbor, warriors wrapped strips of dark wool around their horses' eyes and led them onto longboats with stabling posts to tie them up. Others forked hay and grains onto the boats to help ease the spooked chargers.

"You have done well, mortal," she cooed, returning her gaze to O'Lynn. "I am pleased with you. Arthur Pendragon is ours for the plucking. Even though the Fisher whelp found the Blessed Grail, King Arthur's land still withers. Even now his people grow sick and their bellies roar with hunger."

O'Lynn's body softened at her words and his eyes drank her in––her cleavage rising and falling atop her bodice, her slim waist, the way her hair draped about her shoulders in a waterfall of raven-feathered black strands.

"Our plan is to depart tomorrow," he said. "Our druids predict fair weather to Wales."

"I plan to travel with you. Release the caged crows."

"No, they're necessary should we need to find the closest land point." O'Lynn crossed his arms over his chest. The gold torc around his neck glinted in the afternoon sun. A hint of a sneer curved the corner of his mouth up. "The crows will stay with their masters if released, anyway."

Morgana cocked her head and slitted her eyes. "The crows only stay with their tormentors to feast on their flesh once they die."

O'Lynn's Adam's apple bobbed as the flirtation and challenge in his eyes faded to trepidation.

"I will fly about to each ship to inform the captains, if necessary. Now, release the caged crows. I shall not ask again."

Heaving a resigned breath to cover his fear—a fear that filled Morgana's nostrils with a heady scent that lightened her head with pleasure—O'Lynn grabbed the arm of a warrior passing by. "Tell each captain who sails to release their navigation crows."

"Yer Majesty?" the young man asked, uncertain.

Morgana slid up to the younger man and leaned in close, trailing her sharp fingernail down his cheek. His brown eyes blinked a few times in surprise, though he remained still. "You are a beautiful specimen," she purred. Her nail trailed down his neck to his chest. "Now, be a good lad and do as you're told."

"Yes, Lady," the young man said softly.

Morgana smiled sweetly at him, biting down on her lower lip, a canine bared.

"Anything ye ask of me," he added in an affected whisper before darting away.

O'Lynn glowered at Morgana. Good. He needed a reminder that she was in charge, not him. In a dismissive motion, she turned her back on the older man. She could feel his heated stare before he walked away to finish preparing for their departure at dawn.

Morgana remained on the dock, whispering incantations over the boats for a swift travel, until the sun began to set and a crescent moon began to rise. Only breaking her focus to greet her sister and brother crows who launched into the starry night. Their black wings cut through the air with a song of vengeance. A melody she hummed to the wind.

Sea mist and the whispered prayers of greedy men preparing for war swirled around her. The crow hopped on the dock and peered at the humans who gawked at the sky, mouths agape, fear icing the blood in their veins. The crow then flapped her wings with a loud caw and joined the dark celebration swooping before the goddess moon.

There was nothing that alighted her soul more than impending war and death.

Chapter One

Fionnabhair

I was back in Caerleon. I was home.

The thought struck me like a lightning bolt as we rode through the gates of Arthur's proud keep. I tested the feeling, trying the idea on for size. Yes, this place was the harmony to the joyous song in my heart. Caerleon, and King Arthur Pendragon, and my knights. Strong Galahad, laughing Percival, and infuriating Lancelot. Though Lancelot was as moody as an Irish winter, I missed him like the summer sun. I felt his absence keenly.

Our return to Caerleon should have been a triumphant thing—proclaimed from the hillsides with horns and witnessed by a parade of grateful citizens who tossed flower petals before our horses' hooves. We had done the impossible and found the Blessed Grail. The feat was no small miracle—and yet—I didn't think the enormity of what we had accomplished had truly sank in among our small group. For all we could think of was the dark, grasping curse still seeping through Caerleon's clear waters and flaxen fields.

And the army sailing for our shores.

Arthur had depended on the Grail to breathe new life into his dying lands. A black, creeping death courtesy of his sídhe half-sisters—Morgana, Morgause, and Elaine. The Blessed faerie bowl had almost absolved the dark curse.

Almost, if not for me.

Merlin foresaw how the Grail would heal the land when our group of five each drank from the enchanted bowl. The mystical Grail Maiden confirmed Merlin's theory, the same sovereignty-goddess who had aided us on our quest. She also helped us travel to Avalon, located at the foot of Glastonbury Tor, where we drank from the sacred spring.

Lancelot, Percival, Galahad, and Arthur each drank from Avalon's Red Spring and the land flushed incrementally back to life after each bowlful. But when I drank—the last of us to do so—nothing happened. Not even the wisp of a warm spring breeze or the melodic twitter of birdsong.

I promised myself weeks prior that I would never let Arthur down again. But despite all attempts to prove my worthiness, I had failed him. And, in this misdeed, I felt worse. For I didn't understand why the Grail rejected me. Now, because of my apparent brokenness, innocents would continue to suffer under this wretched curse.

I drew in a deep breath and squared my shoulders against the rocking gait of my horse.

The mood through Caerleon proper was tangibly strained as we approached Arthur's keep. The wary faces of his nobles and common folk alike watched on silently as we dismounted, the jagged look in their eyes a none too subtle reproach for failing to amend the foul magic crippling the kingdom's outlying villages. We had born witness to the curse's dark veins spreading all the way to Caerleon. If something wasn't done, and quickly, people would begin to perish with the poisoned land.

"To my study," Arthur barked, and we hurried after him, leaving our horses with the grooms.

I was eager to visit Zephyr, my beloved mare I had been forced to leave behind while she healed from an injury. But she would have to wait. I knew what Arthur was going to ask me—what we would talk about—and I didn't want to face the truth. My mind spun horrors with every turn of thought. And each possible scenario weakened my resolve to remain mentally and emotionally present.

Why hadn't the Blessed Grail worked on me? What was this strange power thrumming through my body that others seemed to sense but me?

But more so—Arthur would ask about Donal O'Lynn. And this thought was one I couldn't face, not without the red haze of fury covering my vision, setting my fingers itching for a knife.

Donal O'Lynn, Chieftain of the Uí Tuírtri clann, the sworn enemy of my own clann. The man who held my father and sister for ransom and who now sailed for Caerleon with a fleet of ships laden with Dál nAraidi warriors to claim Arthur's crown. With a dark fae priestess on one side. And a new wife on the other. I choked on the latter thought, unable to shove that hellish reality away far enough. At least, far enough away for me to properly focus.

We reached Arthur's study and filed into his room, but no one sat. We were too uneasy, too unsettled. Too lost in our own troubles. I hardly registered Galahad's hulking presence, or Percival's lean, pacing form behind me. Or Merlin's gold-ringed eyes that watched us all with the intensity of a hawk tracking a bevy of field mice.

Arthur rounded on me and I met his fierceness with my own. I knew the anger in his grass-green eyes was not directed at me. But his anger called to me, to the fury pounding through my veins. "O'Lynn," Arthur practically growled, his voice low and deep. "Tell me of him. How many men? Allies? With his new union, could he claim the support of Clann Allán as well?"

His new union. I wanted to retch. *Aideen.* My soul keened my sister's name. I saw her waves of chestnut hair, her kind eyes, her sweet laugh. I knew there was a strength hiding beneath her gentleness, but I feared her courage wouldn't be enough against a man like O'Lynn. How he had managed to claim her as wife haunted me too. Irish women were free to choose their own husband. They could not be forced to marry. So, what could have made Aideen take such a drastic step and agree to marry him? My imagination filled in a parade of nightmares, most of which featured my father. Aideen was tender hearted and loved our father more than any. If O'Lynn demanded Aideen's hand as the price of sparing our father . . . I had no doubt that her consent was a price she would pay without hesitation.

"He will never claim the loyalty of Clann Allán," I said, sure of *that* at least. "There are several strong warriors who would declare leadership over my clann if . . ." I stumbled over the words. "If my father was lost. None of them would side with a snake like O'Lynn. Our clanns have fought and slaughtered each other for generations."

"That's a relief. How many warriors does he have?"

"A thousand, perhaps? But all strong and fierce. Seasoned fighters. They will not be easy to defeat." My hand strayed to my sword, aching to bury the sharp blade into a Uí Tuírtri body.

"How long before they reach Caerleon?" Arthur looked to Merlin, who had relayed the message of the massing ships in Dublin.

"It is unknown," Merlin said calmly.

I wished I could face word of an approaching army with such serenity. It wasn't that I feared O'Lynn and his men. To the contrary, I welcomed a fight with them. But I feared for Caerleon––this soft, gentle land would break under the weight of a war like this. And I feared for my knights and my king. For what I had found in Wales, with them . . . the very thought of losing any part of my life here terrified me.

The druid continued. "It is a three-day passage by boat from Dublin to the Usk River here in Caerleon. Or three days overland to Caerleon on horseback, if they traveled one to two days by boat to Conwy, up north. If they left today, we might have four or five days, a week at best. But I think it is safe to believe they are already en route."

"The messenger who observed the ships in Dublin didn't know when they were leaving?" Arthur asked.

"He couldn't tell. Though he did not think they were leaving for several days. The ships were not manned yet, and provisions were still being secured."

"We must assume arrival is as you say, then—a few days at best." Arthur shook his head in disbelief, gritting his teeth. "There is no way we can withstand a siege with poisoned water and food."

"Ah yes," Merlin said. "The curse. Tell me of what happened at Glastonbury Tor."

"There's something wrong with me," I blurted out.

"Lass, that's not—" Percival began, but I held up a hand, and he fell silent.

"There's no need to protect my feelings. Not at the expense of Caerleon," I said. "We were all there. We all saw. The curse lifted when each of ye drank. Except me."

"Do you know why, Merlin?" Arthur asked. "What went wrong?"

The druid examined me, and I squirmed under the weight of his piercing gaze, as if the man could see right through me. Right into the darkest recesses. Well, he wasn't a man, was he? Only half a man. Half an immortal incubus.

"Alas, I have no answers for you," Merlin said. "But I will cast my runes and see what I can learn. Perhaps there is something that can be done."

"Before the army reaches our gate would be preferable," Arthur muttered.

"And what of Lancelot?" Galahad rumbled. "Apologies, Arthur, but who is to lead your forces while Lancelot is absent?"

Arthur winced at the mention of Lancelot's name. I think we all did.

Lancelot had grown more and more withdrawn from us as our Grail quest continued. And, in the last days leading up to quest's end, we learned why. Morgana had placed a special curse on him alone—a curse that would destroy all Lancelot held dear, but only if he slept with a Gwenevere. A legendary white enchantress that he proclaimed was me.

I let out a hissing sigh as I thought of him. Why had the fool knight carried his burden all on his own? If he had only told me, I would have known why he pulled back from me, why it was important that he did. If by some strange twist of fate I was indeed this Gwenevere, which I believed untrue, I would have resisted the growing connection between us. It's not as though we were animals. We could have resisted our attraction. Though, if I were honest, I hadn't done a very good job at resisting my animal impulses as of late. One glance at the impossibly handsome forms of my king and the two knights surrounding me was all the confirmation I needed, and I cursed the shiver of desire pulsing hot through my body.

Arthur slipped a quiet look my way before finally cutting through the tension and speaking. "Lancelot made his choice. As much as it grieves me, his choice is one we all must accept. With all the trouble bearing upon my kingdom, I do not have time to chase down stray knights. Even if they are ones who are like brothers to me." Arthur loosed a quavering breath, running a hand through his hair. "Galahad." He turned to the brawny Norseman. "Until Lancelot returns, and perhaps even after, I deem you my second-in-command and charge you with the forces of Caerleon. I hope you don't mind the promotion, because things are about to get messy around here."

Chapter Two

Galahad

alahad strode toward the barracks, excitement galloping through his racing heart. Arthur's words rang in his mind like the resounding peal of a bell. *I deem you my second-in-command.*

Was it opportunistic to step into Lancelot's shoes in his absence? His sword-brother had been gone less than a day, and Galahad had already seized his role. But no. Arthur had chosen him—it wasn't as if Galahad vied for the position. And Caerleon needed someone to defend her lands and people after Lancelot abandoned his post. Galahad worked his entire life for a chance like this. He wasn't going to let this opportunity pass him by.

The soldiers in the barracks snapped to attention when Galahad entered.

"Sir," one soldier said, stepping forward. The man was short but well-muscled, a dark brown beard covering his round face.

Galahad wracked his memories for the man's name. "Clive," he said.

The man gave a little nod and Galahad relaxed slightly. It had been a while since he had trained with the soldiers. But now he would need to know them each, especially as he would spend more time among their ranks.

"What can we do for you, Sir?" Clive asked, re-directing Galahad's thoughts. "I was not aware the king's knights had returned."

"Just a few hours ago," Galahad replied.

Other soldiers gathered around, and Galahad swept a calculating eye over each man. They were a well-fed lot, their red linen uniforms clean, their weapons well cared for. Arthur was a kind employer. But still, did these men have the raw power and bloodthirst that Galahad had witnessed among the Uí Tuírtri he had fought near Lord Bronn's manor? Even if so, that detail mattered not. These men were what they had. And they would have to be enough.

Galahad cleared his throat and dozens of eyes snapped to his. "We've received word that a fleet of Irish ships bearing Dál nAraidi warriors is bound for our shores, if they have not already landed."

Murmurs of dismay rippled through the group.

"We must warn the neighboring villages to take shelter within the keep," Galahad continued. "There's no telling what horrors might be visited upon them, if they stay where they are."

"Of course, Sir," Clive replied, dipping his head. "Consider it done."

"Sir," one of the other men, a red-head with a puckered scar traversing his jaw, began hesitantly. "Has Sir Lancelot not returned with you?"

"No," Galahad said simply. "He had other business to attend to. The Pendragon has appointed me as his second-in-command in Lancelot's absence."

Another man stepped forward. They seemed to be growing bolder. "Is the king aware of the strange blackness befouling Caerleon's waters?"

The other men nodded, eyes wide.

"My brother said his entire crop rotted," the red-headed soldier chimed in. "Whatever it is, the black is spreading."

"Rest assured," Galahad said, "the king is aware and doing everything he can to cure this strange sickness. He is consulting with the druid Merlin as we speak. In these difficult times, we must band together and hold fast."

A mutter of affirmations warmed Galahad's core.

"The people should be assured as well," Clive said. "Fear is creeping through the villages. A fear just as vile as the sickness that's infecting our land. The people speak against His Majesty, saying the land has rebelled against him, that his kingship is illegitimate."

Galahad's heart stilled. "You have heard these sentiments spoken?"

"By more than one," Clive said, an apologetic frown pulling on his face.

A sour lurch tightened Galahad's stomach. Likely, the news of an encroaching army would only lower Arthur's popularity farther.

Galahad chewed on his bottom lip, his gaze darting from one man to another. "I will ride with you. Perhaps the presence of a knight carrying the Pendragon's banner will assure the people that their sovereign is doing everything within his power to save them."

It was another hour before Galahad and the soldiers saddled their horses, rode through the keep's gates, and reached the first outlying village. The land, though not as fouled as it had been, still showed signs of Morgana's curse. The row of fruit trees along the village's dirt path were speckled with black spots. The cheerful stream bordering the tiny village showed flecks of darkness as well.

"It's not safe to drink," Clive said. He rode beside Galahad. "The water doesn't kill you, but you'll ail. The villagers have stuck to ciders and ale, but their stores are growing low."

Galahad's spirits sank deeper. After all they had endured to find the Grail—fighting the Twrch Trwyth and the Afanc, facing off against the evil faeries in Eiden's Burgh, journeying through the Otherworld's mist . . . it still had not been enough. What if they couldn't find the final piece of the puzzle before Caerleon starved? The people probably wouldn't wait that long before demanding Arthur's head. And the heads of all his knights.

As Galahad and a half-dozen soldiers rode into a quaint village square, the lime-washed facades bright in the afternoon sun, he did his best to focus on solutions. Arthur and Merlin would find a way to pull this problem out of the fire. They always did.

Galahad swung off his charger and strode toward the largest building in the square, what appeared to be the town's tavern and inn. Taking the steps, he called out in a booming voice, "Gather around, kind people. I have an announcement from your king, Arthur Pendragon!"

Townsfolk sat their burdens before their feet as others came out of the houses—men with wary expressions who should be tending the fields, and women leading grubby-faced toddlers.

"A force of men from Ulster make their way here even now," Galahad called out once more. "Their sights are set on Caerleon, but they will burn, pillage, and raid on their way. We urge every man, woman, and child to come within the keep's walls, where you will be safe until the threat has passed." Another thought occurred to him, and he added, "Bring whatever assures your comfort. Food, ale. If you have herbs or medical supplies, bring them as well. We will set up a makeshift hospital in the keep's Great Hall. Able-bodied women who can help are welcome. Able-bodied men who can fight are welcome as well. Rest assured, your king has the forces and might to defeat these invaders. We only wish to keep you safe until he does."

"And what of the plague on our land, Sir Knight?" someone shouted from the back of the crowd. "Our crops wither. We can't drink the water."

"The king is aware of this blight and has traveled through the Otherworld to fix it. Surely you saw how, just yesterday, the condition of the land greatly improved?"

"Sir, we still can't eat or drink from the land. We'll starve!" someone else shouted.

"It's a sign of the gods' disfavor," someone else yelled. "Arthur isn't the rightful king over Caerleon!"

"Aye!" Another voice. "Uther's bastard shouldn't be our king any longer. He'll drive us all to ruin. The land herself rebels against him. Why shouldn't we?"

Galahad pulled his sword from its scabbard with an ominous ring. When he spoke, his voice boomed. "King Arthur Pendragon is the noblest, mightiest, most honorable man that I have ever known, and who has ever presided over Caerleon. The Lady of the Lake, blessed of the Túatha dé Danann, gifted him the sword Excalibur, confirming his kingship over Caerleon, the Kingdom of Gwent, and over all of Briton. Yes, King Arthur has heavy burdens on his shoulders. Would you wish to be in his shoes? Would you?" Galahad asked, pointing his sword at the men who had spoken. "To defend your people from an army? And defeat a strange magical wasting sickness? No. None of you would have the fortitude it takes to face these grave challenges and defeat them. No other man would either. There is no king for Caerleon but Arthur. And anyone who says otherwise should not hide behind a crowd but should face me man to man. "

The crowd hushed into a tense silence for several beats of Galahad's heart. Then, the ruffle of uncomfortably shifting feet and bodies filled the deafening emptiness at the force of his rebuke.

"Very well," Galahad said. "Then I suggest that you gather your things. And prepare for war."

Chapter Three

Arthur

rthur enjoyed the snug warmth of Merlin's cave. This place of mystery and magic brought him a strange comfort. And today, he prayed this crystal-lined cave would bring him answers.

Merlin approached the wide fireplace, stoking the embers with a poker before adding another log. "Ale?" his friend asked.

"Absolutely." At Arthur's reply, the druid disappeared into the chill recesses of his cave where he stored his food and drink. His friend might be able to light a fire with his thought or travel the currents of time and space with a spell, but he wasn't a show off. Despite having every right to be. That was one of the many virtues Arthur appreciated about Merlin.

The man returned with two horns of ale clasped between his body and forearm while balancing a tray of bread and cheese in his other hand. "You look hungry," Merlin said as Arthur carefully retrieved the ale from its precarious perch. Arthur took a long drink and sighed in delight at the malty flavor. "Gods that's good."

Merlin set the food on a table between them and sat down in the other chair before the fire.

"I am hungry," Arthur admitted. "There wasn't much to eat on the quest, no thanks to the curse. Nor here, it seems."

"Your stores are well equipped enough for a few more weeks," Merlin said. "But before we speak of this . . . do you have the faerie relic?" Firelight flickered in Merlin's eyes, highlighting the gold rings around his irises.

There was no doubt as to what Merlin spoke. Arthur reached into the satchel he had brought and pulled out the Blessed Grail.

Merlin took the bowl reverently with two hands, turning the dish over, gently stroking the embossed, polished surface. "Magnificent," Merlin murmured with awe.

"It's defective," Arthur replied darkly.

Merlin's eyes jerked up, as if Arthur had spoken sacrilege.

"I mean, yes, the Grail is impressive. But this . . . *this* faerie relic didn't break the curse," he practically spat. "And I did everything I was instructed to do. I found the Blessed Grail, battled monsters and shape-changing faeries, and even got *stabbed* by Lleu's spear. . . but it was all for nothing."

"Lleu's spear?" Merlin dropped the Grail to his lap and gaped at Arthur. "Why don't you start at the beginning. Leave nothing out."

So, Arthur told him. He recounted every detail

of their quest, going through two more horns of ale and all the bread and cheese Merlin had brought him. And when he was finally finished, Merlin merely let out a long, "Hmmm . . ."

"What do you think?" Arthur asked. He felt a bit light headed from the fire's heat and the ale's strength.

"Fionna is the key. She has always been the key."

"The key to *what*?" Arthur asked.

"Everything," Merlin replied, now pacing before the fire, his long woolen robes billowing with his movements.

Just everything? Illuminating, Merlin.

"You were magically tied to the land through Excalibur when the Lady of the Lake granted you a sovereign-blessed kingship, Your Majesty. But how you described the land healing incrementally when each of you drank from the Grail . . ." Merlin turned to Arthur, his face alit with excitement. "I think when you knighted each of your knights, laying Excalibur upon them, you tied them to your kingship. Your sovereignty over the land."

"Right," Arthur muttered, furrowing his brow. "That's what knighting is, friend."

"No. Not just by feudal law or duty. *Magically*."

"I'm not sure I follow," Arthur admitted.

"Imagine . . . when you laid Excalibur on their shoulders, a piece of your sovereignty transferred to each of their care. That's why the standing stone spoke of the blessed five. And that's why, though Morgana and her sisters cursed Caerleon and you as the land's king, it took all five of you to drink from the Grail to heal the land. Each knight holds a piece of your kingship. And by extension, each one of you holds a piece of the curse."

Arthur nodded, wishing he had drank one less cup of ale, so his head wasn't quite so foggy. "I believe I understand. So, the Grail healed the portion of the curse held by me, Galahad, Lancelot, and Percival. But not Fionna? Why couldn't the Grail heal her portion of the curse?"

"I have no idea," Merlin said simply.

Arthur threw up his hands up in exasperation.

"I have theories," Merlin continued. "But . . . Caerleon needs better than theories. There is something strange about Fionna. I sensed the Otherworld from the moment I saw her in the arena. She assuredly holds a dormant power."

"Lancelot believes she is a Gwenevere."

"How does Fionna respond to his claim?"

"She says it's madness," Arthur replied. Was Lancelot's belief madness? There was something Otherworldly about Fionna's beauty, as well as her strength and prowess in battle. But Fionna insisted, often, that she didn't possess a magical ability.

"You believe her?"

"I do." And though she had lied to him before about Excalibur, he found he did believe her. Over the past few weeks, she had regained his trust. And had captured his heart well and truly.

"The land has not known a Gwenevere for many generations." Merlin crossed the cave to his desk, where he retrieved a leather bag that held a set of old divination rune stones. "But we live in trying times," his friend offered quietly. "Perhaps it is time for such an enchantress to arise. Give me a moment."

Merlin strode to the empty space before the fire and knelt, closing his eyes.

Arthur watched the druid as he centered himself and called to whatever forces would aid him. The fine hairs on Arthur's arms stood on end, as they sometimes did in the presence of magic. A disconcerting feeling, to know there was something on the air but not able to trust one's senses. Still, if Merlin's magic could discover an answer, Arthur would tolerate just about any strangeness.

Merlin threw the stones and then they both leaned forward to inspect the runes laying face up.

"Interesting," Merlin said, placing a single finger on a rune. One that lay atop all other front-facing stones. "This is *Ur*, or heather."

"What about it?"

"The reading is hazy, but one piece comes through clearly. Heather is used as protection against the evil eye."

Arthur frowned. "The evil eye . . ."

"Yes, indeed. Heather brings only good luck, even symbolizing unselfish love in some Gaelic circles. For heather is immensely infused with faerie magic. Surely you have had heather beer?"

"Well, yes, but—"

"Then you understand the effects of heather. This herb is connected to the Otherworld." Merlin leaned back and met Arthur's eyes.

"Fionna smells of heather, soft and sweet," Arthur said, hoping the flush creeping up his neck didn't reach his face.

Merlin smiled. "You will find the answers you seek in the Otherworld. In the halls of the Túatha dé Danann."

Arthur groaned, his hand straying to his side, where his lifeblood flowed out just days before. "We have only now returned from the Otherworld, and we didn't find the realm of mist particularly friendly."

"The Castle of Maidens was a trap for you within the *In-Between*, not the Otherworld's courts. But, this time, you will know to be on guard. I can better prepare you."

"What makes you think the Túatha dé Danann will even be friendly toward us? Or give us the answers we seek? They've had no qualms about letting Morgana, Elaine, and Morgause wreak all sorts of havoc upon my kingdom. Perhaps they support these wretched curses."

Merlin shook his head. "Vivien gifted you Excalibur and your kingship. She speaks for them more than the ladies of Tintagel do. I am confident these curses were not sanctioned by the Túatha dé Danann leadership or the goddess Danu."

"I don't have time for another quest, Merlin," Arthur insisted. "A fleet of ships is headed our way. This army could reach my keep at any moment. A king cannot abandon his people on the eve of war. Not if he wishes to remain king. The people are already grumbling. Hungry and scared. If I leave now, O'Lynn won't need to take my kingdom from me. My own people will."

Merlin's lined face pinched in thought. "Perhaps there is a second reason to visit the Otherworld then.

The Túatha dé Danann are keepers of another magical relic. The Cauldron of Plenty."

"You wish for us to retrieve a . . . *cauldron*?" Arthur asked.

"Yes, for this *cauldron* is one of the four objects of power in Ireland, where the Túatha dé Danann dwell. And, this *cauldron* is rumored to have healing powers, like the Grail. Even the ability to raise a man from the dead. But importantly—with this magical relic, you can create whatever food and drink you need. Enough to feed all within the walls of Caerleon until the curse is dealt with. Enough to withstand a siege easily."

Arthur considered Merlin's explanation. The Cauldron of Plenty did sound helpful. Though curse its faerie-made iron. The Grail was also supposed to be his kingdom's salvation, and *that* magical relic had proven a disappointment. Could he really go off on a wild goose chase after another mythical object? He had real problems to face here.

Merlin seemed to sense Arthur's thoughts. "What if I found a way for you to travel to the Otherworld quickly. A portal, such as the one the Grail Maiden created for you?"

"You have such magic?" Arthur asked, his eyebrows raising. He hadn't known Merlin to conjure such things before. If his druid could indeed create a portal . . . then perhaps there was time to make a fast trip.

"I have never done such a thing, but now that I know a portal can be made . . . it is only a matter of study. I am certain I could cobble the spell together."

Excitement lit Merlin's face, and a ghost of a smile tugged at Arthur's lips. Merlin was man of magic, but he was a scholar too, much like Arthur. A chance to solve a puzzle like this? Merlin had to be dancing with anticipation, despite his calm composure.

Arthur stood, ignoring how his head spun briefly. He needed a good night's sleep. "Then I will leave you to it. If you find me a way into the Otherworld from Caerleon, I will undertake the journey. Seems my questing days are not yet behind me."

Chapter Four

Fionna

My racing mind wouldn't settle that night. Everything felt wrong. Caerleon still cursed. Lancelot gone. My sister married to O'Lynn. My father . . . he must still be alive. There was no way Aideen would have married O'Lynn, if the bastard wasn't holding my father's life as the alternative. I felt as if the solution to all these hardships should lie with me. Like a brilliant shining moment of insight would occur and loop the disparate threads of my life together in a perfect, victorious tapestry. But Aideen had always had the skill with weaving. All I was good for was killing.

Helplessness squeezed at the air in my lungs. The sensation was like battling in an ill-fitting set of armor. I paced my room for half a candle mark before I decided that I held onto a small remnant of control: I was still keeping secrets. And, at this point, I wasn't sure why. It was time I bared the whole truth to the one person who might know what these burdens meant. I needed to see Merlin.

I made my way down the familiar earth and rock path and into the warm spring night. The once-soothing sound of the river now only served as a reminder of my failure. Black poison churned through those crystal waters, destroying whatever it touched.

I was so lost in my thoughts that I didn't notice another shadowed form coming my way until the figure was almost upon me. When I saw the hooded man, my heart took flight like a startled bird, my hand flying to the knife at my belt.

"Peace Fionna, it's only I, Arthur," he said in the dark.

I sagged with relief.

"Most days you're not so easy to sneak up on," he remarked with a chuckle.

"Most days my mind isn't twisted into *Dara* knots," I admitted.

"I'm distracted as well," he replied softly. "How could we not be, with all that has happened?"

I nodded, peering out into the darkened forest across the river. "I can't stop thinking about Aideen. Tied to that man. His hands on her . . ." I closed my eyes against the horror roiling in my stomach. My beautiful, vibrant sister shouldn't be forced to subject herself to such violations.

"What has happened to your family grieves me deeply. I can't help but wonder if I could have done more."

"And me," I said.

Arthur sighed. "But then I cannot see what I could have done. Even with the benefit of hindsight, the needs of Caerleon came first."

"Ye are the land's king. But I shouldn't have joined the quest," I said. "I should have returned to Ulster and rescued my father and sister."

"No—"

"All I did was drive Lancelot away and fail to break the curse—any curse."

"No, My Lady. You couldn't have freed them single-handedly. And if you hadn't been on the quest, we wouldn't have defeated the Twrch Trwyth or the Afanc. We wouldn't have obtained the key or the stone or the Blessed Grail."

"But—" I began to protest and stopped. Arthur stepped close to me and then stroked the side of my face, enveloping me with his summer scent of green grass and apples. Of home.

The words I had previously spoken had fallen like fallow seeds from my lips. How could I be anywhere but here? Never mind that the price for keeping my head was to join the Grail quest. This is where I had wanted to be. Where I still wanted to be. Arthur was the Caerleon that should be—strong and just and healthy. I cursed the world that punished me for following my heart with Aideen's slavery.

My hand strayed to Arthur's side, where the wound had been. "Ye fare well? No lingering effects from yer injury?"

"I am as healthy as I've ever been."

"Good." My voice tightened. "We couldn't do this without ye. I couldn't—"

Arthur cut off my words with a kiss then, wrapping one arm around my waist, the other around my shoulders. His lips danced across mine—his body an anchor, grounding me to the earth. He was warmth and comfort, and I drank greedily, savoring the taste of him, the feel of being folded within his arms.

It was he who pulled away, but to lay feather-light kisses on the tip of my nose and forehead before pressing me close to him once more.

I leaned my head against the hard planes of his chest with a sigh.

"You go to see Merlin?" he asked, his deep voice rumbling pleasantly against me.

"Aye. I thought . . . I need to talk to him about my past. Perhaps we can discover something."

"He thinks I need to return to the Otherworld."

I pulled back, gaping at him in the dark. "Now? With an army sailing for Caerleon?"

"Yes, that's what he advised. I don't know. I must think on it. Now, you should not tarry any longer. Perhaps Merlin can discover all your secrets this night." He touched his lips softly to mine.

"Can't wait," I said dryly as I pushed away, letting his fingers trail mine as I continued down the hill toward the Usk River and Merlin's cave.

My gaze remained on the windy footpath, but I could feel the caress of Arthur's eyes upon my back. I sighed, reveling in the sensations fluttering through me, even as I approached the cave's entrance. One kiss from Arthur was enough to turn my legs weak with need. From any of my knights, really. But for now, I *needed* to focus.

"Merlin?" I picked my way carefully over the rocky ground and moved deeper into his cave. "It's

Fionna."

The druid appeared suddenly in front of me and I halted my steps with a sharp inhale.

"There ye are," I said, shoving down my annoyance. I swear, sometimes he popped out like that just to seem more mysterious!

"To what do I owe this rare honor?" Merlin asked, ushering me into the main cavern with a welcoming hand.

"I need to tell ye something," I admitted.

"Very well," Merlin said, crossing to sit in one of the chairs in front of the fire. I took the other.

"The night of the faerie wine," I began, words tumbling forth before my nerves got the better of me, "I drank the wine. But it didn't affect me. Not like it did the others."

Merlin studied at me, blinking, his eyes glowing with magic. "Interesting," he finally said.

"I thought perhaps this necklace affected how I felt the wine," I said, picking up the delicate lily pendant that hung from my neck. "A gift from Morgana and her sisters, from the night of the feast."

Merlin leaned forward and picked the pendant up off my breastbone, leaning in to examine the details. This close, he smelled of spices—clove and dried sage and . . . ale? An unexpected scent that was strangely comforting.

He dropped the necklace and leaned back. "There is an enchantment of sorts on the necklace. But I do not think the magic is harmful. It's . . ." he furrowed his brow. "As if the magic is outward facing, rather than affecting the wearer. I will research the origins of such a necklace. But I do not think this piece of enchanted jewelry is what protected you from the faerie wine's effects."

"All right, sure," I said. "Do ye know what did, then?"

Merlin tilted his head and considered me a moment. "I think you have fae heritage somewhere in your family tree," he said. "But the power is blocked somehow. Suppressed."

"So, I'm . . . defective?" I whispered, examining my fingernails instead of acknowledging the piteous look in Merlin's hawk-eyed gaze. I had always been different than my father and Aideen, but I had found my place within my family, the clann. Made my way as a warrior. It was all I had needed. But now, that reality seemed lacking.

"No," Merlin said kindly. "Your magic was suppressed on purpose."

I looked up sharply. "What do ye mean?"

"I sense there is an enchantment over you. Of a kind I cannot see or recognize. And that makes me think the magic is fae born."

"There is a faerie enchantment on me?" I jumped to my feet, my heart in my throat. "Well, get it off!"

"It's not that simple. The one who put the géis on you is also the one who will need to remove it. And do not be so alarmed. If the enchantment protected you from the wine, then perhaps this magic is benevolent." He paused a beat, the gold ring around his eyes flashing. "A ward against the evil eye."

"Benevolent, evil eye, or no, I want this géis removed. This magic has something to do with why I couldn't use the Grail, doesn't it?"

"We must assume so," Merlin said.

"So how in the hell do I find out who put a faerie charm on me?"

"I think this enchantment has been with you for many years. Perhaps since you were a babe. Your best chance of unraveling this mystery is to speak to the only other human who might have been there."

My mind spun, and I fell back into the chair, lightheaded. "Ye mean my father."

"I believe you are not the only Allán with secrets."

"But my father is in enemy hands," I protested. It was ironic. I spent years living under the same roof as my father, and never thought to ask him why I looked so different from Aideen. In truth, I had never wanted to know the answer. And now, when I was desperate for the truth, he was out of my reach.

"I suppose it is luck that the enemy is bringing him to us, then," Merlin countered, bending to pick an *Ur* rune up off the rug before the hearth—a rune mark for heather.

"Yes," I said slowly, a kernel of an idea blooming to life inside me. "Yes, luck indeed."

Chapter Five

Lancelot

Lancelot led Cheval onto the ferry, his stomach bobbing with the longboat. He was a man of one-and-twenty the last time he had set foot on the Isle of Man. Following that visit, he had sworn never to return. Now here he was, four years later, coming back with his tail tucked between his legs. A man of twenty-five years, crying to his foster mother for help.

The ferryman, a gruff little man—with a face covered in sharp, gray stubble, and a short reed sticking out from between yellowed teeth—secured the rope behind him. The ferry was an old, less-than-sturdy-looking clinker with red ochre paint, now chipped and faded from years of exposure. Luckily, the passage was short, and the craft was faerie enchanted to keep the boat from swamping—the only way Lancelot would even think to climb aboard this rotting pile of heap.

The night was dark and strangely cloying. A sickening sweet scent he normally associated with magic. Low clouds crowded out the sliver of moon while grasping fog swirled around the boat. It was always misty on the approach to Man. He wondered if the weather phenomena was just some strange quirk of geography, or if it was a spell cast by his foster mother to disquiet anyone who approached. Probably the latter. There was no such thing as coincidence when it came to the fae.

Lancelot stood by Cheval's head, idly stroking his velvety neck, savoring the connection to something real. The mist seemed alive. And Lancelot swore he could see shapes materialize and dissipate. Figures. He left his horse and strode the short distance to the edge of the ferry and then peered out into the darkness.

"Careful," the man said. "Folks always see strangeness in the fog. Don't think the Lady likes visitors."

"I'll consider myself warned," Lancelot murmured.

He pulled his black, woolen cloak tight against the wind, when a flicker of an image coalesced before him. He drew in a sharp breath as he beheld a vision of himself as a lad of eighteen, writhing atop a maiden behind a hay wagon during a Beltane feast. Shame heated his neck and face as he remembered ducking around the keep for weeks to avoid that same girl until she finally understood his disinterest. What was her name?

The shape changed again, flashing images of him whispering into a lady's ear in the Great Hall; his face pressed into a woman's bosom in a dark hallway. That knight from Morganwgg whom he had shared a wild night with. Lancelot's mouth went dry as he saw the man beneath him, Lancelot's hand fisted in the knight's blond locks. The images flashed faster now, and he wanted to turn away, to close his eyes against the assault. All he had ever done—those he had hurt—laid bare before him. The mist was accounting for his every misguided attempt to find connection. To numb the emptiness within him.

The fog flashed Fionna's ethereal face now, sorrowful and tender. Even she could not fill this void, the gaping hole created by the two mothers who had abandoned him. He was a burden from his very first breath, even as he breathed now. On his ride north from Glastonbury Tor, Lancelot had thought long and hard. Picking apart his psyche piece by twisted piece, turning toward the darkness he normally shied away from. A shadow self he normally tried to hide. But he would do anything to be worthy of Fionna.

Even face his own demons.

And he thought he finally understood. This mist, it too understood. The enchanted fog showed him exactly who he had been. Perhaps the price to return to Vivien's kingdom was nothing less than brutal honesty as to the man he became, the people he hurt. He had been living a half-life—seeking comfort by filling his days with training and sex and even his friendship with Arthur. Being Arthur's second-in-command had made him feel worthy—finally—but not deep down, where it mattered most. The twisted part of him knew, from the beginning, how he didn't deserve such an esteemed responsibility over others. And so, he had sabotaged the honor, tarnishing his reputation and reliability time and again. But no more. He would find his way out of this dark place, no matter the cost. No matter how long it took. This was his new mission.

The ferry bumped against the dock and Lancelot blinked in surprise. They had already made the crossing?

He tossed the ferryman a coin and then led Cheval onto the creaking, log-hewn dock. The cool smell of the Isle of Man greeted him—the brine of the sea mingled with the sweet scent of gorse and blaeberry. He swung onto his horse, riding the familiar path through rocky outcroppings and tough, wild grasses to Vivien's stone keep.

Two guards in Vivien's blue and silver livery snapped to attention at the open gate, their delicate pointed ears and pale skin marking them fae. "Sir Lancelot here to see the Lady of the Lake," Lancelot announced.

They nodded him through and Lancelot urged Cheval forward, his horse's hooves resounding on the cobbled stones beneath his feet. At the keep's entrance, Lancelot swung down and then strode inside, shivering from the dank, cold journey, all-the-while surveying the castle where he had grown up. He suppressed his nervousness as he walked toward the gathering hall where he suspected Vivien entertained.

Her main residence looked no different from his memories—fantastical trees and beasts adorning the stone walls in ornate carvings and tapestries, faerie nobles in strange finery who were wrapped around each other in dark alcoves, their cups of sweet wine forgotten. Human servants moving about, as if invisible—cringing when a faerie passed by. His mother didn't mistreat her servants, but a faerie court still wasn't the safest place to serve as a mortal. The fae turned from whimsical and lighthearted to cruel and manipulative in the blink of an eye. It was part of what made growing up here such a holy terror.

Music and light emanated from the end of the hallway—the sounds of laughter and chattering hanging on the air. Lancelot took a deep breath and then walked into the room, squinting at the brightness.

"Lancelot!" Vivien cried out when she sighted him, launching from her throne before flowing down the stairs toward him like a rushing river. Her dark brunette hair was arranged beneath a jeweled headdress he hadn't seen until now, and her cerulean gown was also new. But everything else about her was just as he remembered. She was as smooth and cool as ice, lovely as a spring's thaw—as unpredictable and deadly as one too.

"My son!" she reached him and placed one chilled hand upon his cheek, a rare smile gracing her lips. He almost flinched at her bright display of happiness. "To what do I owe this rare pleasure? I thought perhaps you were so secure in Caerleon, you would never again grace your poor foster mother with your presence."

Lancelot's eyes narrowed. She rarely used the word "mother" around him, let alone in front of an entire gathering. He peered over her shoulder and glimpsed a handsome man of obvious stature sitting near her throne, looking on. Men often crawled out of their gilded hovels for political favors from the legendary Lady of the Lake. Though, by her buoyant behavior, Lancelot guessed Vivien sought this man's patronage. To increase her status and wealth among the human nobility and, thus, more influence and power within the faerie courts. Always scheming and maneuvering, his foster mother.

"I'm sorry I haven't visited in several years," Lancelot replied with all the pleasantness he could muster. It was good to see her, in a strange way. She was familiar, if not exactly comforting.

"You are forgiven," she said sweetly—too sweetly. "You must be hungry from your journey! Thirsty?" She gestured at a servant, who materialized at their side, a cup of wine on a tray before him.

Lancelot eyed the goblet. He was parched, but not parched enough for faerie wine, even from Vivien's cellar. He waved away the cup and returned his focus back to his foster mother.

"I have a few questions for you."

He looked around at the glittering nobles of Vivien's court. Though they continued to chat and dance as if nothing had changed, he could feel their eyes on him. As a human foster son to a faerie, he had been an aberration when a boy—especially when titled "faerie prince." But now, as the second-in-command to the High King of Briton . . . he garnered even more interest. Like the man who awaited Vivien's company to negotiate political alliances with the Túatha dé Danann.

"Could we speak privately?"

"Of course," Vivien said, threading her arm into his. "Come."

They walked back up the steps of her raised dais and then through a door leading to Vivien's private meeting room.

She settled herself behind a desk, one situated by an open window.

Lancelot shivered. "Mind if we sit by the fire?"

She let out a little annoyed laugh. "I forget how sensitive to hot and cold you mortals are," she practically grumbled. Still, she stood and crossed to a chair beside the fire.

Lancelot stoked the low-burning flames, throwing on another log. "Just one of the many inconveniences of humanity."

"Ask me your questions, dearest Lancelot. I'm *dying* to know why my princeling is here."

"For court gossip, *mother*?"

"I will not spill a word of what you share without your permission, I swear it."

Lancelot took a deep breath and plunged forward. "Do you know what has transpired between Morgana and Arthur? And . . . me?"

"I know I received a wedding invitation, and then another card soon after, expressing regrets for the cancellation."

Lancelot grimaced. "Yes. Morgana didn't . . . take the cancellation well. She and her sisters cursed Caerleon. And me."

Vivien clucked her tongue. "Such children they are, those three, playing with curses and retribution.

If you wronged her somehow, she should have just killed you."

"Thanks," he muttered dryly.

"Well, she obviously didn't." Vivien waved her hand. "You're here for assistance to break the curse, I imagine?"

Lancelot nodded.

"Tell me of the magic's nature."

"The spell was more like a prophecy. Morgana declared that I would fall in love with a Gwenevere—"

"A Gwenevere?" Vivien's head whipped up, her dark blue eyes widening.

"Yes. But if I lay with her, our joining would ruin all I love."

Vivien laughed, full of innocent humor and black wickedness. "And do you deserve this . . . prophecy?"

He scowled. "Will you help or not?"

One delicate brow raised. "If you are here to break this curse, then it must also mean that you have found this 'Gwenevere.'" She cocked her head in an inhuman, predatory way. "You honestly believe you have, don't you dearest Lancelot?"

He clenched his jaw but remained silent.

"If this is so, then I'm afraid you have an even bigger problem."

"What do you mean?" His heart sank into the churning, bubbling cauldron of his sickened stomach. They were already battling several fairly large problems.

"A Gwenevere, a white enchantress, only arises when the High King of Briton faces powerful, Otherworldly challengers to his throne, and thus needs more than a relic, like Excalibur, to claim and maintain his sovereignty. He needs a blessing from Danu herself, Mother Goddess and queen of the Túatha dé Danann. A Gwenevere is a direct conduit of power from Danu to physically marry a king to his land."

"And the Gwenevere is this . . . blessing?"

Vivien leaned forward and placed her hands on either side of Lancelot's face, gently cradling his face. And ignoring his question. Typical faerie. She closed her eyes, murmuring quietly in a language he didn't understand.

Lancelot held his breath.

She opened her eyes, leaning back. "Whatever curse was upon you has lifted. You are clean of enchantments."

"Truly?" Lancelot's pulse leaped within his chest. Drinking from the Blessed Grail must have cleansed him of Morgana's curse!

His foster mother dipped her head in a dignified nod. But he didn't care about decorum. Instead, he whooped and then pulled her into an embrace, spinning her around, shouting, "Thank you!"

Vivien laughed, her head thrown back. Lancelot stared at the points of her canines as he set her gently down on her feet. As her giggles tapered, she ironed out invisible wrinkles over her gown with fluttering hands. Then she squared her shoulders and leveled a cool gaze—girlish whimsy out and scheming, maneuvering Vivien back in control. "Shall I take this to mean that you are in love with this woman? The one you suspect is the Gwenevere?"

"More than anything." Lancelot ran a hand through his tussled curls. "But . . . how do I know if she really is an enchantress? She insists that she has no magical ability."

"That is odd." Vivien frowned, her dark blue eyes sparkling with mischief. "Well, there is only one way to know for sure."

"Which is?"

"I shall have to meet her."

Chapter Six

Fionna

I was in Zephyr's stall, explaining my absence to her very accusing black eyes, when I felt a pair of strong arms encircle my waist.

I whirled, a dagger in hand, the sharp point laid deliberately along the interloper's jugular.

Galahad quirked a brow. "If you can't tell my touch from that of a foe, then I didn't leave enough of an impression." His words ended in a laugh, a deep rumble in his barreled chest.

I snorted as I lowered my dagger, flipping the small blade in my hand before sheathing it at my side. "Didn't anyone ever tell ye not to sneak up on a woman?"

"Yes, but where's the fun in that?" he asked, his broad hands re-circling my waist and tugging me to his hard, chiseled body.

I knew I should scold him, or ask him about his ride through the villages, but his wild, blond hair was down, tumbling about his shoulders, and his eyes were fixed on my mouth. The urge to taste him simmered hot within me, smothering all higher thought. I rose on my tiptoes and claimed his mouth with mine, melting into his warmth as his arms pressed me even closer to him, one hand roving up to tangle in my hair, the other roaming down to grip my arse.

The Grail quest's final days were a blur. Had it really been since Betws-y-Coed that we kissed like this? The night he and Percival and I—the thought of our shared intimacy sent a curl of heat through me. I shuddered at the memory. With a knowing smile, Galahad's mouth angled against mine expertly, his tongue darting playfully between my lips. Goddess above, he tasted divinely of honey and adventure and sex. I reached up to grab his head and pull him closer when a huge, velvet head butted against my back.

I pulled back and looked over my shoulder, shooting Zephyr a dark look. "Do ye mind?" I asked, to which Zephyr gave a whinny and a stamp of her hoof in reply.

Galahad chuckled. "Seems I'm not the only one starved for a little attention." He reached out and scratched Zephyr's forehead. Zephyr shook her head in delight and I resisted the urge to roll my eyes.

"Ye do have a way with the lasses," I muttered dryly. Reluctantly, I extricated myself from Galahad's embrace.

"Is that jealousy I hear?" Galahad grinned, and it was like the whole stall brightened. He rested his hands on my hips and placed a kiss on the tip of my nose. "Once we trounce O'Lynn and these faeries, we'll have all the time in the world for me to demonstrate how you have nothing to fear. There's no woman for me but you."

I opened my mouth to reply and the words stalled on my tongue. I couldn't say the same, could I? Guilt reared its ugly head. An unwelcomed and far too frequent a visitor as of late. True, Galahad hadn't appeared to object to sharing my affections in the past, but our feelings were all so hopelessly tangled. Could I really think that my love for these four men wouldn't end in broken hearts and a broken fellowship? As Lancelot shared? I quieted the ache in my chest. We needed to focus on the task before us. So, I seized the distraction eagerly.

"How was yer visit to the villages?" I asked.

A shadow fell across Galahad's handsome face, dimming the light his earlier smile had cast around the stable. As though the sun had suddenly set.

"The people are unhappy. They speak out against their king." He folded his arms across his chest. "I don't think we have much time."

"Rebellion?" I asked in rising horror. "At such a time? Don't they realize Arthur is their only hope against Morgana and the Uí Tuírtri?"

"I fear logic and reason are not the going currency in such a time. Fear seems the champion today."

I huffed in frustration. "Have ye told Arthur?"

Galahad nodded.

"Where is he?" I asked. "I should go to him . . ." I trailed off. I didn't know what I could do, only that Arthur had to be suffering, and I wanted to be at his side.

"He's inspecting the fortifications," Galahad said.

I hesitated.

"Go," Galahad encouraged. "If anyone can help Arthur right now, it's you."

I smiled at him, grateful for his understanding.

"Zephyr and I will keep each other company," he said, patting my mare once again.

"No moping in my absence," I replied, my smile twisting wider.

"No promises." Galahad smushed his face next to Zephyr's and then angled a long, mopey frown and big, puppy dog eyes my way.

I shook my head with a laugh as I hurried out of the stable.

I found Arthur walking the walls of the keep, speaking quietly with soldiers and tradesmen alike. I watched him for a few moments from the shadow of the wall. I think he was trying to convince every inhabitant of Caerleon individually of his worth as king. My heart softened at the sight. Sometimes I worried—could a man in Arthur's position care so deeply and so genuinely? Surely the cruelties of this world would break him by now. My fists tightened at my side. That's what we knights were for. I would not let this world destroy the man he was, while I still had breath in my body to stop it. I would protect him and his kingdom.

I felt the wrongness first—the faint lift of hairs on the back of my neck. An awareness that I couldn't account for. My hand flew to my sword and the newly sharpened blade was out of its sheath before I even knew why.

But then I saw the reason. A smoky whiteness, filtered by slanting afternoon light, billowed up from the earth like steam rising from a great cauldron.

Magic.

My first instinct was Arthur. In just four paces, I was between him and the strange growing cloud, the mist pouring into the space where only air and grass and sunshine should be.

"What?" I heard Arthur pounding down the stairs behind me from the wall, the ring of Excalibur's steel. My eyes stayed fixed on that unnatural mist. "Stay back," I called, throwing my arm out.

A figure stepped through. Tall, wearing a tunic of blue . . . with dark hair . . .

My mouth fell open. "Lancelot?" My sword drooped in my hand, my pulse still not sure if he were real or an apparition. His hair was tousled, and he wore a look of contrition on his face that was as unfamiliar to me as the mist that had delivered him.

Arthur stepped up beside me, sheathing his sword. "I take it you found your foster mother," Arthur said. His voice was hard—wary. I knew Arthur regretted what had passed between him and Lancelot when they last spoke, but the pride of men and kings especially was a funny thing.

The thought fled my mind as another stepped through the mist. A faerie female, tall and willowy as a reed. She was like a black alder tree in winter, her dark hair was the rich hue of bark, her pale skin milky as new-fallen snow. Long dark lashes fringed eyes wide and granite gray-blue as Lancelot's, though I knew they were not related. For this had to be Vivien, his foster mother. Lady of the Lake. She was a legend brought to life.

Arthur gave a slight bow. "Welcome to Caerleon, My Lady," he said. "To what do we owe this pleasure?"

The Otherworld evaporated behind the two mist-born wayfarers.

"Lancelot shared your unfortunate predicament with me," she said, gliding nearer, moving with preternatural grace.

"Are you here to assist?" Arthur asked, a hopeful ring to his question.

She blinked, then cocked her head, her fangs bared as she seemed to examine the mortal standing before her. "I'm afraid there is little I can do that the Grail did not, Little Dragon King. But . . ." Her gaze flicked to me, pinning me where I stood. "When Lancelot told me how Morgana spoke of a Gwenevere, I had to see this mythological creature for myself."

She approached me and, without asking, placed ice-cold fingertips on either side of my face, then closed her eyes. I froze in shock, standing stock still as a shiver passed through me from my toes upward to my head, leaving a tingling in its wake. I tried to quiet my thundering pulse, to shake the feeling that I was being weighed and judged by this female, that she was turning me inside out. Did she find me wanting?

Her eyes snapped back open and she withdrew her hands.

"Well?" Lancelot asked.

Vivien cocked her head at me—similar to how she had with Arthur—as if I were a five-fold knot her ancient faerie mind couldn't untangle. "She appears mortal. Yet . . . there *is* something. Something magical that lies deep, a power that is more than human. Waiting."

"Is she the Gwenevere?" Lancelot asked. "Can you tell?"

I opened my mouth to object to being discussed as if I wasn't right before them, but Vivien spoke first. "There is only one way to tell. Ask her parents."

"What do ye mean?" I asked, finding my voice.

"A Gwenevere is a great enchantress, yes. But she is more than that. She is the daughter of the goddess Danu, conceived when she lays with a mortal king on Beltane. Is your father a king?"

"Aye," I whispered, my throat a pile of dry, brittle leaves. *Daughter of the goddess Danu?* My mouth fell open, again, and my eyes widened.

"And your birthday?" Vivien asked, heaving a dramatic sigh. She fluttered a look of longsuffering patience at Lancelot. When I continued to gape at her, she huffed, "Well, when is it, so-called White Enchantress?"

"Fe-February third . . ." I trailed off, doing the math in my head. Nine months after the new spring. Everything in me wanted to look at Arthur, to see if he figured the math out as well. But I didn't. Instead, I continued to stare at the Lady of the Lake in fear and in wonderment.

Vivien lifted a single eyebrow. "I cannot account for your appearance. Though you are pretty-ish for a mortal, I suppose."

"How can we know for sure?" Lancelot asked.

"If she is pretty-ish?" Vivien asked with a girlish, baiting smile, and cool, glittering mischief twinkling in her unnatural eyes. "What say you, Sir Knight?"

Lancelot groaned. "No faerie tricks. You know of what I ask, *mother*. Is she the Gwenevere?"

I glared at him, my idiotic fish-gape quickly turning into a scowl. Why did the fool man need to know so badly if I was a bloody Gwenevere? Was this still about the third curse? I had no compulsion to sleep with him right now, that's for damn certain. Did any other thing ever cross the man's irritatingly obsessed mind?

"Like I said, dearest *Lancelot du Lac*." Vivien punctuated each word. "Ask her parents." Then she shifted toward me. "Your father."

I swallowed thickly. "My father is held captive by my clann's enemy." This faerie was the second individual today to proclaim my father as the one who held the answers I sought. I longed to see him again, to talk to him, to storm into that bastard O'Lynn's camp and fight my way to him. To take my family and leave only a path of destruction in my wake.

"A shame," Vivien replied with an elegant shrug of her slender shoulder. Then, as if bored with the conversation, she slid a glance my way and said, "Danu would be the only one who could tell you for certain, then. Too bad she hasn't been seen in twenty years."

"What?" Arthur exploded. "I thought she held court in the Otherworld?"

Vivien shook her head, then lifted a hand to fuss with a loose curl. "It's not common knowledge among mortals." She hissed the last word with sizzling disgust over our kind. "But a regent presides over her court. In her absence, obviously."

The earth goddess was missing? The earth goddess . . . and possibly . . . my mother?

It was madness.

This was all madness.

Life made sense before Caerleon. Now it was all curses and faerie relics and magic beasts and mists that transported people.

Madness.

Chapter Seven

Percival

Percival strode through the hallway, his mind racing with the events of the past weeks. They had found the Blessed Grail. Part of him had never thought they would do it, even as fevered as Arthur was about finding this relic . . . and as hopeful as he had been when Fionna joined them. Percival still had doubted. Until signs from the Grail Maiden began to appear, he thought that the legend of the Grail—the legend of the Fisher King—was just one more cruel twist of fate in the long line of tragedies shadowing the noble lines of Pendragon and Caer Benic. But they had found it. And now he was free.

True, the Grail Maiden had bid him return to Caer Benic and take up his place as the Fisher King. And perhaps one day he would. When he wasn't needed here. But, for now, he was needed. And he was wanted. And gods, did *he* want.

Images of Fionna filled his mind and tightened his breeches. Her features, delicate and soft as a feather—so incongruous with the skill of her blade—combined with the fire in her eyes. Compelling yet kind. Hard and soft—yielding as butter in his hands yet strong as stone when she faced monsters the likes of which he had never seen. Fionna was the most powerful woman he had ever known. She would strip his chastity from him with a power and gentleness that was all her—and the thought exhilarated and terrified him in turns. He wanted to please her. To make her moan the way she had for Galahad—

"Fionna!" he said as she ran full into him.

"Percival," she said at the same time, stumbling back. Her hand pressed to her breast as she breathed out. "My mind was elsewhere, my apologies."

"The fault was mine, dove," Percival said, studying her. Her silver eyes darted about, her breathing was shallow. "Is everything all right, lass?"

"Aye." She shook her head, closing her eyes. "No. I don't know. Lancelot is back."

"Well that's good," Percival said with a whoop.

"Indeed," Fionna agreed. "He brought Vivien. Arthur invited her to dinner."

"Vivien." Percival's elation dimmed, and he peered over his shoulder. "Is it just me," he whispered, "or have ye had enough of faeries for a spell?"

She let out a hard laugh. "Nay, not just ye. She brings riddles. I don't know. I need to change and put on something more suitable for evening's feast."

"I'll walk ye," Percival said, falling into step beside her. "Did Lancelot get any answers about the third curse?"

Fionna shrugged. "He didn't say. Vivien just put

her hands all over me to discern if I was 'the Gwenevere.'" Fionna made marks in the air with her fingers. "I'm starting to hate the word."

"I know the feeling," Percival agreed. "Being the "Fisher King's son,' 'heir to the Grail' isnae any more fun."

She looked at him softly. "I don't think I realized how hard it was on ye."

"Och, we'll get this sorted, ye'll see," Percival said.

"How can ye be so optimistic?" she asked.

Percival tucked strands of hair behind his ear and shrugged. "I dinnae ken. The feeling is just more pleasant than the alternative."

"That simple?"

"Not everything has to be complicated." They had reached Fionna's door, and she turned to face him.

"Tell that to the possible mortal/immortal daughter of a goddess, who or may or may not be a Gwenevere, yet very certainly screwed up the Grail's healing of Caerleon."

Percival fought a smile. "That is a mouthful. I think I'll just stick to 'dove.'"

Fionna grinned at him, giving a playful roll of her eyes. "What would I do without ye?"

Percival took her hands in his and kissed the backs of each one. "Ye shall never have to know, fair Lady." He dropped his hands but didn't let hers go. Even her hands were so Fionna—pale and slender and soft on the backs, yet with hard callouses covering her palms. His thumbs traced two circles on the backs of them. "Fionna—" he began, finding himself suddenly tripping over each sound and syllable in just her name.

"I must dress for dinner," she said, pulling back her hands, clearly impatient. "What do you need?"

He cleared his throat, banging a fist softly against her doorframe. *Out with it, Percival!* "My vow—" he murmured, silently cursing his stupid tongue.

"I'm not sure I heard you?" Fionna asked.

He looked up then, meeting her eyes. If he wanted her, he needed to claim her. No longer a boy. He was a man. He was the Fisher King. Percival cleared his tightened throat again. "We have found the Grail, ye ken? I am now released of my vow. And the thought of my newfound freedom, it burns within me, lass."

Fionna's mouth opened in a little O as she realized what he meant. Then she closed her eyes, letting out a little sigh. "Percival, my head is in knots over everything that has happened right now. The curses, and Vivien, and my sister."

"Of course." Percival swallowed thickly, fighting his disappointment. "I didn't mean to come off as insensitive, or meant this very moment . . . I just . . ." his face heated.

He didn't know what he had been thinking. Coming here, asking her like a hound begging for a treat, then allowing his needs to have a voice after he knew she was upset. Sometimes he wanted to hide in a hole over his own awkward ignorance.

"Percy," she began, almost as though a big sister rather than a lover. He stilled. Did she only see him as a friend, then? The other men were handsome and virile and strong. But he? Was he only good for cheering up his friends? Fionna reached for him, but he stepped back. "It's not a no. It's just . . . not now."

He nodded stiffly at the tone of her voice. He wasn't a wee bairn, nor did he need her sympathy. Had he misread what they had shared in Betws-y-Coed? These past weeks? No, she cared for him. He was sure of it. Though, perhaps Fionna still saw him as a lad. A little brother to laugh with. Her tone certainly suggested so. But he wasn't that boy anymore. He had earned the adder stone and pleasured a witch of Byzantium and claimed the Blessed Grail for himself. He was capable, a man among men. But he just needed to prove it to her.

An idea bloomed to life inside of him.

"I wonder," he said, "If there is something I can do for ye . . ."

Fionna's cheeks reddened. "Oh Percival, that's very generous—"

"Nae, not *that*," he said hastily. "Though, I would happily serve ye in such a way, whenever ye wish for pleasures between a man and woman. Rather, I meant . . . I would like to make a gesture of my favor. Prove to ye the depth of my regard for ye, and my worthiness. To lie with ye and . . . to love ye."

"Ye don't need to earn my favor," Fionna said, threading her fingers through the ends of her braids. "Ye already have my affections."

"Please, I want to, dove," Percival said. "There must be something I can do for ye."

Fionna's expression grew thoughtful, and then a conspiratorial smile crept over her face. "I've half a mind to do something dangerous," she quietly confessed. "Something that rides the borderland between bravery and stupidity."

Percival's heart soared, and a mischievous smile crested on his own face. "Go on . . ."

Chapter Eight

Arthur

Entertaining a faerie always proved disconcerting. Arthur had felt uneasy around the Túatha dé Danann since boyhood. For he was the product of a vile act against the children of Danu when his conniving father, Uther, had arranged others in the front lines of war to slaughter Gorlois—Arthur's mother's first fae husband. His half-sisters never forgot or forgave. And with Uther now dead, their vengeful attentions turned Arthur's way.

His steps dragged as he made his way to the Great Hall from his room. Freshly bathed and wearing a tunic of emerald green, Arthur was physically clean. But nothing could wash away the worry that clouded him. A fog swirled about in his mind, thick as the Otherworldly mist of Castellum Puellarum, paralyzing his reason and quick wit. Everything was spinning out of control. The curse, the broken Grail, war, rebellion, his errant knight come home. His love, the daughter of a goddess? Half fae? Certainly,

Fionna was no ordinary woman. It was as plain as day. But he had always attributed her unique grace, beauty, and battle prowess to the wonder that was Fionna herself, not some undeserved gift of divine parentage.

"That look can't be good," a deep voice called out.

He looked up and found Lancelot striding toward him. His knight and sword-brother met him in the hallway outside of the Great Hall, wearing a tunic of grey trimmed in silver.

Arthur forced a laugh. "I admit, there is much on my mind as of late."

"A large piece of the blame lies with me," Lancelot said. "And for all the pain I have caused you and Caerleon, I am deeply sorry." Lancelot dropped to one knee, his head bowed.

"Lance—" Arthur began, but Lancelot interrupted him.

"You must let me make amends, Your Majesty. I wronged you. I wronged you all, by keeping the secret of the third curse. Though my motives were to keep the burden from you . . . my desires were selfish too. I wounded you a second time when I left. But I have returned with aid from my foster mother, and glad tidings. The Blessed Grail's magic washed the third curse from me. Morgana's prophecy hangs over our head no longer. I wish nothing more than for you to give me another chance. To be your second-in-command once again. To earn your trust again." Lancelot peered up at him, his eyes red and glossy with building emotion. His voice grew thick.

"Arthur, I will do *anything*."

Lancelot's words warmed Arthur like a roaring hearth on the coldest of winter nights. Yes, part of him remained angry. But he no longer desired to be at odds with his dearest and oldest friend. His brother. He needed Lancelot, now more than ever.

"Stand, Sir Lancelot du Lac," Arthur said, and Lancelot did. "I'm afraid you've underestimated the depths of my feelings on this subject."

The anxious thoughts racing behind his friend's ice-blue eyes flashed bright with grief, the muscles in his jaw working. "I understand," Lancelot whispered, gritting back the tears. "It's nothing less than I deserve, Your Majesty."

Arthur laid a hand on Lancelot's shoulder, his friend's body a tense, coiled spring. "I love you far too much, brother, to let your fool-headedness tear us apart."

Lancelot let out a gasp of disbelieving laughter, his head curling down. He nodded, and a hand strayed to cover his eyes as his shoulders began to shake. Arthur pulled him into an embrace, and Lancelot shuddered against him, before he wrapped his arms around Arthur, his hands fisting in Arthur's tunic. Arthur clapped his friend's back, his relief at Lancelot's safe return forming into something harder. Something strong and unyielding as granite. His enemies could take his sword, the health of his land, even his kingship. But they could never take the *loyalty* of those Arthur loved. Lancelot and Galahad and Percival and now Fionna—he would lay down his life for any of them. And he knew in the marrow of his bones that they would each do the same for him. For each other. The Celts believed that a cord of three strands was not easily broken. *Well, Morgana,* he thought, the fire stoked within him—*try five.*

Lancelot pulled back, wiping his eyes.

"Do you fare well?" Arthur asked. "For I have need of my second. One who is clear-headed. No more doubts. No more letting faeries play upon our weaknesses. Each of us must be ready to do what needs to be done, if we are to get through the days to come."

Lancelot's smile was grim and his voice hard. "Let them come. We'll be ready."

"Do I sense a spring thaw in the ice of yer fated brotherhood?" Fionna asked, striding up the corridor in a stunning gown the color of plum. The dress dipped low, revealing the slender curve of her neck, the spill of her cleavage where the lily necklace gifted by Morgana's ambassador still nestled. Her hair was freshly braided at the crown of her hair, the rest falling free down her back in a waterfall of white. Lancelot slid him a questioning look and Arthur smiled his assent.

"A man can do naught but burn inside in the face of your beauty," Lancelot said with a grin, taking Fionna's hand and bowing over her fingers with a kiss.

She quirked a brow. "Just returned and ye're already back to full form I see."

Arthur motioned them inside. "You have no idea Fionna. You've been stuck with crabapple. If the old Lancelot is back, get ready for interesting times ahead."

Lancelot offered Fionna his arm, which she accepted, and then they all moved into the candle-light-warmed Great Hall.

"Back with a vengeance and ready to kick some faerie arse," Lancelot said with a laugh, before realizing his foster mother and Merlin stood inside the dining hall. "Er, sorry Mother," he said.

Vivien patted him on the cheek, grinning in such a way that her canines appeared. "Perhaps it best you stick to *kicking faerie arse* for a spell, rather than doing anything else with it."

A booming laugh sounded behind them, and Arthur turned to see Galahad and Percival joining their circle.

"Too right, My Lady." Galahad greeted the Lady of the Lake with a bow and a kiss on her delicate hand.

"Fair Galahad." Vivien studied him with a gleam in her eyes before she caressed one of his sizable biceps. "My son has spoken of you. Time has treated you well. And Percival! Our very own Fisher King, in the flesh."

"Welcome, Lady," Percival said, with a wide smile.

Arthur couldn't help the grin that now stretched across his face. Gods, it was good to have them all back together, here in his keep. Despite all that faced them outside these walls, inside, things were finally as they were supposed to be.

"Shall we sit?" Arthur asked, gesturing to the head table.

Murmurs of affirmation rounded the group and they made their way to their seats. Until Vivien grabbed Fionna's wrist, her glittering blue eyes growing wide. "What is this you wear?" Vivian half-whispered, her hand straying to the necklace at Fionna's throat.

Arthur halted all movement, his instincts on alert.

Fionna shot him a wild look as the Lady of the Lake picked up the pendant hanging from Fionna's neck and inspected the lily.

"How did you come upon this necklace, child?" Vivien asked.

"The ambassador Alworn delivered this gift from Tintagel," Arthur said. "When we knighted Fionna."

"The chain won't come off," Fionna admitted. "No matter what I try."

"You did not mention this during our discussion," Merlin quietly said.

"Nor me," Arthur added. "I wish I had known, so I could have sought your relief sooner."

Fionna gnawed the inside of her lip. "There were far more important matters at hand than troubles with a silly necklace."

"This *silly necklace* was stolen from me," Vivien hissed. Her eyes darted about the room, resting on each person in turn. "And missing for months from my keep on the Isle of Man."

Horror flickered across Fionna's face. "I'm so sorry, I didn't know, My Lady. Please, take the necklace back." Fionna fumbled with the clasp, letting out a growl of frustration.

"Relax child, I care not that my property was here

in *your* safekeeping. Tintagel, however . . . I shall deal with the dark sisters." Vivien grasped the necklace, closing her eyes and murmuring under her breath.

The clasp of the necklace sprang apart, and then the silver chain slithered down from around Fionna's neck and into Vivien's hand.

Fionna released a gasp, feeling her bare neck. "Thank ye!"

"Little Dragon King, your half-sister's meddling was more than just idle," Vivien said. She loosed a laugh, but her blue eyes held little mirth. There was something foreign in her gaze that made Arthur's stomach clench in fear. Pity. She looked upon him with pity. "Rather clever, actually. A curse on my dearest Lancelot, declaring ruin if he fell in love. And a necklace enchanted to ensure he did."

Silence blanketed the room, thick and heavy.

"What do ye mean?" Fionna whispered, her hand still on her throat.

"This necklace is enchanted with a love charm. Whoever wears this pendant and corded chain will be irresistible to the opposite sex. Whatever men cross her path will have no choice but to fall madly in love with her."

Chapter Nine

Lancelot

Vivien's words settled over them like a drenched wool cloak, heavy and stifling. Lancelot looked at Arthur, and saw his own shock mirrored on his king's face. The necklace made a man fall in love with the wearer? So . . . were their feelings for Fionna . . . false? Lies spun of faerie enchantments? Had the last weeks, the fire that had burned hot within him—

"I think it's bollocks," Percival cut in, marching across the room. He took Fionna's hand and began walking toward the head table, saying, "A man need no enchantment to fall for our fifth knight. If her beauty and wit weren't enough, the might of her sword arm would capture him completely." Fionna followed Percival to her seat like an obedient child. "I for one am certain that my feelings are my own."

Fionna shot Percival a grateful look as she sank heavily into her chair.

For once, Lancelot envied Percival's quick thinking. While he stood stock-still, processing his doubts and shock, Percival had proven his loyalty.

"Agreed," Galahad said, sinking into his chair as well. "No faerie trinket can confuse my heart."

His foster mother was watching this all with a twinkle of impish amusement in her eyes.

"Thank you, Vivien," Arthur said quietly, "for removing the necklace. Perhaps now we are almost rid of Morgana and her sisters' magical meddling."

"But not quite." Vivien sank gracefully into her chair between Merlin and Arthur, and then cocked her head at Arthur in that inhuman, animalistic way of hers. "The Blessed Grail failed to eradicate the curse upon your land."

"A mystery, that," Merlin murmured, leaning in toward Vivien eagerly as his pupils narrowed into reptilian slits. "I would relish your ancient wisdom on the matter, My Lady. When each of them drank from the Grail, the land healed. Except Fionna's portion."

Fionna's face remained downturned, her eyes fixed on her empty trencher.

Lancelot reached under the table and grasped the fingers of one of the hands resting limply on her lap. She slid a glance his way beneath lowered lashes. Shadows darkened her eyes and doubts carved lines into her face. He squeezed her hand in a weak attempt at comfort. Still, he believed they would sort this mess out.

"Very peculiar indeed, druid," Vivien mused. "The Grail should have wiped away all magical enchantment, like with Lancelot. Although . . . perhaps the Grail's healing properties could not affect a more powerful enchantment."

"But what could be more powerful than the Grail?" Merlin asked.

"The magic of a goddess, obviously." Vivien huffed in irritation. Lancelot knew this look. His foster mother grew weary of mortals. But she continued when Merlin dipped his head for her to explain further. "Such as the goddess Danu. If Princess Fionnabhair Allán is the Gwenevere, then perhaps her mother placed a spell upon her that even the Grail could not break."

Merlin's eyes flashed gold as he turned toward Arthur. "I am telling you, Your Majesty, our answers lie in the Otherworld. With the court of the Túatha dé Danann."

Arthur sighed, taking a sip of wine. Servants were bringing out trays of food now, filling the room with the smell of spices and fresh bread. "I fear you are right. But we still do not have a way to travel there quickly."

"You seek the Otherworld?" Vivien asked, eyebrow arched. "As I already shared, you will not find Danu there. A steward holds court in her name. Though, I fear that after years of her absence, Danu would scarcely recognize the place."

"Answers from Danu would be a bonus," Merlin said, "but I have advised Arthur that the Cauldron of Plenty may be able to help feed the people while the curse lingers, as well as aid us if Morgana's armies lay siege."

"The Cauldron is rumored to have healing properties, as well," Vivien remarked, though somewhat distracted. She sniffed at the leg of lamb placed onto her trencher and wrinkled her nose. Lancelot resisted the urge to roll his eyes. His foster mother's focus was like a butterfly, flitting and fluttering about endlessly.

"If the rumors prove true," Arthur said, "that would be a helpful fact. Only, we don't have the time. With an army approaching, I cannot leave my keep."

"Can the Lady of the Lake assist?" Galahad suggested. "She did transport herself and Lancelot here by magical means, did she not?"

"Of course," Vivien purred, looking at Galahad with an appraising eye as she licked sauce from her fingertip. "But my power transports you between locations on the mortal plane. You would still need a key to enter the Otherworld."

"They have such a key," Merlin said. "Carved from the tusk of the Twrch Trwyth."

"And you mention this now?" Vivien nibbled on a bannock, melodramatically peering up at the rafters of the Great Hall, as though in great thought. "Then," she added after swallowing, "I could see you there, Little Dragon King. Entering the Otherworld would be as simple as stepping through a door."

"Truly?" Arthur set his goblet of wine down and leaned toward her. "Your assistance would help us greatly. This Cauldron, if the magical properties are true, could solve several of our problems efficiently."

"Which only leaves us with several other problems to contend with," Percival said cheerfully around a bite of chicken leg. Vivien grinned at the younger man and then side-eyed Lancelot. She knew. His foster mother sensed Lancelot's tether to Percival. How? He wasn't sure.

"Quite right, Percival." Arthur's gaze darkened. "Fionna, I should like you to accompany me. The Otherworld might hold answers for you as well."

Fionna's head snapped up and she stared at Arthur, eyes wide and unblinking, as though a startled deer. "As ye wish, Yer Majesty," she managed.

"If I may," Vivien interjected, practically cooing. "I would not take Fionna, if I were you."

"Why not?" Lancelot asked. His foster mother was always scheming and maneuvering, and he didn't trust the glimmer in her eyes.

"Do you mortals ever listen? As I said, the steward who rules over the court of the Túatha dé Danann has sworn fealty to Danu, but I fear over these years . . . her allegiances may have shifted."

"You didn't share this latter piece of information, mother," Lancelot muttered.

"No? Well, then listen now." Vivien's hand fluttered through the air as she giggled before turning solemn once more. "There could be faeries at court who are no longer friends of Danu. If Fionna is the Gwenevere, and if Danu placed a géis to shield her daughter's true nature, then she had reasons for doing so. Delivering Fionna to those who may be hostile toward her could prove dangerous."

Arthur's brow furrowed.

"Lady Vivien speaks sense," Merlin said. "Until we can untangle the truth of Fionna's heritage, and her powers, she is safest within your keep."

Fionna swept a heated gaze across the table, the fire in her finally rekindling. "I am no wilting maiden who needs protection. I am safe so long as I have my sword at my side and my knives in their sheaths," she snapped. Then she took a long, slow breath, seeming to re-center herself. "But I am happy to remain here, if everyone thinks it best. I have tasks to attend to here, anyway." She hurried on. "Ye know . . . assisting in the defense of Caerleon. I have the most knowledge of the Uí Tuírtri battle styles and tactics."

"Of course," Arthur said. "Merlin didn't mean to imply you couldn't protect yourself. Right Merlin?" Arthur raised an eyebrow, to which Merlin nodded in apology to Fionna.

Vivien ignored it all, continuing. "May I suggest . . . young, virile Galahad?" She turned to the brawny knight. "Elathia, Danu's regent, has a weakness for handsome mortals of his *persuasion*. His presence could prove useful."

"I will seize any advantage." Arthur sent a sly look to the knight in question. "What say you, young, virile Galahad?"

"Travel to the Otherworld as faerie bait?" Galahad sighed, blowing a loose strand of hair out of his face. "Of course, Your Majesty. Sounds like romping fun."

"Then it is settled. Galahad shall come with me. Lancelot, you are reappointed as my second-in-command. Percival and Fionna will assist in defending the keep and leading our men. Merlin, keep searching for cures or clues to Fionna's condition."

Percival hoisted his glass. "To the next mad adventure that will likely get us all killed."

Lancelot laughed darkly. "I'll drink to that."

They talked plans and strategy late into the night, as the dishes grew cold and the wine dwindled. Arthur was understandably hesitant to leave his keep with an imminent threat on the horizon; so, Lancelot forgave him his over-managing, his insistence of going twice over every piece of their defensive plans and fortifications.

Vivien and Merlin spoke of the Otherworld and what Arthur and Galahad might expect there, as well as speculated on the mystery of Fionna's condition. The night ended with many theories but no answers.

Fionna had grown quieter and more introspective until she finally excused herself, pleading exhaustion.

Indecision warred within Lancelot as Fionna's lithe form disappeared into the dark shadows of the corridor. There was much he wanted to say to her. There was time, but . . . he didn't want to wait. He needed to clear the air—now.

Lancelot stood. "Excuse me as well," he said, then strode after her. He didn't want another day to pass without telling her how he felt.

"Fionna," he called after her.

But she didn't slow. If anything, she sped up.

"Fionna!" He broke into a jog, catching up with

her as she neared the hallway that led to her room in the North wing. He grabbed her arm and gently swung her around to face him. "Fi, speak to me."

Tears glittered on her white lashes and slipped down her cheeks.

Alarmed, he towed her into a darkened servant's hallway and away from prying eyes. "Why do you cry?"

She pinched her face up, her eyes closed, fighting the tears. "I betrayed my father and sister to stay here in Caerleon. Aideen is married to a bastard, the foulest man I've ever known. Because of me." She jabbed her thumb at her chest. "Because I forgot my duty and threw aside my honor to follow my heart. I acted like a foolish lass, one who put love over family. And now . . . that love was false!" Her voice cracked, and she clapped a hand over her mouth. "Every moment was false. Yer feelings, all of them, they were magic. A cruel faerie joke. Well the joke's on me."

Lancelot took her face in his hands, wiping her tears with his thumbs. Even with her face red and puffy, her nose streaming, she was beautiful. The most beautiful and powerful woman he had ever known. "If it was all a cruel faerie joke, and you no longer wear the enchanted necklace, then why do I still love you?"

She stepped out of his embrace and threw her shoulders back, head lifted high, her silver eyes rippling with anger. "Do not mock me."

"You think so little of me?"

"Ye once asked to know my love and then ye pushed me away. My heart cannot bear another game, Lancelot du Lac. No more lies."

Lancelot advanced toward her in such a way that she had no choice but to back up against the stone wall. "The only *lie* I want to know with you is the fiery, passionate truth between our bodies. Our souls."

"Is this your cock speaking or yer heart?"

"Both."

A furious laugh escaped her flushed lips. "Oh please, woo me more with your pretty words, prince."

The snappish reply was meant as an insult, but he glimpsed the challenge in her daggered gaze—a test. From the very first day, their every spark was born of weaponized words. Sparring wit and emotions and stubbornness. Her steel was his equal—in moments such as these and with real swords in hand.

Placing his forearm on the stone wall by her face, he leaned in close and whispered, "What I feel for you is more real than the ground beneath my feet. Than the air I breathe." Her breath pulsed hot on his lips, her breasts rising and falling in a seething tempo. With a devilish smile, he moved toward her ear and continued in moonlit whispers. "The love I feel for you was not born of magic. You were the only spark needed to kindle this blaze. And there is no man or magic who can tear it from me."

A disbelieving sob escaped Fionna, and her body tensed against more tears. She fisted the front of his tunic, her red-rimmed eyes locked onto his lips. "Ye wish for passion-filled *lies*?"

"Only if those *lies* seal the truth of us, princess."

A single tear rolled across her mouth as a raging heat billowed between their bodies.

"Show me."

Lancelot smirked. "Is this your cock speaking or your heart?"

"Both."

A soft laugh escaped him as he pulled her mouth to his.

Chapter Ten

Fionna

His mouth collided with mine, his fury begging me to meet his ferocity. Darkness had always danced between us. And I welcomed his grief as I fought my own. Lancelot was a flinted passion, a Winter Solstice's bonfire—cold when distanced yet breathtakingly hot when close. Unlike Galahad's honeyed sensuality, Arthur's tender romance, and Percival's laughing kisses, the man who pressed me to a stone wall in a dark, rarely-used hallway was seductive wickedness and hidden moonlight. In a word: dangerous.

His lips left mine to explore my neck as his hand slid up the silk skirt of my gown. Calloused fingertips caressed my thigh, moving higher and higher. Determined. Then a single teasing finger paced a line between my sex and my slit when he discovered that I wasn't wearing any undergarments.

I couldn't breathe, my chest gasping for air at the fire of his touch.

"You want pretty words?" Lancelot murmured

into the skin of my neck.

Gripping the back of my thigh, he yanked my leg up and around his waist, while his other hand pushed the neckline of my bodice down my arm until my breast sprang free. Rippling folds of my plum-hued silken skirt fell toward my stomach and exposed me further.

"I will claim your body first." He rocked his hip into me and I shuddered. The lightning strike of his bulging cock against my throbbing clit thundered through my core. My breast bounced with the rolling movement and he lowered his head, flicking his tongue against my nipple. "Gods woman, you taste sweet . . ." His murmured words trailed away as he took my breast into his mouth.

I stifled a sharp cry of pleasure as his teeth nibbled on me, his tongue roughly sucking my pebbled tip before releasing my breast to the night's chill.

He dragged his lips back to mine, whispering, "I want your anger," before seizing my mouth once more in a bruising kiss.

Heady, I pushed him back and leveled a glare. "My body isn't enough for ye? Goddess above, ye arrogant, infuriating boar."

The side of Lancelot's mouth tipped up. Still holding my thigh around his waist, he stroked my exposed skin with his hardening cock. Continuing to do so even as he began unlacing his breeches.

"I want *all* of you, Fionnabhair Allán," he said, and then I felt the crown of his smooth skin sliding across my swollen sex. "Your pain." The fingers of his free hand snaked up my torso to my breast and pinched my nipple. Molten iron pooled between my legs as his cock teased my body into submission simultaneously, sliding back and forth, back and forth.

I moaned, clawing at the front of his tunic, unable to contain the aching pang of pleasure. Furious and ecstatic that he could play my body as expertly as a bard plucks the strings of his harp.

"Your grief," he whispered next, softly kissing my jaw, my cheek, and each eyelid.

His tongue swirled patterns down my throat, as if he were writing his name on my skin. The very thought stoked the bonfire in my pulse and sparked embers flew into my veins.

"And I want your passion."

Lancelot bit down where my neck and collarbone met as he thrust his cock into me—deep, hard. I sucked in a sharp, ragged breath. Gods above, he felt incredible. And he didn't move, allowing me to feel the thick size of him as he stretched and filled me. Starlit waves of pleasure rushed between my legs, intense and leaving me breathless. An orgasm was building. But I wasn't ready yet, wanting more. *Needing* more.

Heat flared where his teeth gripped my skin, a feral pain that ignited a wildness in me. A soft whimper escaped my lips. This is how the fae claimed their lovers, I had heard once. A thought that left me wanting to become animal, to crave every forbidden carnal delight. To furiously take his body as he raged into mine.

And rage he did.

Grabbing my other leg, he hoisted me up—his

shaft still buried to the hilt inside me—and then he pressed me harder against the stones digging into my back. I was now completely at his mercy, my legs dangling in the crook of his arms and spread wide for his taking. His hips crashed into mine.

I groaned, angering when I felt the hard length of him slide away, leaving me bare and empty. My hands loosened their grip on his tunic to clutch the soft, black curls around his head. Our eyes met, mouths parted in heaving breaths as his muscled, unyielding body crashed into mine again and again, filling me and leaving me, his hips grinding into mine with each thrust.

"Tell me you want me," he whispered between stirred breaths.

Those words pierced my heart as I understood. This was the dark pain he protected. The love he sought and feared to never know.

"I want ye."

His breath caught as his eyes fluttered closed. "Say it again."

"I want ye, Lancelot du Lac."

"Again," he breathed.

"I want ye all my days," I whispered before touching my mouth to his in a sweet, gentle kiss.

With our lips connected and his cock still buried inside me, Lancelot pulled away from the wall and carried me a few steps toward the stairs, where he softly laid my body down across the steps. He knelt on the stones, straddling my hips. Moonlight from a nearby latticed window dusted him in silvers and blues. My Winter Prince, all fire and ice. Breathtakingly gorgeous, with frosted blue eyes peering at me through curling black strands that fell over his flushed cheeks and swollen lips. Reaching behind his back, he pulled his tunic over his head and then flung the garment to the side.

Fingers of light caressed his muscled chest and torso, and I drank in the sight of him. He was tall and lean and well-built, with veins roping around his forearms and ink dancing across his skin in swirls and ancient patterns. The length of his cock glistened from our passion. Jealous of the moon's intimate knowledge of this man's body, I reached up and brushed my fingertips along the tattoos. "What do they mean?" I asked.

"Runes," Lancelot whispered back. "Ones that mark me as a faerie prince of the Túatha dé Danann."

"Ye are, truly?" My gaze locked with his. "I always thought 'faerie' was in jest or to mark yer upbringing."

"I am a prince of two realms, mortal and immortal, though not one of power or consequence in either. Any I have is only by the good favor of others." He angled his head away, as if in shame.

I cupped his cheek and drew him to me until our lips touched. "Ye have power over me, Lance. And . . ." I swallowed back the rising emotion. "And I not only love ye, I *choose* ye."

A tear slipped down his cheek and he hoarsely whispered, "I promise you, Fi . . . I promise to never intentionally hurt you again or push you away. I'm sorry. I'm so very sorry."

"Claim my heart, Lancelot. I am yers."

"And Arthur's?"

I smiled. "Aye, I'm Arthur's and Galahad's and Percival's. Just as yer heart also belongs to Percival."

He bit his bottom lip, a look both shy and sensual. "You don't mind my affection for Percival?"

"No, ye belong to each other too. But this moment is ours, only ye and me." The energy between us surged again, and another tear rolled down Lancelot's cheek. My hand traveled down his jaw and neck to his chest, over his pounding heart. "I *want* ye."

His eyes closed once more as he shuddered under the weighted truth of my confession.

"You've claimed my body," I said, running my hands across the beautiful, olive-toned skin of his chest. "Now lie with my heart."

And there, on the stairs, we joined once more. This time every moment slow, each touch to savor the beauty and wonder of the other, each whisper shared as though our souls entwined intimately too. This man made me so mad—both in fury and in adoration for him. But most of all, he humbled me. For I knew his heart wasn't a gift he gave easily or often, if ever until now. Nor did I doubt him: his love wasn't born of magic but freely given.

Delirious with pleasure and utterly drunk on his kisses, I yielded completely to him as I whispered over and over, "I want ye."

Chapter Eleven

Galahad

Galahad wasn't eager to reenter the Other-world. But he was a knight, and a knight went where his king commanded.

His sleep had been fitful the night before, filled with images of faerie maidens with sharp ears and even sharper teeth. Through his dreams they tormented him, stabbing Arthur, twisting into Fionna's lithe form and back again, taunting him and his peasant origins, laughing at his mortal attempts to fight back.

Finally, he rose before dawn, stumbling toward the stable yard to pound at a straw man until sweat coated his entire body and the sun had risen. Until his dreams grew hazy and his body sore.

He then bathed and changed into a fresh tunic, letting his damp hair fall about his shoulders to dry. He was to meet Arthur, Merlin, and Vivien in Arthur's study, where the Lady of the Lake would open a portal. The familiar corridors of the keep comforted his troubled thoughts, as did motion. Moving always helped calm his agitation.

Before turning down another hallway, he crossed paths with Fionna. "My lady," he nodded to her. She looked like she had known little sleep as well—purpled shadows smudged the fair skin under her eyes. But her eyes, though worried, were strangely bright and alert. "Here to see us off?"

"I don't like this plan," she said, grabbing his hand and pulling him to a stop.

"What's to like?" Galahad turned to her. "But we must. For Caerleon."

"I know." She gnawed the inside of her lip in that adorable way of hers. "Promise ye will be careful. Don't do anything gát."

"I can make no such promises. They don't call me gallant Galahad for nothing."

Fionna snorted. "No one calls ye *that*." A smile hinted at the corner of her lips. "Yer nickname is chipmunk."

"Then I have little to concern myself with other than gathering for the winter. Perhaps I can find an acorn here?" He pulled her into his arms, burying his nose into the crook of her neck, kissing the soft skin there. "Or here?" He nosed up to her ear as she squirmed in his arms.

"Galahad!" she gasped, shrieking in laughter.

Someone cleared their throat and they flew apart, Fionna's face going as red as a huckleberry in spring.

Vivien and Merlin stood nearby—Merlin amused and Vivien with a mischievous and oddly curious glint in her dark blue gaze.

"They are a spirited bunch," Vivien remarked.

"You have no idea, Lady," Merlin replied.

"Are we ready?" Arthur strode down the hall between them and then ushered them into his study. He seemed full of nervous energy as well.

"We are, Little Dragon King," Vivien said.

Galahad nodded, pushing his hair back from his face and straightening his tunic. Play time was over.

Fionna watched from the corner, her arms twisted before her. "Arthur . . ." she hurried forward and pulled him into an embrace. He buried his face in her hair, just as Galahad had done moments before. "Be careful," she whispered.

Galahad observed the feelings within him, studying them with careful scrutiny. There was a hint of jealousy there, but it was fading. His king was a good man who deserved Fionna's love. Arthur's affections for her were clearly genuine and ran deep. Just as his own did. In his own way, Galahad was . . . happy for Arthur and Fionna. Just as he was happy when he was with her. There was an unease there too. But that was understandable. Arthur had declared that Fionna would make her choice, which they would all respect, but kings weren't known for sharing. Would Arthur someday claim Fionna as his and his only?

He shook off the thought. His worries about Fionna would have to wait. He needed all his wits about him for where he and Arthur were heading.

Vivien stood before the fireplace, waving a hand, whispering words he couldn't hear, and no doubt would not understand, even if he could. The air before her appeared to shimmer, and smoke billowed from the nothingness before them, forming a sort of door.

"You have the key?" Merlin asked.

Arthur patted the pouch dangling from his belt. "We will be able to return. I am taking the adder stone too, just in case something is not as it seems."

"Wise. The door will only respond to you alone. When you're back through, Merlin has the means to banish the portal." Vivien cocked her head and grinned until her canines showed. "Good luck Little Dragon King. I hope you find what you seek."

"Thank you for your wisdom and aid, My Lady," Arthur said with an incline of his head. "Come Galahad. Let us plunge once more into the unknown."

Stepping through the door was like stepping into a dream. They exited into a dark forest glen illuminated by faerie light. Tall trees soared above them, blocking out the sky, if there even was one to see. What stars adorned the midnight tapestry of the Otherworld's sky? He knew not. Glowing purple fireflies winked in the air and lush flowers bloomed all around them, dripping nectar that glowed with magic.

"We stay together," Arthur said, stepping over one of the many vines that climbed around them like living things.

They followed the path of light as it joined with a tinkling river. A fish jumped in the water beside them, brilliant in shades of magenta and silver. Its brethren seemed to glow within the water, giving off more preternatural light.

"A beautiful place, that is for sure," Arthur said.

"When it comes to faeries—the more beautiful

they seem, the more dangerous they are," Galahad quietly commented.

"What a remarkable sentiment," a melodic female voice said. "Is the same true of mortal men?"

Arthur's and Galahad's hands flew to their sword hilts as a female emerged onto the path before them. She wore a draping dress of the deepest purple, and her hair, through light like Fionna's, was a shade of violet Galahad had never seen on any creature, human or fae. She was exquisitely beautiful, her face round and perfectly symmetrical, her figure generously proportioned. *Dangerous*, he reminded himself.

"I am King Arthur Pendragon and this is my sworn knight, Sir Galahad of Swansea. We seek the regent, Elathia," Arthur said, dropping his hands to his side.

"You have found her," Elathia said, a secret smile curving on her face. She stepped closer to Galahad, her bright violet eyes examining him from toe to nose. He stood his ground against the obvious attentions. Vivien had said the faerie enjoyed the company of mortals. That was why he was here. Bait. He tried to ignore the fact that it never ended well for the bait.

"Come. Let us speak," she purred.

They followed Elathia down the path to a clearing. Before them, a massive rock face rose up amongst the trees, the stone's surface encrusted with glowing crystals in a rainbow of hues. Rivulets of water, shimmering in a prism of light, dripped down the face, gathering in a sparkling pool that fed the river they had passed. It was an impressive backdrop to the throne of vines and branches that sat below on a gentle mound of grass and moss.

As Elathia settled herself onto the throne, white blossoms—bright with vibrant magic—burst open around her, silhouetting her form. Galahad swallowed thickly. This faerie was not one to trifle with. The casual display of such magic demonstrated that as much as Vivien's warnings.

Other faeries drifted into the clearing, females with dresses of mesmerizing fabrics, handsome males with swords at their sides. Goblins and hobgoblins, brownies, and red caps. Even a monstrous creature with grey mottled skin and tentacles for arms that Galahad couldn't even begin to identify. It was as if it had crawled out of a sea abyss or deep crevices of the earth—like a Fomorian. But he knew that was ridiculous. Fomorians were mortal enemies of the Túatha dé Danann. Such a creature wouldn't peacefully grace this court. Still, Galahad shifted uncomfortably as the fae-born crowd silently filled in the ranks around Elathia. There was no way they could fight all these faeries, if things turned ugly.

"What brings you here, mortals?" Elathia asked.

"My land is ailing under a curse. My people begin to die of starvation. They cannot drink from the streams," Arthur said. "We seek the Cauldron of Plenty to feed them. If you could just loan this relic to me for a time, I would return it to you when the business is done. You have my word."

Elathia laughed, a sweet sound. "The Cauldron is one of the four relics of the Túatha dé Danann. It is not 'loaned' out for use. Danu did not appoint me as regent over her kingdom to simply allow mortal kings to walk out with our most precious treasures."

Arthur ground his teeth. "Is there nothing I can say to change your mind? I am trustworthy. Appointed as king over all of Briton by the Lady of the Lake herself."

"Your mortal kingship means little here," Elathia scoffed.

"Perhaps a feat of strength, to prove my worth—"

"My answer is no," she snapped.

Arthur inclined his head stiffly. "I apologize for wasting your time. Thank you for your hospitality." He turned on his heel, motioning to Galahad. Arthur's shoulders were hunched. His king was clearly furious, but Galahad saw little that they could do. If the faerie wasn't inclined to help them—

Galahad's feet stuck in the ground, and he fell forward onto his knees.

Arthur spun around too. Excalibur pointed out straight behind him, as if pinned by thin air.

"I did not excuse you," Elathia's voice cracked like a whip, and then she stood, stalking across the grass toward them.

"What is the meaning of this?" Arthur asked, his voice low and hard. "We came here in good faith. We have not wronged you."

"But you have something that belongs to us . . ." Elathia said, halting at their side. She reached out and stroked the length of Excalibur's sheath with one graceful violet-hued fingernail. Then she stroked that same finger down Galahad's arm, tracing the ripples of his muscles. He held back a shiver. Her sharp nail felt more like a claw. ". . . And something we want."

"Explain yourself," Arthur barked, drawing himself up to his full height.

"You're free to go, Little Dragon King," she said with glee, "but the sword and the knight stay."

Chapter Twelve

Arthur

The heat of anger burst through Arthur like greedy flames through dry tinder. How dare this faerie think to hold them here against their wills. They had done nothing to earn her ire, save the misfortune of being born mortal. He turned to her, wanting nothing more than to lay Excalibur's sweet edge across her milky-white throat. To *make* her listen.

"Excalibur is *my* blade," he practically growled, "given to me by the Lady of the Lake, appointing me with the blessing of your sovereign, the goddess Danu. The sword stays with me. And as for my knight Galahad, he is a free man, belonging only to himself. But he has sworn himself into my service. He stays with me too."

Galahad crossed his arms over his chest.

Elathia grinned, licking the points of her fangs. "You do not seem so impressive to be crowned king over all Briton. Indeed, you cannot even defeat a simple holding spell. Perhaps Danu made a mistake."

"Perhaps we should ask her," Arthur countered.

"Alas, she has not been seen for many years." Elathia didn't even appear upset over this. Rather, a secret smile curved her face.

"I'm not leaving here without my sword and my fellow," Arthur insisted.

"Then it seems we are at an impasse," she snapped back, stepping forward, and draping one hand over Galahad's shoulder. The other reached up to lift a tendril of his golden hair, examining the strands with interest.

Galahad stiffened beneath her touch, his mouth fixed in a firm line.

"We shall have to find a way to while away the hours," she murmured, her eyes making a leisurely assessment of Galahad's form and profile. Then she giggled, a sound of malicious joy that seemed innate to all faeries. The one that always sent crawling fingers of ice up Arthur's spine. He pressed his resolve further.

"Your actions here go against the will of your goddess," Arthur said, trying to draw her attention away from Galahad. "They will not be without consequence."

Elathia scoffed, and the faeries who had gathered around laughed, a harsh and raucous sound. "If you are the darling of Danu, perhaps you should prove yourself so." She cocked her head and locked her predatory violet gaze onto him.

"What do you propose?" Arthur asked carefully.

"If you are sovereign-blessed as you say, then you should pull the sword from the Stone of Knowledge.

For surely, if the Sword of Light belongs to you, Excalibur will yield to your touch like an eager lover." She stepped close to Arthur now, running her finger along Excalibur's cross-guard. She smelled of berries and nightshade, of the lusciousness of death. "Prove your worth, Little Dragon King."

Galahad's deep blue eyes rounded with concern. "Your Majesty," he said, his voice low and careful, ripe with words unspoken. Arthur knew the thoughts racing through Galahad's mind, for they raged through his as well. Do not make a deal with faeries. It is a trick. They cannot be trusted. All of these cautions were true, but what better choice did he have? He and Galahad had no magic. They had only their convictions and the courage to face these mad creatures head on.

Arthur nodded. "If I allow you to drive Excalibur into this stone you speak of, and if I pull my blade back out, you will allow us to freely leave? With the sword?"

"I will allow you to leave with the sword." She smiled. "Your friend however—"

"I cannot abide by these terms," Arthur barked.

But Galahad held up a hand. "Free my feet, and I would offer my own wager, fair Elathia."

Arthur's eyes widened, but Elathia appeared intrigued. She waved her hand, and Galahad stepped forward.

"I do not find the company of a beautiful faerie to be distasteful," Galahad purred, taking her hand, and laying a soft kiss upon her long, delicate fingers. "To the contrary. Think of the pleasures we could enjoy together, if I were to stay of my own free will."

What the hell was Galahad doing? Arthur wanted to protest, to order him to silence, but the warning flash in Galahad's eye told him to stay steady. To trust him.

"Go on," Elathia said, her gleaming eyes fixed on Galahad.

"If Arthur pulls the sword from the stone, we leave with Excalibur *and* the Cauldron of Plenty." Her face darkened but Galahad pulled the female toward him, twisting her body so her back hit his broad chest. One of his arms snaked around her waist, the other splaying across her ribcage just below her breasts. He murmured into her ear, "If Arthur fails, then I stay behind of my own free will, and I will devote myself to your desires." He lay a soft kiss on the crook of her neck and her tongue flicked out, dampening her lips.

"An intriguing wager." Elathia pulled herself from Galahad's grasp and spun on her heel to face them both. She threw back her shoulders, haughtiness falling over her like a heavy rain. But the heaving of her bosom revealed the truth—she was affected by Galahad's seduction. Gods, Arthur himself had practically been moved by the display. Galahad was masterful.

"Your offer is one I accept," she said. To Arthur, she held out her hand and said, "The sword."

Arthur ground his teeth as he turned the jeweled hilt toward the faerie, offering her his beloved blade. Every fiber of his being shouted against the action, shouted at the wrongness. He was not supposed to be parted from the sword.

Elathia took Excalibur from him, a smirk on her face. "Follow me, mortals."

"What the hell was *that*," Arthur hissed as they joined the silent train of faeries who gathered in Elathia's wake.

"If you don't retrieve that sword from the stone, we're both stuck here," Galahad whispered back. "So, I figured I had better make it mean something when you do."

Arthur pressed his lips together. "A fool thing, to freely bind yourself to her. A brave thing, but a fool thing."

"Only if you don't pull the sword," Galahad countered. "And you'll pull the sword, right?"

"I had bloody better," Arthur muttered. Doubt reared its head, a monster dark and vicious. Vivien had granted him Excalibur, but so much had gone wrong since then. Morgana, the curses, a stolen Excalibur, now an invasion from Ireland. What if Danu was rethinking her blessing? What if all he had proven in the last years of his kingship was that he wasn't worthy?

"Watch for tricks," Galahad said. "With faeries, things are never as they seem."

Arthur nodded, swallowing back his nerves. He was either worthy or he wasn't. Today he would find out the truth, whether he was ready for the answer or not.

They climbed a harrowing path up the rock face to the left of the waterfall, following Elathia and the others. When they summited the craggy steps, they found themselves in a grotto aside a crystalline pool.

Tall trees bowed around the clearing, their leaves the blues and greens of gemstones, glittering with dew. A white owl swept across the space of the lake, alighting on another tree branch. The bird, known as the bride of death, drew Arthur's eye for a moment, but his gaze and his thoughts—his very future—quickly came to rest on the boulder perched in the center of the lake. Glowing toadstools floated along the surface of the lake in a path leading to the stone—a path Elathia now walked, graceful as a queen. She took the two steps up to the top of the boulder, and then, with a movement of her lips, raised Excalibur and plunged the tip into the granite below. The sword's blade was buried halfway to the hilt, its red ruby pommel winking at him in the low light.

Elathia turned, her eyes bright with delight. "Come Little Dragon King, show us what you are made of."

Galahad squeezed Arthur's arm as Arthur pushed forward, past the prying faerie eyes. Arthur kept his gaze straight forward, his features impassive. He could do this. Claim his birthright. His kingship. The honor was his already. The familiar weight of Excalibur had hung at his hip for years. This sacred blade belonged to him, and he belonged to it.

Arthur balanced across the strange toadstools and took a step onto the boulder. The stone shivered beneath him, and then a deep voice called out, "Whoso pulleth out this sword from this stone shall be king born of all Briton." Arthur's heart raced in his chest at the words. He looked back at Elathia—had the stone's magic been her doing? He could not be certain. She clutched her hands before her chest, a smile on her face as though she were giddy about the day's turn of events.

Anger roared within Arthur once again. It was time to end this. He took a steadying breath and reached for the sword. And—his hands passed right through the pommel.

He lurched forward as the unexpected absence of the sword unbalanced him. He caught himself on the rough rock, sweeping his hand at Excalibur's hilt. His fingers passed straight through the pommel again, as if the sword were a ghost.

"Uh oh, looks like the sword is playing hide and seek," Elathia crooned behind him, giggling. Her faerie court laughed, the sound mocking and harsh to his ears.

He looked back at Galahad and noted how his knight's face had drained of blood. His stomach churning, Arthur turned back to the sword, his anger shifting to fear. A faerie trick. Why had he expected Elathia to fight fair? How could he pull the sword out, if he couldn't even touch it?

Arthur's mind raced for a solution, even as another part of him spun horrible scenarios out like cloth from a loom. Him and Galahad, stuck here indefinitely. Caerleon—a sick and blackened land. Fionna, Lancelot, and Percival, speared on Uí Tuírtri blades. No, gods, this future could not be. But what could he do, when he couldn't even see what was real?

A thought blazed bright and clear through him, and he plunged his hand into his pocket. His fingers closed around the adder stone, Percival's bloody magic rock. Instantly, the scene before him transformed. Excalibur's hilt stuck out from the stone, but a foot behind where he had been reaching. She had cast a simple glamor over the stone, making it look as if she had plunged Excalibur into the stone somewhere else.

Arthur smiled grimly as he reached out and seized the real sword's hilt. And began to pull.

Chapter Thirteen

Percival

A knock echoed against Percival's chamber door, and he flew across the wooden floor. He paused for a moment with his hand on the iron ring handle, taking a deep breath to steady himself. He pulled the door open, schooling his face into what he hoped was an expression of suave nonchalance. "Come in, lass."

Fionna strode into the room like she owned the place, spinning on her heel to face him. When she saw him, a burst of laughter escaped her rosy lips. "What are ye wearing?"

Percival looked down at himself, at the black tunic and dark breeches he had donned. "What? Are we not infiltrating an enemy camp? I wanted to look the part."

She crossed her arms before her. "Ye know it's near high noon. Don't you think someone might get a wee bit suspicious if you walk out into the sunshine like yer off to the god of the Underworld's own funeral? Change."

Percival's cheeks heated, but he covered his embarrassment with a grin. "Lass, if ye wanted to get me naked, there was no need to come up with such a contrivance. Ye need only ask, ye ken?"

Now it was her turn to flush. "We don't know how long Arthur and Galahad will be gone." She strode to the window, turning her back to provide him privacy. "We must be quick."

"Understood," Percival said, unbuckling his sword belt and pulling off his tunic. He grabbed another from the chest at the end of his bed, one boasting a deep green hue, and then pulled the garment over his head. He caught Fionna's silver eyes, peering over her shoulder, before she whipped her gaze back toward the window. He hardened at the reality of her—here in his room. "Why dove," he crossed to stand beside her, brushing a few of her braids over her shoulder. "Did I catch ye peeking?"

"I don't know what yer talking about," she said, though her neck arched as if she appreciated the soft brush of his fingers on her neck. "My eyes are firmly affixed on our task. We must find the enemy camp and acquaint ourselves with its layout."

"So, we can rescue yer father," Percival finished.

She nodded, her lush lips set in a thin line of determination.

"Fionna, ye know what we attempt is likely a dangerous folly that could get one or both of us killed. If the others discovered our—"

"Which is why they won't," Fionna said. "Not until we return with my father safely in hand. And the answers he holds. I know what Arthur would say

. . . Lancelot . . . it's why I only trust ye with this."

"I will do everything in my power to prove that trust is not misplaced." He nodded. "Lead the way, My Lady."

Their clandestine mission painted the palace in a new light. Every servant they passed made his heart leap into his chest, as if they could see his very thoughts, discern his secret purpose. "I feel as if I might jump out of my own skin at the slightest surprise," Percival murmured. "Is this what it was like for ye those first days, when ye were set upon your mission to take Excalibur?"

"This, and a thousand times worse," she replied. "I only hope that I see the chance to drive my sword through O'Lynn's gut before this is all done."

"Och, I hope ye get that chance too," Percival said, as they crossed the open space to the stable. And caught sight of Lancelot coming toward them. "Dark and stormy, headed our way," Percival murmured.

"Curses," Fionna muttered, though she arranged her features in greeting.

Something had shifted in Lancelot, and though the change was subtle, Percival knew his sword-brother's moods and mannerisms well enough to recognize the difference. The tense shadow that had draped over him since Morgana had lifted. Once again, his eyes were bright and sharp, his chiseled profile held high. He wore a tunic as blue as the sky, the neckline unlaced to reveal the lean muscle there, the pattern of ink across his skin that longed to be traced by gentle fingertips. And skies above, he wanted to explore those dark swirls and patterns. Percival swallowed and brought his mind back to the present. Lancelot was a cursed man no more. Arthur's proud second-in-command had returned to them, and just in time.

"You look as if you're heading somewhere." Lancelot stopped before them, his keen eyes locked onto Fionna. "Out of the keep?"

Percival looked to Fionna, for the lie that would roll smoothly off her tongue. But she seemed at a loss for words. "We—" she managed, clearing her throat.

Percival jumped in, his mind whirring. "Fionna wanted to take Zephyr for a short ride. To . . . test her leg. I thought to accompany her. We're, um, going to inspect the wall, to ensure there are no areas ripe for a breach."

Lancelot's gaze flit back and forth between them. "Wise idea," he finally said, slowly drawing out the words. "We haven't inspected the wall yet. Be careful though. Reports put O'Lynn's men on our southern shore, perhaps less than an hour's ride. There could be scouts."

"We'll be watchful," Fionna said, a grim smile on her lips.

"See me when you return," Lancelot said. "Some of the men who have come in from the villages are willing to fight. I could use your aid in outfitting them as well as putting them through a few rounds of basic training."

"Of course," Percival said brightly, pulling Fionna past. "We're at yer disposal."

Lancelot arched an eyebrow but let them pass.

"Och dove, I thought ye were a better liar than

that," Percival whispered.

She shook her head wearily. "I've had enough lies for a lifetime. I think they're all spent."

"Ye'll have little need of them when this is all done."

"I hope yer right."

Percival and Fionna rode through the blighted countryside in silence, tense and alert. Lancelot's warning was fair. Caerleon wasn't safe anymore. There could be enemies at any turn. As they rode closer to the gray waters of the Severn Sea, Percival felt as if a hand seized his chest, squeezing tighter with each step. Surely, they were upon the invaders by now.

Fionna reigned in Zephyr, looking ahead with a peculiar expression. A grassy hill topped with a thicket of trees arose to the left, and the road curved around the slope, disappearing into the distance. She nodded up to the left. "We should have a good vantage point from up there. Let us get off the road and see if we can spot the enemy."

Percival wasted no time directing Kit with his knees to head up the hill. "I feel something," Percival said. "Perhaps it's my imagination, but it's . . . cloying. Almost a strange thickness in the air too."

Fionna nodded. "I feel it too. It feels like—"

"Magic," they said together, sharing a disquieted look.

They trekked around the shadowed-side of the hill, to avoid being spotted. Once arriving at the hill's backside, they walked into overgrown trees and across a blanket of thick ferns and mossy ground. A scattering of trees showed blackened signs of the curse's blight, but mostly they were surrounded by greenery.

"Let's dismount and leave the horses here," Fionna said. "I don't want a stray whinny alerting anyone to our position. The horses should be well-hidden."

Percival nodded and dismounted. They tied their horses to a tree and crept toward the front edge of the hill. Toward a view he had hoped never to see on Caerleon's fair lands. An invading army.

From the shadow of the canopy, the O'Lynn camp was stretched out before them. Hundreds of tents hugged the circumference of a small port town, one that looked overtaken by the enemy. Flags of blue and yellow with a snarling wolf fluttered in the breeze.

Fionna growled beside him, as though she were ready to surge down the hill, sword bared.

"Patience, dove. We must be smart about this. Now, do ye have any idea where yer father might be held?" Looking down below, their task suddenly seemed even more of a fool's errand. To bumble about amongst thousands of hostile warriors, searching for one man . . .

"O'Lynn is a warrior," Fionna said. "But he likes his comfort. He has injuries that pain him. He will have taken up residence in the grandest home in the village."

"The inn then," Percival said, gesturing at a three-story timbered building perched below. "Full larder, warm fire, comfy beds."

"He would keep his prisoners close by. Would a town like this have a gaol?"

Percival shook his head. "Nae. Only the stocks here."

"Then, he would keep him somewhere easily closed off. Out of the way."

Percival wracked his brain. "Like a cellar?"

Fionna's eyes lit up. "Would there be a cellar beneath the inn?"

"Aye."

"The cellar beneath the inn, then. That's where we'll find my father."

It seemed a thin thread indeed to stake their lives on. "Fionna—" he began.

"Let's head back to the horses," she said, striding into the trees.

He followed. "I know he's yer father . . . but if we defeat O'Lynn, we'll free him soon enough. Perhaps we should wait."

"Ye heard what Vivien shared. My father may be the only one with answers about my mother. Whether . . ." she trailed off.

"Whether ye are borne of a goddess," Percival finished.

She gave a curt nod. "If I truly have some power, then we may need my magic to defeat O'Lynn and Morgana. We can't wait."

"I ken, lass. But to walk into the middle of an enemy camp—" Zephyr and Kit whickered in greeting as they emerged back into the clearing where they had left them.

Fionna rounded on him, her face a twist of emotions. "I shouldn't have asked this of ye, Percy. I took advantage of yer feelings for me, for I knew ye wouldn't say no. But I can't ask ye to risk yerself. Ye should go back to Caerleon. I'll do this alone."

Percival stepped in closer, taking her face gently between his hands. "If ye think that the only reason I'm here is because ye tricked me, then ye ken me less than I thought. And if ye think I could leave ye here to go in alone . . . well, then ye don't ken me at all."

She tried to look down, but he held her face gently, tilting her chin back so she was forced to meet his eyes. "I am here, dove, because yer cause is just, *and* because I love ye. Ye don't have to carry these burdens alone anymore. I will help ye find the truth of yer past, just as ye helped me find mine."

Her chin quivered as she pressed her lips together. She closed her eyes, her white eyelashes brushing her soft cheeks. "I don't know how to thank ye," Fionna eventually said. And then her eyes snapped opened, and a different light glowed in them—a gleam he had seen only once before. "That's not true. I do know how to thank ye."

Then she surged against him and pressed her lips to his. A crow startled into flight from a branch above them—the last thing he saw before losing himself completely to her kiss.

Interlude

Morgana

The crow glided over the forest surrounding Caerleon, wings aloft with giddiness over finding a male and female who belonged to the Little Dragon King. Alone.

Just over the crest of maples, birch, and evergreens, an encampment came into view. Hide tents surrounded a small village. Smoke curled from thatched, lime-washed homes as well as from the inn and several fire circles dotting the premises. In the distance, longboats moored up the banks of the River Usk and against Caerleon's coastline along the Severin Sea.

Landing between a cluster of ferns and a moss-draped tree, the crow called upon the shadows of the forest and the blood-thirsty prayers of the nearby warmongers. Leaves and fallen lichen swirled around her until her female form materialized beneath a canopy of sun-dappled green maples. She then eased from the forest's edge and into the encampment. Dirt and sea grimed warriors—men and women both—stopped what they were doing to watch her swaying body walk past. Her skin fairly glowed in the pale sunlight, her face and clothing unblemished from travel or camp set-up.

The guard before O'Lynn's tent moved to block Morgana, but only for half a heartbeat. Bowing his head, he stepped aside and allowed her to enter. Incense wafted to her nose as she stepped through the flaps and into the lantern lit space. In the corner, the older man glanced up from where he sliced an apple from a crudely made corner table beside his cot. A cot occupied by the Allán waif, Aideen. Dark circles bruised her seasick gaze and Morgana smiled.

"Feeding your pet?" she asked O'Lynn.

"She must earn her food," he muttered under his breath as he went back to slicing a chunk of apple. "So far, the lass continues to displease me."

"Poor man," Morgana cooed. "I bear news that will surely please you."

At that, he looked up and arched an eyebrow. "Do ye now?"

"The witch is just over the hill with that Fisher whelp."

The younger woman gasped before she whispered, "Fionnabhair . . ."

"Yes," Morgana hissed, drawing out the sound. "Your sister is in the woods with a young lover. Did you honestly believe she would come and rescue you?" Morgana laughed low in her throat. "Poor lamb. Your hope is a foolish waste of the energy you barely can spare. Especially as your name is not the one leaving your sister's mouth in a breathless gasp right now."

O'Lynn pushed from his chair, throwing Aideen a glare, before marching to the tent's opening. When alone, Morgan sat on the edge of the cot and tilted her head. "He is a beautiful lad, the Fisher King. Copper hair, dark earthen eyes framed by long lashes, a boyish smile, and a fine, muscular body. Just two years older than you, I believe. And he loves her. The stench of his pheromones perfumed the trees and moss." Aideen turned her head toward the tent's wall, blinking back the forming tears. "And she fancies herself in love with him too. All of them. Including the abomination of a king, Arthur Pendragon. All this emotion, all this falling in love while you waste away beneath the hateful hand of your husband."

"Lies," Aideen spat. "All ye speak are lies."

"Then why do you cry?" Morgana arched to a stand, satisfied with the girl's roiling pulse and seething breaths.

O'Lynn stomped into the tent with a handsome man at his side. "This is Níall, one of my finest warriors. He'll take one of my fiercest fianna to kill her."

Morgana flashed a delighted glance at Aideen's teeth-bared expression as the girl strained against her chains in fury, and then she gracefully slinked toward Níall, examining the warrior. "The witch is a capable warrior," she said to O'Lynn. "Sending a fiann crashing through the forest will only serve to alert her and send her scampering back into the safety of Caerleon's keep. He should go alone. Or perhaps with one other." To the warrior, she said, "Come upon her quickly and with stealth, while she is otherwise engaged. This is how you shall end her.”

"Very well," O'Lynn said grudgingly. His obedience training was coming along nicely. "Tell him exactly where ye last saw the witch and he'll run her through and then dump her carcass before King Arthur's gates."

"Follow the crow, she will guide you."Arthur stifled another sigh. "I hadn't realized my thoughts were so plain."

Chapter Fourteen

Fionna

Sunshine poured into my body as Percival tugged me closer, deepening his kiss. His warmth permeated every part of me with a bubbling urge to frolic and tease and laugh. But instead, my body yielded completely to the dancing rhythm of his lips and the gentle hands that roamed my back.

Until he lost his balance and jerked out of our embrace.

I yelped as he fell into a bush only to laugh a heartbeat later when Kit nodded his head up and down before nickering his displeasure. Percival's horse nudged him through the leafy boughs with his nose, stamping an impatient hoof.

"Aye, I see ye. Dinna fash yerself." Percival brushed dead leaves and twigs from his breeches and hair as he climbed out of the underbrush. Kit nickered again, and Percival rolled his eyes. "Ye know ye're the only one for me." Percival blocked Kit's view with a hand and then winked at me. I bit my bottom lip to stifle my snicker. "Here," he cooed and offered up an apple from his saddle bag. Kit lipped the apple, then wuffed at Percival's cheek, before taking the apple from his hand, turning his attention to his treat.

"The stallion fancies ye," I taunted in a sing-song voice. "A jealous male, if ever I saw one."

"A wee too leggy for my taste." Percival flashed me a cheeky grin. "Smothering hen too. A lad needs his freedom."

"Leggy?" I pretended to be outraged. "With such criticisms, I wonder what ye must think of me."

Percival stepped close—a good head taller than me, no less—and narrowed his eyes as he slowly inspected my legs, arms, torso, and face. "Open yer mouth and show me yer teeth." Not expecting this request, my mouth parted in shock and Percival's lips twitched. "A little wider. Cannae see the back."

Realizing my mouth was agape, I clamped my jaw shut and then smacked him across the upper arm. "Ye brute!" His laughter filled the woods around us and my heart soared at the rascally sound. Still, I placed fisted hands on my hips and glared at him. But he laughed only more. So, I picked up a handful of leaves from the forest floor and threw them at his face.

A leaf fluttered directly into his mouth, to my wicked delight. He sputtered, spitting brittle pieces out while batting at the others hitting his face, hair, and chest.

Now I laughed. "Yer lucky I didn't knock ye back onto yer sorry arse."

"Och, ye'll pay for this, dove," he declared, then pounced at me.

I spun away with a shriek, but not fast enough. He grabbed my arm and pulled me to him until his mouth collided with mine in a triumphant kiss. Gods, his lips. They were Otherworldly and full of impish magic. But I couldn't give into his attempts at distraction, even if his very touch was bliss. Which encouraged an idea. A plan that would be too easy, for I knew he felt the same as me. And, as expected, he deepened his luscious kiss and melted against my body, just enough that I could place my leg between his and then kick his heel out from underneath him. Percival's arms flew out in surprise, a waterfall of leaves splashing into the air as he landed with a satisfying *thwump*.

And then I ran.

I charged into the forest, ripping through ferns and undergrowth, unable to contain my glee. But I didn't get far. Percival hooked me around the waist and yanked me to a stop. An embarrassingly girlish squeal escaped me as we tumbled to the ground in a fit of laughter, his body settling atop mine.

Silken, copper strands curtained around my face as our mirth faded into soft smiles. His dark brown eyes crinkling with affection. My fingertips tracing along his jaw and then across his bottom lip. My chest heaved for breath and I wanted to moan with the arousing feel of my hardened nipples brushing against my chestplate. Memories of his stomach muscles, limned in candlelight, and the way he stroked himself as Galahad pleasured me teased my growing need.

Part of me knew this was foolish to give in to our carnal urges at this moment—that we were exposed here, so close to our enemy's camp. But the wood was thick and gnarled, and I felt safe here, with the tall trees standing sentinel over us. We had seen no signs of Uí Tuírtri scouts coming this way while we watched the camp. And we had hours left until dark. I could think of no better way to pass the time.

So, I tucked strands of chin-length hair behind his ear, then kissed him. Long. Slow. Every sensation languorous and yearning.

Pulling away, he caught his breath and whispered, "I ache for ye."

"Make me yers," I whispered back.

A crooked smile flitted across his lips. "Why did we wear so much armor?"

"Protection against me, of course."

"Aye, ye weaken me senseless."

"Let's remedy that."

"My weakness for ye?"

"No," I said with a roll of my eyes. "The armor."

From my position beneath him, I began unfastening his leather chest piece. Then I unlaced the bracers tightened at each wrist. I ran my fingers along his well-sculpted arm—an archer's forearm—calling back images of him on horseback while shooting from his longbow, his burnished hair tossed about in the wind. Heat kindled in my belly at the feel of his hardened body. Slowly, I moved up his abdomen and pectorals to his collarbone, where I unclasped the leather armor around his neck.

I would be his first, the one to awaken his body to a form of pleasure unlike any other. A part of me wanted to roll him over to gain control. To ride him until his every muscle tensed and shuddered with release. Until he moaned and clawed at the dirt and painted my bare skin with the earth stained on his fingertips. But this moment was his to control, his to navigate and discover. And mine to enjoy. For he chose me, and I would not disappoint the man who gifted me with his laughter and his heart.

His innocence.

He smiled sweetly, dipping down for a kiss. "I've waited my whole life for ye. I would search for the Grail and fight monsters all over again, just to prove myself worthy of yer love."

"Percy . . ." My heart clenched at his confession. "Ye have always been worthy of my love. There is naught to earn, ye silly goose."

"Sure, but I'm not made of tree trunks like Galahad or an experienced lover like Lancelot or as dreamy as Arthur."

"Dreamy?"

He quietly laughed. "Ye think he is, admit it."

"Sir Percival of Caer Benic, Fisher King and Grail Prince, the only matter I'll discuss right now is how much I fancy ye." I tried to hold a straight face, my voice even as I added, "Which is unmeasurably more than Kit."

"I dunno," he replied, a silly grin in place. "We have history."

"Kit has good taste in men. For a horse."

"He doesn't like to share my attentions."

I arched an eyebrow and flirtatiously whispered, "I would share ye. Perhaps, next time, I'll roll on the forest floor with ye and Lancelot together."

Percival shivered, his eyes shuttering for a wild heartbeat as his hand traveled southward to the bulge pressing against the laces of his breeches. "Och, I might end before we begin, if ye keep up this talk."

"Then no more talk."

I placed my hand over his, massaging his cock by moving his fingers over his own body. He moaned, increasing the friction. With my other hand, I cupped his hip and dragged him back and forth against my sex, pressing his hardening length to our joined hands. Long copper lashes brushed along his cheeks as more soft moans escaped his mouth. Unable to take my eyes off every flutter of pleasure coloring his face, I slipped my fingers beneath his and then gently stroked up and down his throbbing cock. His eyes snapped open, his breath hitching. This was the first time someone had touched him in this way. And I wanted nothing but the feel of skin and sweat and pleasure-laden breaths between us.

But I was still in armor.

Removing my hand, I began unfastening my chestplate. At first, he frowned until he saw what I was doing and then he began to help. In a matter of minutes, we had both undressed, reveling in the feel of each other's nakedness.

I sighed and sank into the feathery moss as Percival explored the curves of my breasts. Goddess save me, his lips—full, soft, and playful. Made for kissing. My pulse trilled when his mouth met mine once more, his kiss gently reverent yet gloriously fevered.

I had never longed for a man like him before, one who was as seductive as he was boyishly innocent. But he had captivated me from first sight, his masculine beauty the kind that made maidens jealous and men take notice. And men did, often. I had caught Lancelot shooting dark, possessive glares at several interested men during our travels. Percival, as usual, was unaware of his own bewitching attractiveness, or how his magnetism drew people to him. His guileless affect only added to his allure.

Arthur, Galahad, and Lancelot were intense lovers—emotional and serious, always. Intimacy was more a race to release the building energy between our attraction. But, with Percival, my body felt young and untouched. As though this was also my first time with a man. Every breath, every caress, every soft, enthralling sound of pleasure, was filled with wonder and beauty, as if I were falling in love with him all over again. And again. Losing myself to an endless cycle of discovery and reverie.

My heart halted a beat.

I loved Percival. *Loved* him, truly, and had for a long time, I realized. From the beginning, he has been my champion and my haven. I could talk to him about anything and he always provided the words and humor and acceptance I needed to remain strong. Nor has he ever felt intimidated by my sex or my battle prowess, unlike the other men. Rather, he was almost always the first to offer his support and forgiveness.

A sob tightened my throat as joy warmed my

chest. What did I ever do to deserve such a man? Tears threatened to spill, but I pushed them back by smiling into our kiss.

"What, lass?" he asked, smiling back, caressing my cheek.

"Ye make me so happy," I whispered. "I love ye, Percy."

He kissed me sweetly. "I love ye too. Until my dying breath." His words bolstered me, filling me with tangible relief. The necklace was gone, but Percival's love remained. His love, too—like Lancelot's—had been true.

I gripped his hip tighter, lifting my thighs off the ground to deepen the sensations from our rocking rhythm. His head fell back with a rumbling moan. I could watch him savor every delicious sensation forever. And I longed to memorize the aroused, soft look of him when his body joined mine.

Releasing his hip, my hand tugged on his cock, my palm sliding up and down his velvety shaft. Skies, he was long. And hard. His Adam's apple bobbed and a hot, heaving breath rushed from his body. The muscles across his chest and shoulders rippled and his stomach flexed. The heat of anticipation curled through me as I guided him to my opening.

Percival pushed in slowly, gasping for breath. Pleasure tensed every muscle in his face, a rosy hue warming his neck and cheeks. With mouth parted, lips swollen, and every muscle tight with need, his hips began to move. Unsure at first, but then he found a rhythm and I moaned with the wondrous feel of him.

"Gods," he breathed.

His eyes pinched shut as he thrust harder, his hips rolling in the most erotic grinding motion I had ever felt. A move that liquified the blazing heat in my core. I felt as though magic swirled in my veins each time we joined. The feeling was so incredibly intense, I sank my fingers into the loamy soil beneath my body just to ground myself. The landscape of muscles across his blushed body tensed into defined lines as his shaft slid in and out, the soft skin and fiery curls of his pelvis rubbing along my clit with each smooth, sensual pumping motion.

The earth cradled my floating body. Vibrations tingled across the skin pressed into the moss, ferns, and leaves. Percival increased his rocking motions, the thighs touching mine flexing with each thrusting arc of his narrow hips. I explored the undulating ribbed muscles of his stomach as he ground into me—deep, hard—his balls slapping my sensitive skin, my swollen clit groaning with each caress. I grabbed his arse with both hands and dragged him harder across my pelvis until a lance of pleasure arrested the wild beat of my heart. I felt myself shattering into a million scintillating beams of light. I wanted to keep shattering until I was nothing but glittering ash.

Tilting my hips and spreading my legs wider, my fingernails digging into his soft flesh, I pulled him tight to me and held him there. I became rippling, spasming sensation. My core tightened around the length of him until his thick, hard body ignited my every nerve ending.

The ground began to gently tremor. I cried out

as a soft rush of energy surged through me, my body becoming all the elements, the moon and stars, and the sun's golden fire.

"Oh gods," he moaned loudly. "Oh gods, oh gods . . ." His body stiffened despite the desperate, crazed rhythm of his pounding hips. Goddess, the way he moved. He was sensual grace and erotic bliss. His frenzied moans faded into breathy grunts until he cried out, "Fuck!" Followed by, "Foos yer doos!"

I almost orgasmed again, watching him peak. He was mesmerizing.

Wait.

I stilled, my brows furrowing as I pushed up on my elbows. "Foos yer doos?"

His eyes opened on an embarrassed smile, his cheeks reddening. "Uh, aye," he said, nodding his head comically, as though his awkward slip was intentional. "It means, 'how are yer pigeons.' In Doric, that is. It's the Gaelic language we speak where I'm from. Our way of asking, 'how are ye?'"

I stared at him for one more confused heartbeat before falling back to the moss in a fit of laughter. "My pigeons are cooing at present. Ye've made them quite happy." I laughed again, unable to help myself. "Foos yer doos?"

A silly, lopsided grin stretched across his handsome face. "Aye, peck'n away, peck'n away." Then he rolled his hips once more, before flashing another cheeky grin.

"Kiss me, ye fool man."

"Anything ye want, dove."

His lips returned to mine, both of us trying to

hold back our sputtering laughter.

And then I heard a human sound nearby. A throat cleared, and I stilled. "Don't move," a man with a gravelly voice said in Gaelic—Irish Gaelic.

Chapter Fifteen

Fionna

Percival's head snapped up from where he was kissing my breasts. His eyes rounded as the tip of the man's blade came to rest just below Percival's Adam's apple.

My eyes darted to-and-fro, surveying the scene quickly. The man with the gravelly voice was as tall as Percival, and well-muscled, with dark brown hair braided down his back. Though he wore a thick beard, he was young. Younger than I. And quite convinced of his superiority, his immortality. He would be impetuous. Stupid and cocky. Another warrior circled us too, perhaps ten years older than me.

I grabbed the edge of my cloak and pulled the wool over my naked form as best as I could, not wishing to give these men—these Uí Tuírtri warriors—any more sight of me than they had already enjoyed. Which appeared, from the one man's lewd grin, and the other's quiet intensity, was everything.

"Enjoying the afternoon, were ye?" the other said. His voice was as low and quiet as his placid features, but his tone held a hint of mockery. Fairer than his companion, twisting tattoos ran up arms that were lean with muscle and sinew. His dark brown leather armor was well-cared and oiled, but the nicks showed how he had seen many battles. Bright blue eyes examined each of us, picking us apart piece by piece. Goosebumps rose on my skin as he watched me. A hunter, catching the scent of prey. Here was the more dangerous man of the two.

Our weapons were beyond arm's reach, buried beneath the hastily discarded pile of our clothes and armor. I could get to my sword, but not before the man speared Percival through. What idiots we had been, utter and complete fools! To get so wrapped up in each other when Uí Tuírtri camped mere leagues away. I wanted to rail at the tall trees—at the forest creatures—for not warning us. But I knew it was no one's fault but my own.

"My lady and I were enjoying a private retreat in the country," Percival said, his voice managing to sound imperious, regal. Like a king.

I wanted to cringe, to tell him that nobility would only get him speared more quickly here. Better to be common, low born. Beneath notice. Though, without clothes on, we were unrecognizable—perhaps the only blessing of being found naked by enemy soldiers. I prayed this small silver lining at least bought us a few moments before they spotted my Dál nAraidi armor and the birch tree ogham rune of clann Allán etched into my sword's hilt.

"Methinks your fair lady is in need of more of a man than ye." The younger man stepped closer, trailing his blade's edge to rest on the side of Percival's throat while gazing at me.

My hand itched for my sword, for my knives. To crush this man who looked at a woman and saw only a thing to have. To take.

"We have no quarrel with ye," Percival replied in Gaelic, his brown eyes flashing angrily. "But I will not allow ye to mistreat my lady in word or deed."

Gravelly-voice laughed, a cruel, mocking sound. "Hear that Níall? He won't *let us*."

Percival stiffened at the taunt, and then the other man—Níall—spoke. His words were soft as he stepped forward. "Haven't ye heard? The Uí Tuírtri rule these lands now. Not yer bastard-born king. And we take what we want." His gaze flicked back to me.

Percival growled, his muscled form tense, as if ready to spring.

"Don't feel left out," gravelly-voice said, looking over his shoulder at Níall with a smirk. "Ye're pretty enough. We have some lads back at camp who would love a turn with ye."

The moment the warrior looked away, Percival surged forward. He knocked the warrior's sword aside, barreling into his chest like a storied Greek wrestler.

I scrambled for my blade, the protection of my cloak forgotten. I seized my sword belt and whirled, only to see Níall club Percival over the back of his head with the hilt of his sword.

Percival crumpled in on himself, his strong form now limp.

A sharp gasp escaped from my lips as the younger warrior shoved Percival off him with a roar while jumping back onto his feet. Spitting on the ground beside Percival's body, he pulled his sword from its sheath. And coiled back, preparing to stab Percival through.

"Wait," Níall barked, putting a hand out. The gravelly-voiced warrior lowered his sword slightly, waiting for his superior's instructions.

Níall's eyes were fixed upon me. Upon the sword belt in my hand. Upon my naked form. My skin crawled beneath his assessment, and my rage burned brighter within me.

"Drop the sword belt, princess," Níall cooed. "Ye don't want to hurt yerself." The word buffeted me like a gusting, biting wind. Did this man know who I was? Or was princess merely a term he used to ridicule? Indecision wracked me. I wished for nothing more than the chance to spear these men through. But Percival was unconscious. At their mercy. It would only take one vicious thrust and my sweet Percival would be torn from this world forever. I would endure whatever I must in order to save him.

"Drop yer blade and I will spare him," Níall said, and the decision was made for me, even though I didn't know if I could trust his word. I could only pray that they were too intent upon their sport of claiming me to dispatch him.

I let the leather slip from my clammy fingers. And I kept my face slack, letting him see what he wanted to see. The poor, helpless maiden, ripe for the plucking. Let him be blind to the truth. That even without a blade, I was not helpless.

"Watch him," Níall said, striding toward me. He crossed the distance between us in three strides and then loomed over me. Even knowing myself, knowing my skill, I was momentarily struck still with a sense of vulnerability I had never felt before—being bared before my enemy. My pulse pounded in my ears, drowning out the other clannsman's words, most likely complaints of having to go second.

My hands crept up on their own accord to cover my nakedness, a gesture which only made Níall grin. "Ye are a rare beauty, lass," he said, his eyes glittering. "I shall enjoy ye until my balls are empty. And then again as payment for all my men who were cut down by clann Allán."

When his last word finished, he gripped me, leaving me no time to process his comment. Or that he knew who I was. His hand fisted in my hair, yanking me back down to the earth where Percival and I had just shared the most beautiful gesture of love. Pain bit into my scalp, into my skin where the weight of the warrior settled upon me. The sharp buckles of his armor dug scratches into my body. But I ignored it all: the foul stench of sour ale on his breath, the sea's grime still on his skin, the vile feeling of his rough hands pawing at me. For I was focused on the one point where I knew I would find my salvation.

There was one thing clann Uí Tuírtri and Allán shared, and that was the design of our armor. And the sheaths for our knives. My hand reached around the man as he struggled to unlace his breeches, far too intent upon his task to pay attention to the creature he was about to violate. And so, he moved far too slow to stop me as I grabbed the knife sheathed at his hip, the one I plunged directly into his spine.

He stiffened atop me and, with a scream, I shoved at his bulk, jerking the bloodied knife out with the movement. But he was a hardened Dál nAraidi warrior, and such men don't die easily.

He lunged at me. One large hand closed around my throat while the other clamped around the wrist that held his knife, arresting my movement before I was able to stab the sharp point into his eye.

We grappled, but he was strong. I wheezed in air, struggling to draw breath. Then the hand around my windpipe squeezed even harder. His other hand gripped my wrist until I thought the delicate bones might snap from the pressure. I let out a garbled scream of frustration as the knife dropped from my numb fingers.

"Ye bitch," the other warrior was screaming now.

He thundered toward me, his sword blade gleaming. I tried to wrench my body to the side, but I was unable to move much. The older warrior held me fast and sure. *Oh goddess.* The darkness of unconsciousness began to claim me. I wasn't going to be able to fight my way out of this situation. And, this time, there was no pregnant pause giving me a chance to consider my life, my choices. Or the men I loved who I would leave behind. There was only one quicksilver realization—I was going to die.

But . . . I didn't feel the sword pierce me through. Not when I expected it. Instead, the sound of blades clashing met my ears. My attacker—distracted by whatever new challenge had presented itself and weakened from my inflicted wound—loosened his grip on me. In a vicious blow, I twisted my arm up and brought my elbow down onto the forearm holding my throat. His grip on my burning throat broke. I gasped large breaths of precious air, trying not to grimace with pain.

Without wasting another beat of my still-living heart, I lunged toward my sword. My hand closed around its hilt, the supple leather in my palm as welcome a feeling as I had ever known. I pulled my blade from its hilt and, with a smooth, powerful arc, severed Níall's head from his shoulders.

Instinct had my sword up before me and my body crouched in a defensive position, even as my mind tried to catch up with what had happened. My eyes locked onto the younger Uí Tuírtri warrior, now slumping to the ground. Dead.

And then I focused on the blessed vision of Lancelot standing behind him, sweat dripping down his face, bloody sword in hand.

Chapter Sixteen

Lancelot

Lancelot's chest heaved as he surveyed the scene before him—his mind barely able to comprehend the horror. How close he had come to losing Fionna. Percival.

"Percival," Fionna cried out, running to the young knight's prone form, caring little for her nakedness.

"What happened?" Lancelot leaned down to wipe the blood from his sword on a patch of moss.

She gently rolled Percival onto his back. The copper-haired knight moaned. Fionna deflated in relief and scrubbed at her face with shaking hands, before murmuring, "The Uí Tuírtri caught us unaware."

"I can see that," Lancelot snapped.

He sheathed his sword and then knelt next to Percival, probing gently at the clot of blood that was forming on his temple. One of the warriors must have hit him with something blunt. The wound didn't look too bad. Percival was already stirring. Good. Because now he could level both to the ground for their foolishness.

"The real question is," he began, "what in the bloody hell were you two doing out here?"

"We came to rescue my father." She raised her chin a notch.

"Naked?" Lancelot shot back.

"We . . . had some time to kill." She dropped her gaze to a cluster of ferns near her bare foot, crossing her arms beneath her supple breasts. It took all of Lancelot's focus to keep his attention on the lecture she deserved, rather than the beauty of her lean form.

"So, you thought you would just enjoy yourselves, here within a stone's throw of the might of Morgana's and O'Lynn's invading army? My gods Fionna, you're smarter than this. I would expect this idiocy from a green warrior, but not seasoned ones like you and Percival."

Heat suffused her face. "The Grail Quest is over . . ."

Lancelot's anger softened ever so much at that. Of course, a virile young man like Percival would be eager to take advantage of his new-found freedom.

She narrowed her eyes to slits. "I don't need this from ye," she hissed, pushing to her feet. "It's not like ye've never made a mistake."

"I paid for my mistakes." Lancelot followed her while she gathered up her clothes, her armor. "I pay for them still."

"So did we." Fionna dramatically motioned at Percival, and a shadow crossed over her face that gave Lancelot pause. He looked back at the two corpses, then Fionna, who now stalked behind a tree with a bundle of clothes and boots and armor in hand. "They didn't—" he cut himself off. Burning anger filled him at the very thought of those unclean animals defiling their Fionna. His Fionna.

She turned from the copse of trees. "No." Her voice was hard. "But not for lack of trying."

Percival groaned and Lancelot turned back to him, grateful for the distraction. He couldn't bear the thought of what the Uí Tuítri had tried to do to her. What they might have done if Lancelot hadn't trusted his gut and followed after Fionna and Percival's hoofprints.

Lancelot knelt at Percival's side as his sword-brother's eyes began to flutter open. His copper lashes were long and as soft as silk, dusting the sun-kissed apples of his cheeks. Percival's muscled body was stretched out before him, and though Lancelot shoved the thought to the back of his mind, a part of him appreciated what a fine body it was. Full of the coiled energy of youth and health.

Percival sat up with a curse and then groaned again, his hand flying to his injured temple. "Fionna," Percival cried out, his eyes wild and unfocused while attempting to surge up to his feet.

"Easy." Lancelot grabbed Percival's shoulder to hold him down gently but firmly. "She's safe. The men are gone."

"They were going—" Percival sucked in a sharp breath, unable to finish, seemingly lost in the horrible moment.

"It's okay. We stopped them. They're dead."

Percival looked at him, his eyes clearing as he

registered Lancelot's presence. "Crabapple? How are ye here?"

Lancelot's mouth twisted in a smile at the name. What had once infuriated him, he was coming to regard with . . . fondness?

"Something struck me as off about your and Fionna's explanation. I had a bad feeling. I went to find you beside the wall, and you were nowhere to be found. I followed your tracks."

Percival sprang at Lancelot, pulling him into a crushing embrace. "Thank ye, Lancelot. If you hadn't followed . . ." The words were choked.

Despite his surprise, he wrapped his arms around Percival's strong back, gently rubbing a circle between his shoulder blades. Percival's skin flushed with heat beneath his touch. "It's all right. All is well."

Percival clung to him for a moment longer, before pulling back slowly. But he lingered, leaning his forehead against Lancelot's with a heavy sigh, one hand pressed to Lancelot's chest.

Lancelot's own hand settled behind Percival's neck, tangled in the soft strands of his hair. He had known other men before. But he had never yearned for another man like he desired Percival. A man who owned his heart. A man he never once believed could be his, even though he flirted and teased. And, for years, a man whom Lancelot secretly ached to touch in this way.

The moment on the stairs at the Castle of Maidens rushed back to him, and his pulse quickened. Heady with the enchanted feast, and silly with wine, he had kissed Percival. It had seemed a moment of levity at the time, silliness. They were all growing so close, their lives and stories becoming more intertwined by the day. But now, with Percival's sweet citrus smell washing over him, their lips mere inches apart . . .

"You have to be more careful," Lancelot whispered hoarsely. "Arthur would never forgive me, if I let anything happen to you."

Percival looked up then, his brown eyes filled with something that Lancelot thought he recognized as disappointment. "Right. Arthur," Percival said. He touched his wound and winced, before examining the blood on his fingertips.

"Not . . . just Arthur," Lancelot choked out, looking away.

"What do ye mean?" Percival whispered back.

"I would miss you Percival." Lancelot swallowed thickly, his breath coming in quick. Fionna had helped him pull down the walls used to shield his heart, and the remnants were still crumbling. No more running. No more hiding. "You bring light into the shadows of my life. Your jokes, and your stupid nicknames, your smile and laugh . . . they warm me."

Percival reached out a trembling hand and tilted Lancelot's chin, forcing Lancelot to meet his eyes. "I still remember the first moment I saw ye and Arthur ride into the forest, where I lived with my mother. The first time I had seen men in years. Arthur was majestic on his horse, every bit a king. But it was ye I couldn't take my eyes away from. I still can't."

Lancelot smiled. "I remember. You were so . . . *beautiful*. Gangly as hell, but you've always been the most beautiful man I know."

Percival laid his hand against Lancelot's breast-plate. Warmth filled Lancelot's chest, radiating out from where Percival touched him. The gesture was an invitation—one which Lancelot wasn't going to squander, despite the lecture he had just given Fionna. Lancelot closed the gap between them.

Their mouths touched tentatively at first—curious and light. But a kindling spark quickly caught flame and the roar of heat blazed hot between them. Percival mouth was warm and sweet, his tongue soft as velvet. Unable to help himself, Lancelot tugged Percival closer until their chests pressed together. The younger man moaned. A sound that aroused Lancelot instantly, the hardening bulge in his breeches growing even tighter. Percival's hands moved up Lancelot's chest to cup his face. Percival's thumb traced along his cheekbone, his jaw, softly brushing along his stubble.

The forest was fading from Lancelot's awareness. All he knew was their tongues intertwined, their mouths moving in a fevered rhythm, their breaths mixing, their bodies caressing each other's in delicious strokes. And, in this stolen moment, Lancelot swore that Percival's heartbeat galloped in tandem beside his own trembling pulse.

A gentle, feminine throat-clearing sounded behind them, and Lancelot pulled back, more than a little reluctantly. Percival peered up at Fionna with a silly grin, his eyes almost sleepy.

"Ye appear to be well, Percy," Fionna said, a hint of a smile brightening her otherwise stoic expression.

She stood, clothed and armored once more, a few feet from them.

"Aye, I will be," Percival replied. "My head is pounding, but Lancelot relieved my discomfort fer a spell. He's better than bitter willow bark tea."

Lancelot arched a humored eyebrow. "You may sip from my cup any time you wish."

Percival coughed, and then pushed to his feet, suddenly shy. "I should dress." As he stood, Lancelot took in his beautiful body, including the cock as hard and as throbbing as his own. Then, with a look that seemed to say that what had started in this grove would be continued—Percival grabbed his things and began dressing.

Lancelot pretended to inspect the surrounding woods, feeling a bit sheepish as he said to Fionna, "We need to get the hell out of here. We don't know when O'Lynn plans to move."

"Not until morning, surely," Fionna said. "And we can't leave yet. We haven't rescued my father."

Lancelot eyes rounded slowly, incredulity dawning. "Surely you're not still intent upon that mad plan."

Fionna stiffened. "I wasn't aware saving a king of Tara and one of the only two family members I have left in this world was mad. If we retrieve him, we'll manage to remove one of O'Lynn's major bargaining chips."

"It's too dangerous." Lancelot arched an eyebrow. "That army is two thousand strong. And we don't even know where they're keeping him."

"We have a strong suspicion." Percival had his

pants and boots on now and was pulling his tunic over his head. "And Fionna knows how they organize their camps and keep watch. We'll be in and out like ghosts."

"No . . ." Lancelot drawled the word out, long and slow. He couldn't believe how they persisted in carrying out such a dangerous task. "Caerleon needs you back in the keep. Arthur does. *Your King*. What happens if our king comes back and finds you two captured? Talk about handing O'Lynn a bargaining chip!"

"Then we won't get captured," Fionna said.

"I forbid it, soldier," Lancelot snapped.

"Good thing no one asked you," Fionna shot back, squaring her stance to face his.

Lancelot took a step toward Fionna and leaned in close to her face. "I am second-in-command of the knights of Caerleon. And you are a knight of Caerleon, last I checked. Unless you betrayed our king *again* while I wasn't looking."

Percival winced at that, and Fionna narrowed her eyes to slits.

Lancelot knew as soon as the comment escaped his lips that it was a bridge too far. But why couldn't she understand? He had just witnessed her near-violation and murder by two foul Irishmen! And now she wanted to walk into a camp of *thousands*?

Percival finished buckling on his sword belt. "Perhaps this isn't the best place for a shouting match."

"Agreed. We go back to the keep," Lancelot gritted out.

"I'm not going," Fionna said, her grit matching

his. "I feel him within my reach. I'm not giving up on my father."

Lancelot closed his eyes, willing patience. How to convince her? How to make her see sense? Why was it even so important to her? He understood that he might not have the closest connection to family, and of course she worried for her father, but he had been a prisoner for months. Why now? Fionna was normally so pragmatic. He breathed out slowly. He didn't want to fight with her anymore. He didn't want that to be their relationship.

"Why . . . why is this so important to you?"

Fionna and Percival exchanged a glance.

She took in a deep breath and let it out slowly. "Because of what Merlin and Vivien shared. That my father is the *only* person who can tell me about my mother. Whether I really do possess a strange sort of power." She hurried on. "If we are to war against the might of O'Lynn's clann and Tintagel, if there's a way my power could help . . . we need to know. *I need* to know."

Lancelot chewed on his bottom lip, his gaze flicking from Fionna to Percival. Percival nodded imperceptibly at him, his expression asking Lancelot to understand. This was why the other knight was here. He had seen the importance of Fionna's mission. What the information could mean for them all. It wasn't just a personal quest for a family reunion. If Fionna was a Gwenevere, if she was sovereign blessed, then her joining with Arthur would secure his kingship in a time when he desperately needed it. And if she was a Gwenevere, she had power. Perhaps even surpassing that of Morgana and her sisters.

Rescuing Fionna's father could be the difference between winning and losing this war. Between losing all they held dear or saving it. Lancelot muttered a curse. Damn it. They would have to infiltrate their enemy's camp and rescue a king.

Chapter Seventeen

Fionna

Lancelot was weakening—the indecision play-ing across his face. I pulled in a breath, not wanting to say something that might cause him to dig in his heels—again. After my and Lance-lot's wild intimacy, I was now truly beginning to understand our dark second-in-command.

He was entirely too much like me.

"Fine," Lancelot said with a hiss of exasperation, raking a hand through his curls. "We'll rescue him."

"Thank ye!"

I hardly recognized the delighted squeal that es-caped my mouth as I threw my arms around his neck. My gratitude was palpable. I felt unsteady and filled with the adrenaline of our near miss, and Lancelot's solid presence grounded me. He would be the need-ed counterpoint to Percival's optimism and my des-peration. Together, the three of us could pull this off.

Lancelot squeezed my torso, burying his nose in my hair. His fresh scent and warmth permeated my being, and my body reacted, need blooming low and hot. I was still turned on after watching him and Percival kiss with barely restrained passion. Gods, I almost joined them, if not for the feel of my freshly dressed armor and boots and the corpses' bloody mess nearby. But it was easy to forget the dead with the relief of being alive and relatively uninjured. The rush of emotions was overwhelming. I couldn't fault Lancelot's slip in kissing Percival after his high-and-mighty speech.

I pulled back reluctantly, pressing a kiss to his cheek, doubting that I could control myself if I fastened my lips to his. Memories of our coupling in the hallway and on the stairs heated my cheeks, setting my blood to racing again. I glanced at Percival, who was once again exploring the goose egg on his temple with gentle fingers. What was it about these knights that robbed me of my good sense? When I was around them, I was little more than a wild woman buffeted by the winds of her desires—the demands of her body. And her heart. She was diametrically opposed to the warrior—the brutal fighter that I had cultivated so carefully over these years. And yet . . . I wanted to be both. I was both. Surely there was a way to reconcile these parts of myself.

I shoved my troubled thoughts aside, together with the fear that throbbed at the sight of the dead Uí Tuítri bodies on the ground. How close Percival and I had come . . .

"Percival," I said softly, clearing my throat. "Will ye be up to a fight, if it comes down to it?" I walked over to him and brushed the strands of his copper hair back gently, examining the wound. The injury wasn't too bad. Thankfully, it wasn't bleeding any longer. The bruise was concerning, though. Especially as he had been rendered unconscious.

"Aye, I'm feeling much better, dove." A sly smile crossed Percival's face at my nearness, and I fought an answering smile. His was the languid look of a man who had known a woman for the first time, and my heart was gladdened to see such a blissful expression. He continued, "Better than I've felt in some time, actually." He reached out to stroke my cheek and I pushed off his chest, turning. We didn't have time to go down that road again.

"He can fight."

"So, what's the plan?" Lancelot asked.

I filled him in quickly on our rough plan, wincing at the parts I knew sounded shaky and full of holes. I expected Lancelot to scoff and tear the plan to shreds. But he merely nodded. As if he were in for a pinch, in for a pound.

"We will wear the armor of these men." Lancelot gestured to the two dead warriors. "Fionna's armor looks similar so long as no one looks closely. It's your hair that will draw attention."

Dusk had fallen over the camp below us, and fires and torches were winking to life like will-o-the-wisps.

"I'll keep my hood up," I said. "Unless ye have a better idea, *Faerie Prince*."

"You're the *Gwenevere*," he shot back, and I scowled, opening my mouth with a crude retort on the tip of my tongue.

"Shall we get changed?" Percival popped in-between us, cheerful as ever.

Lancelot grunted stiffly.

We dragged the two warriors deeper into the shelter of the trees, pulling off their armor and cloaks. I vacillated between watching the quiet camp and watching them don the attire of my enemies—a mix of unease and gratitude swirling within me. The dark leather armor didn't suit them, these brash knights of Caerleon. These two princes. I didn't know when it had happened, but something had shifted within me. The boiled leather of the Dál nAraidi looked crude to my eye, the dark burnished buckles dim. I had grown used to the bright color and shining beauty and finery of Caerleon and Arthur's court.

I swallowed back a forming knot in my throat. Every thought of seeing my father again made my stomach clench. Would he see the changes in me and scorn them? I had set out for Caerleon to save him and Aideen, to save the life I had built for myself and the clann that I loved. And, somehow in the process, Caerleon had changed me. Arthur and his knights had changed me. I had found a new family.

"Ready?" Percival asked quietly, stepping up beside me.

I softly smiled, grateful for the distraction.

Lancelot flanked us, his cut profile shadowed by his hood. "Swift and silent as a wraith. If we are identified, we must abort. There is no way we can fight our way out of this camp. It is stealth, or nothing at all."

"Agreed," I whispered. As much as I wanted to protest, Lancelot spoke sense. Arthur needed us alive even more than I needed my father. An all-out fight was a risk we couldn't take.

We padded down the hillside, our cloaks swathed around us to keep the light from glinting off our buckles or swords. The tents stretched around the village like a vast sea. I shoved aside the part of me that needed to count, needed to assess. So many had come to pluck the ripe fruit that was Gwent. To take what wasn't theirs.

We paused in the shadow of a massive oak as two sentries strolled by, their words carried off into the night air. The guards didn't seem particularly concerned with security. *That* could work in our favor.

Lancelot motioned us forward as the man passed, and we darted across the stretch to the nearest tents, pausing between two. "We stay out of sight. If we're spotted, act like we belong."

Percival and I grunted our assent. Part of me prickled at Lancelot seizing control of this mission, but I knew that was foolish. He was second-in-command. And if it was the price of him being here, it was a price I was happy to pay.

My heart galloped like Zephyr in an open field as we snaked between tents and cookfires, making our way into the outskirts of the village. The familiar sounds of a Dál nAraidi camp should have soothed me, but they set me more on edge. I wiped my palms on my breeches, cursing silently to myself. Give me a fair fight any day. But I was not cut out for sneaking around like a silent assassin.

My nerves were frayed to a single thread by the time we reached the village center, where the proud inn stood. Candlelight poured out the leadened window panes, together with the sounds of carousing. The Uí Tuírtri were clearly enjoying Caerleon's bounty. Hopefully they were now well into their cups.

One warrior stood guard before the cellar doors, and I smiled grimly. Percival and my deduction had been correct. Someone was in there. I turned to Lancelot to find him already moving, silent and quick as the wraith he had prompted us to be. In a few heartbeats, Lancelot had run up behind the man and slit his throat, catching his body and then dragging him into the dark shadows of a nearby alley.

Percival raised an eyebrow and we darted out to help, grabbing the deceased's legs and carrying him out of sight. The man's eyes were open as his lifeblood poured out, but I considered him little. This man was guarding my father. Perhaps starving him. Beating him. He deserved no quarter.

I fumbled along the man's belt with numb fingers until I was rewarded with a ring of keys.

Rising as one, we poked our heads out of the shadow of the inn and surveyed the square. Two Uí Tuítri warriors were strolling across the dirt expanse, horns of ale in hand. I exchanged a wide-eyed glance with Lancelot. Would they notice how the guard was missing?

But the warriors passed through with a loud guffaw of laughter, and I let out a breath, my lungs burning for air.

"Now," Lancelot said.

We darted out into the open square, and I felt as

exposed as I had while standing naked before those foul Uí Tuítri bastards. My hands shook as I tried one key and then another. The key's jangling sound seemed deafening in my ears, and I cringed. Any moment, I swore the inn's front door would crash open with a cry.

One of the keys slipped into the lock and turned with a click. I hauled open the door and Lancelot and Percival hurried inside as I urged them on.

I followed, pulling a knife from my belt as I heaved the door shut behind us with a muffled *thunk*.

As the door closed, we were swallowed completely in darkness. My senses roared to life as I gripped the dagger tightly. The smell of earth washed over me, the leeching cool of being underground pebbling my skin. We hadn't considered this. We didn't truly know what would await us in the dark.

"Who goes there?" A thin voice called out. "Is this a new game?" *That voice*. Recognition roared within me. Followed by relief.

"Father?" I called out, taking a blind step forward.

"Fionnabhair?" His voice—my father's voice. Alive. Here.

A sob escaped me, and I sheathed my knife, shuffling forward.

"Fionna," Lancelot hissed. He reached for my shoulder, but I shied away until his grip slipped from me.

"Da," I said, my hands out before me, reaching for the familiar form I longed to touch again, the wiry beard, the strong shoulders.

And then another hand made contact and cold,

gnarled fingers twined with mine. We crashed together like a wave against the rocky shore, and hot tears spilled past my self-control to roll down my face. My senses told me he was thin and weak and dirty—but none of it mattered. He was my Da. He was alive. And he was *here*.

Chapter Eighteen

Arthur

The path from Elathia's throne back to Vivien's portal had transformed. Gone were the gentle scenes of faerie lights and fantastical flowers. Their path was now overgrown with thorns and gnarled brambles. Though it seemed Elathia was holding true to her side of Galahad's bet—letting Arthur, Galahad and the Cauldron of Plenty leave her court—she clearly wasn't pleased about it. And, therefore, didn't intend to let them go easily.

Arthur and Galahad navigated through the tangle of rambling limbs, ignoring the thorns tearing at their tunics and rending sharp slices across their arms and chests. Though no words passed between them, it was clear a similar sense of urgency gripped them both. They needed to get the hell out of here before Elathia changed her mind.

Galahad clutched the Cauldron of Plenty to his broad chest, as if it were the most precious possession he had ever held. For perhaps it was. This strange silver bowl—the shrunken cauldron—was the very relic that would save Caerleon. And Arthur's kingship. If they could only get through these cursed thorns!

Arthur was about pull Excalibur from its sheath and set to work like a common woodsman when the dense thicket cleared.

"Thank the gods," Galahad said.

"I'm not sure the gods have sway here anymore," Arthur muttered. "We go together," Arthur added. He grabbed Galahad's wrist and then they pushed through the portal Vivien had created.

And landed back into the Great Hall at Caerleon.

Arthur leaned over in physical relief, his hand on his stomach.

"The portal closed," Galahad said, heaving a sigh while running a hand through his long, wild strands. "Just like Vivien said. They can't follow us."

"We did it." Arthur laughed. "I can't believe we bloody did it." He turned to Galahad. "You bold son of a bitch. I can't believe you bet yourself."

"Well, I knew you weren't leaving Excalibur, and I wasn't leaving you." Galahad grinned. "So, I figured we might as well get comfortable."

"Did you see the look on Elathia's face when I crossed back over the lake with Excalibur?" The faerie had practically spit at him, pointing her finger like a spear. "*A bet well made. Now take the Cauldron and go.*"

Galahad guffawed. "I thought she had downed a tankard of vinegar! She was *not* pleased with you, Your Majesty. Not one bit."

Arthur laughed, reveling in how the tension drained from him each time he did so. They were back. They had the Cauldron. And with this relic, their chances of defeating O'Lynn and Morgana's army increased tenfold. Allowed them to feed Caerleon until they could figure out how to cure the curse for good too. "Shall we go find the others?"

"I'll make sure to regale Fionna with tales of your brave deeds." Galahad grinned again.

"And I yours," Arthur said, clapping Galahad on the back.

But the others were nowhere to be found. Not Lancelot, nor Percival, or Fionna.

Arthur and Galahad finally found Merlin. The druid stood atop one of the keep's towers with eyes glowing in the darkness.

"You have returned," Merlin said. He raised an eyebrow. "And with the Cauldron of Plenty, though smaller than I expected. I see Danu's steward is friendly to our cause."

"Not exactly." Arthur exchanged a wry look with Galahad. "We have a bit of a tale to tell. Do you know where my other knights are?"

Merlin nodded out into the darkness. "They return anon."

Arthur frowned, squinting into the night. "They're not here? But I left instructions—"

"I suspect they have a tale to tell as well," Merlin interrupted.

"How fares the keep?" Galahad asked, ever the diplomat.

"Preparations for war are coming along well. But, if I may—" Merlin reached out a hand for the Bowl "—we need provisions. I will set up in the Great Hall.

Galahad, please have all manner of food available brought to me?"

Galahad handed over the Cauldron stiffly, nodding. Arthur understood. After what he had almost sacrificed to gain this relic, he must feel a bit attached.

Hoofbeats reached Arthur's ears, and he leaned over the wall to identify the riders. Fionna and her dappled mare Zephyr came into view first, their white and silver hair and coat appearing like a specter in a distance. But . . . there was someone behind her on the horse. A man.

A story to tell indeed. "Come," Arthur said. "Let us meet them."

Arthur and Galahad were standing in the courtyard when the keep's thick doors were cranked open. Fionna, Lancelot, and Percival rode in. Guilty expressions colored their faces when they spotted Arthur and Galahad.

"You've returned," Lancelot said carefully, swinging down from Cheval.

"You, too, have returned," Arthur said dryly. "Though from where, I'm uncertain—"

"This was my idea," Fionna hastily interjected, swinging down from her own horse. Lancelot was crossing to help the man dismount behind her. When the older man's feet touched the ground, his knees buckled, and it was only Lancelot's strong grip that kept him from falling.

Fionna crossed to the older man's side and drew his arm around her shoulders gently, and with reverence. Together, Fionna and Lancelot helped the man forward, to stand before Arthur.

"Arthur, meet my father. His Majesty, Brin Allán, King of Tara, Chieftain of Clann Allán."

Arthur's eyes widened. Fionna's father! How in the ten hells . . .

The man shrugged off Lancelot and Fionna's help and drew himself up to his full height. He was dirty and clearly malnourished, but there was a well of strength there that Arthur recognized. The man was as tall as he, and broad of shoulder, with a warrior's carriage. He looked to have a handsome face beneath the dirt and beard, the crinkled lines around his brown eyes speaking of laughter and kindness, in a time long past. "Forget all the formalities. I haven't been king of a pile of cow shit since O'Lynn took me. Call me Brin, lad." He held out a hand to Arthur.

Arthur laughed, and then took his hand, shaking it. This man was Fionna's father. This man, if Arthur had his way, would be his father-in-law. He was struck by the importance of this moment. "I see where Fionna gets her fire."

"Och, between her and her sister, it's a wonder the lasses didn't burn my keep down."

"Da," Fionna chided, but her eyes shone with happy tears, her face rapt.

"Welcome to Caerleon, Brin. I suspect you have need of food and a hot bath, though in what order, you may choose."

"Thank ye for yer hospitality, King Pendragon."

"Please, call me Arthur."

Brin inclined his head. "Arthur. If it's all the same to ye, I would like to drink an ale, catch up with my daughter, then plan how we're going to beat the shit out of O'Lynn and that faerie bitch at his side."

"Hear, hear," Lancelot murmured.

Arthur grinned. "Brin Allán, you are welcome indeed."

Fionna

I didn't want to break contact with him. My father. I held tight under his arm as we walked slowly toward a chamber next to mine, where Arthur's servants were already arranging a meal, a hot bath, and a change of clothes.

"I'm gonna lose my fingers if ye keep squeezing so tight." He looked at me sideways, a hint of mirth in his eyes.

"Sorry," I said ruefully, only loosening my grip slightly. "I think I'm still in shock that ye're actually here."

"Ye and me both, my duckling. When I heard yer voice in the dark . . ." he trailed off, his eyes growing distant. "I was sure it was another of that witch's foul tricks."

The mention of Morgana set my pulse pounding. "Did she mistreat ye? Did he?"

"No more than ye might expect. There was mocking and humiliation, and drunken nights where the Uí Tuítri thought I would make a fine punching bag. A man comes into this world naked and without pride. I supposed it was too much to expect that I would depart for the Otherworld any different."

"And a woman?" I asked softly, but he never answered me. We had reached the chamber next to mine and walked through the open door slowly as servant hurried about making his room ready. I took all the activity in, afraid to ask the question on my lips. "How is Aideen? Did . . ." I didn't know what to ask. Visions of my vibrant, sweet sister at the mercy of those monsters colored my vision blood red.

Brin sighed heavily. "They held her apart from the men, thank the gods. She got the taunts and the jabs twice as bad as me. As much as I hate to say it, O'Lynn taking her as a bride might be the best thing that could have happened to her."

"How could ye say such a vile thing?" I snapped. "The man's a foul brute!"

"Aye, but she's his now. And, thus, off limits. She'll be treated with respect, cared for. As much as I hate the thought of that man's hands on her, Aideen is strong. A woman can endure one man's unwelcome advances for a time. Without losing herself."

The servants poured the last of the steaming bathwater into the copper tub and curtseyed their leave. "Spoken like a man who's never had to endure such advances," I muttered under my breath, thinking of the Uí Tuírtri warrior scrambling atop me, believing he was entitled to my body. I didn't know what trauma Aideen would have suffered in O'Lynn's hands. But I prayed Brin was right. That she was strong enough to endure it.

"Let me help ye," I said as he took unsteady steps toward the bath.

"Help me by grabbing that ale I asked for," he replied gruffly, pulling his impossibly-dingy shirt over his head, before leaning one hand on the tub's rim.

The sight of his back stole my breath. Beneath the film of dirt and grime, his skin was crisscrossed with dark bruises and scabbed cuts. His once muscled form had shriveled from malnourishment. For the first time, he looked not like a King of Tara, the proud Brin Allán who had helped Brian Boru, then High King of Ireland, subdue the Norsemen out of the Kingdom of Dublin in the Battle of Clontarf. Now he looked like an old man. "Oh Da." The words slipped from my lips, and he stiffened.

"I don't need yer goggling, I need that ale!" he barked, and I turned to the tray of food the servants had left, giving him some privacy to finish undressing.

When I turned back with his blessed ale, he had slipped into the tub, a look of bliss on his face. I handed him the drink and he took a long swig, before releasing a satisfied sound.

"By the goddess," he murmured. "Thought I might never feel such pleasures again. A hot bath, a good ale. The sight of my beautiful Fionnabhair." He looked up at me, and I thought I glimpsed a flicker of emotion within his eyes, before the warrior's shield slid down once again.

"Do you want me to leave ye?" I asked, though I had a list of questions as long as my arm that I was desperate to ask him.

"Nay, don't leave, daughter," he said. "I've need of ye yet. Pull up that stool." So, I did, pulling a stool up beside the tub and perching upon it. "Hold this," he said, and I held his ale while he ducked under the water all the way, running his hand through his matted hair. The bathwater was already gritty and gray.

He came up for air and took his ale back. "Get me one of those chicken legs, eh?" He nodded back toward the tray of food.

"I see why ye want me here," I said but my words were gentle, and I retrieved the requested chicken leg for him.

"Not just that," he said. "I want to hear yer story. Why the hell ye're—why we're—in Briton. How ye became a knight of Caerleon. How ye came to live in this fine keep with the favor of a High King." He waved the leg around.

"How about a trade?" I offered. "Because I have questions for ye too. Ye ask one, I ask one."

He inclined his head. "Start talkin'. And while ye do, grab me a piece of that bread."

As he munched on the bread, I told him of Morgana and her sister's hatred for Arthur and Lancelot, as well as their three curses. O'Lynn's deal with me—to steal Excalibur from Arthur in exchange for their lives. I told him how I failed—how the knights stopped me on the road to Brunanburh in Northern Wales. But how they spared my life. Because they had learned I was a key to finding the Blessed Grail.

"And them sparing ye had nothing to do with how they all look at ye like lovesick whelps?" My father asked, now gnawing through a piece of roast venison.

My cheeks heated. "We have . . . come to care for one another. It played a part." I was reluctant to share the extent of how. Not that I thought he would judge me for loving four men—having multiple lovers, especially among warriors, was as common as clover in Ireland—but for fear that he would judge me for putting my heart over his and Aideen's safety. Their very lives, even. For how could he not? I cursed myself for this predicament daily.

"So," he said, "somehow, we bumbled into the middle of a faerie war, and that idiot O'Lynn is merely a piece on the game board?"

I nodded. "That's a fair summary." I sighed. "I suppose I'm a piece too."

My father shook his head. "You were. But you've made yourself indispensable to these knights of Caerleon and their king. You will be a queen soon enough."

My blush deepened as my father voiced my secret hope. But also, if it was indeed true that I was a Gwenevere, then he already knew I would become queen one day. A queen destined to save a king.

"My turn," I said, voicing the question that had been crystalizing in my mind for weeks. I was grateful that I could speak the words without wavering. "Who is my mother?"

My father froze with the ale horn halfway to his mouth. He lowered his drink slowly, his brown eyes penetrating my own. "I always knew we would visit this topic someday." He swallowed. "First, know that my wife Catríona loved ye. She loved ye like her own daughter."

A numbness overtook me at his words. Catríona Allán wasn't my mother.

"It was, eh, twenty-one years ago now. I was riding through the woods near Aghanravel. Beautiful spring day. The buds were bright on the trees, birds flitting about. I came upon a woman. As beautiful as a field of wildflowers. Hair brown as loamy soil, skin soft as cotton-grass. Just standing there in the middle of the forest, wearing this gown of white. No horse, no possessions, just standing there. Like she was waiting for me. I stopped to see if she needed assistance. Things were fairly peaceful then, but still, there were dangers that could face such a fair maiden alone. She told me her name was Danu, and that she was waiting for me."

I hissed in a breath. "The goddess?"

He nodded. "I couldn't tumble off my horse and onto my knees fast enough. I begged her pardon and offered myself to aid her in whatever way she needed. She told me . . . she needed a daughter. Mind ye, I wasn't a young stag in my prime anymore."

My mouth parched like the poisoned land as he continued his tale. "I loved Catríona with all my heart. She was my wife before the law, but also my soul's lover. But when a goddess makes requests, ye serve. I laid with Danu in that very bed of wildflowers. When we were done, she thanked me, and was on her way. I told Catríona everything that evening, falling on my knees in apology. She pardoned me, so long as I forgive her should she lay with a handsome god who presented himself to her in request."

A smile ghosted his lips. "I don't think she really believed me. Not until nine months later, when Danu appeared at our doorstep with a bundle in hand." He met my eyes. "That bundle was ye, a daughter she had named Fionnabhair."

"The White Fae," I whispered to myself as the heat of tears fell down my numb face. "Ye never told me . . ."

He shook his head. "She swore us to secrecy. The goddess shared how her enemies were moving against her, and that the child would be key in defeating them. A Gwenevere, as the Cymru call her." My heart nearly stopped beating. "But also, that the foretold White Enchantress needed to remain hidden. So, she placed a géis over you in protection against all forms of enchantment, and to disguise yer true demi-goddess form, as well as yer magical powers."

"A géis?" I asked, my mind struggling to process. "Who were her enemies?"

He shook his head. "I don't know, my duckling. No one ever came for ye. Not yer mother or those who opposed her. But if Morgana tried to pit ye against her enemy King Arthur by forcing ye to steal Excalibur, I suspect the secret might be out and that he is also the foretold High King who needs such a queen."

Chapter Twenty

Galahad

The mood that hung over the knights at breakfast was a strange one. Arthur was absent, seeing to Merlin's work with the Cauldron of Plenty. Lancelot and Percival were far too quiet for comfort. Well, Percival was far too quiet. Silence from crabapple was not out of character.

But the two kept exchanging pregnant glances that told Galahad that something had passed between both men last night. Had the tension between them boiled over into something more? But no . . . it wasn't quite the type of the secret smile he would expect if the two had spent a night together.

"Out with it," Galahad finally said, setting his tankard down with a thunk. "You two are as bad at keeping secrets as the maids when doing the washing together. What are you hiding?"

Fionna and her father appeared in the doorway, her father much changed from his condition last night. He was bathed, shaved, and clothed in a fresh tunic and pants. He still looked gaunt and shadow-eyed, but there was more spirit in him than before.

Fionna was the one who answered Galahad's question, even as she ushered her father to a spot at Galahad's side. "Our rescue last night didn't go entirely according to plan."

"What do you mean?" Galahad furrowed his brow.

"Our presence wasn't . . . unnoticed," she replied. "We killed two Uí Tuírtri warriors. I think one was a man of some importance."

"So, come daybreak—" Percival said.

"They'll know we poked the bear," Galahad finished.

Lancelot grimaced.

"The man Fionna spoke of, Níall. He was one of O'Lynn's oldest friends and most trusted leaders," Brin said.

"Ah, you didn't just poke a bear. You stirred the hornet's nest." Galahad let out a muffled curse. Even with the cauldron, the keep's fortifications and preparations weren't complete. They couldn't afford an all-out assault.

"In our defense, they were going to attack anyway," Percival said. "It's not like we turned an ally into an enemy."

"His Majesty will need to be told," Galahad said, sliding a look Brin's way. Honorific titles were needed now that they were in the presence of a foreign king.

"I'll tell him," Lancelot said at the same time as Fionna said, "Let me handle that."

The two exchanged an irritated glance.

"No one needs to tell me anything," Arthur appeared in the doorway, his face pinched. Galahad and his fellow knights rose to their feet and bowed their heads in respect. Arthur lifted a hand in appreciation then gestured to their chairs. "A messenger just arrived," he said as they returned to their seats. "O'Lynn is on the move. And burning everything he passes."

Curses of dismay rounded the table. "The villages should be mostly empty, Your Majesty," Galahad said.

Arthur nodded grimly. "It's a small consolation. But those homes, crops, livestock? Caerleon will need them if we are to have anything to harvest, and homes for our people to return to. We must stop what we can."

"So, we ride," Lancelot said, a determined smile crossing his face, perhaps grateful for a foe of flesh and blood rather than mist and magic. "I won't mind facing those Uí Tuítri bastards again. And showing Morgana that the might of Caerleon is not to be trifled with."

Arthur frowned, narrowing his eyes slightly while running a hand through his hair. Galahad knew that look of stern consideration: Arthur the strategist.

"Would O'Lynn move all of his forces out?" Arthur turned to Fionna. "Would he himself be among them? Morgana?"

She shook her head. "If they're just razing and burning, O'Lynn will likely be sitting back, fat and happy. Real battle, however? He would ride out among his warriors. But this . . . we will likely find him in his camp. Morgana too, if she is with him."

"We will split up, then," Arthur said. "Sir Percival, I'll send you with a force to meet the raiders. Harry them, draw them out, pick off the stragglers. Do not *fully* engage. Just distract them so they don't return. Lady Fionna, Sir Galahad, and I will take another force into their camp. We'll bring Merlin too. I'm sick to death of being on the defensive. It's time to take the offense to O'Lynn and Morgana. See how they like being blindsided by magical attacks for a change."

"Will Merlin fight?" Fionna asked. "I didn't know he used his magic in battle."

"Merlin was quite a fighter in his youth," Arthur said. "He will fight."

"And what of me, my King?" Lancelot asked.

"The most sacred task falls to you," Arthur said. "I need you to see to the defenses of Caerleon. You must hold this keep, whatever comes."

"Hold the keep?" Lancelot was incredulous. "Perhaps you've forgotten, Your Majesty, but it's not the king's role to be on the front lines. Let me win this battle for you. I gladly offer my services as your champion. You need not risk yourself."

"Dál nAraidi clann chieftains ride to battle at the front of their hordes," Brin said. "If King Arthur Pendragon does not go, even for a raid, it will be seen as a sign of weakness. Practically an admission of defeat."

"Says the king who was captured in battle by his enemies," Lancelot shot back.

Fionna's eyes narrowed at Lancelot's slight, though Galahad had to admit, it was a fair point by their second-in-command. Brin arched a humored eyebrow and smirked at their dark knight's fire, before glancing at his daughter, who just rolled her eyes back at her father.

Galahad lifted a hand to his mouth to hide a humored smile of his own. Fionna and Lancelot were too much alike at times, there were really only two acceptable reactions. Irritation or humor.

"I will not do anything rash," Arthur reassured. "Sir Galahad and Lady Fionna will be by my side. But I must see. I must take this man's measure. If we can cripple him and Morgana today, it could buy us the time Caerleon needs to figure out how to break this final curse."

"And to awaken my magic," Fionna added.

"What magic?" Galahad asked.

Fionna exchanged a glance with her father. "I had a chance to speak with my father last night. It turns out . . . Danu is my mother."

Silence fell over the room.

"I bloody knew ye were a goddess!" Percival finally said, slapping his knee with a laugh. "Any man could see that ye are no ordinary woman." The way Percival purred the words, and how Fionna's ears turned pink as a smile crept onto her face . . .

Galahad's eyes widened. The Grail Quest was over . . . had Percival claimed more than Fionna's heart?

"Indeed," Lancelot murmured. "If you are the daughter of Danu, then you are a Gwenevere. The first in a millennia. I told you, Fionna. The third curse didn't lie. Morgana said I would love a white enchantress. And here you are."

Fionna's cheeks reddened to a pretty hue and Galahad swung his head to take in the smug grin twisting Lancelot's mouth. The way his eyes rested on her, as if she were his. As if he knew every hidden place and secret whisper of Fionna's beautiful body. "Odin's beard, woman!" Galahad cried out, looking from Lancelot to Percival to Fionna. "We were gone for less than a day!"

Arthur frowned. "What are you talking about?"

Fionna full-on flushed now, as scarlet as a ripe cherry. "Stay on topic, *Sir*," she said pointedly to Galahad, then chanced a furtive glance her father's direction. "The important detail to discuss is how I do indeed possess magic, but my access has been locked up by Danu within a géis. To protect me from her enemies."

"A géis," Lancelot practically spat. "My foster mother thought as much."

"Danu's enemies?" It was Galahad's turn to exchange a look with Arthur. "The faerie we encountered in Danu's court was not . . . friendly. I think it's possible that Danu's enemies have already come home to roost."

"What enemies does an earth-goddess have?" Percival asked.

"The Fomorians," Arthur said slowly. "The curse over the land reminded us of their dark magic. Danu saw fit to hide her child from someone . . . and the Fomorians are the ancient enemy of the Túatha dé

Danann." Arthur turned to Lancelot. "Can a Fomorian shift into the form of another faerie?"

"Why do you ask?"

"Well," Arthur drawled out, as if deep in thought. "I wonder if a Fomorian took on the shape of the faerie Danu had planned to appoint as regent in her absence? I cannot imagine she would just appoint anyone, let alone a Fomorian."

"Possible, I suppose," Lancelot answered. "Faeries can shift into animals or make themselves appear more human. Fomorians are beastly and quite ugly. Only halflings, a child of Danu and a child of Domnu, possess humanoid fae beauty."

Galahad ran a finger along the rim of his tankard. "Elathia, Danu's regent, was beautiful."

Lancelot curled his lip in disgust. "Bloody faeries."

"But if the Fomorians have returned from the sea's abyss," Arthur considered, "perhaps we have bigger concerns than O'Lynn and Morgana. We will consider all these things with Merlin when we return. Lady Fionna, I will see that the druid gives all his attention to breaking this géis over you." Their king swept his gaze across the table. "We will not solve this mystery over breakfast. Not when we have a battle to win."

Brin lifted his tankard into the air. "Aye, victory will be ours, Pendragon."

reakfast was forgotten as they scrambled to rally their soldiers and prepared to ride out. Lancelot scowled darkly but obeyed his king's command.

Several hours later, Galahad found himself mounted on his charger, riding through the countryside between Fionna, Arthur, and Merlin.

"What can you tell us about their war strategy?" Arthur asked Fionna.

"If we ride upon them quickly, they'll fight like banshees to defend their turf," Fionna answered. "In a more traditional engagement, they would try to strike fear into our hearts with war cries and horns. For those who have never heard a Dál nAraidi force crying out, it can be terrifying indeed. Then the foot soldiers and lightly-armored horsemen would charge us, to break our ranks. But, if we're able to hold rank, they will likely flee. Then the foreign Gaels will attack."

"The foreign Gaels?" Galahad asked. "You mean intermarried Gaelic Norsemen?"

"Aye, I do. They fight with the Danish axes ye're familiar with, together with our own Irish bows and darts. The foreign Gaels will hit us with the force of Odin's hammer," Fionna said, giving Galahad a weak smile.

"So," Arthur began, nodding thoughtfully, "we must ensure they don't have a chance to reach their mounts or weapons."

"There's no honor among Dál nAraidi, Your Majesty," Fionna stressed. "Such an attack won't surprise them much. O'Lynn's warriors will rally a defense quickly."

As Fionna spoke, they crested a forested hill and the Uí Tuírtri camp came into view below them. Galahad tightened his grip on his horse's reins. Thousands of warriors swarmed Caerleon's green rolling hills and the valley the peaks cradled. In the far distance, black smoke plumed into the sky where a village burned.

Arthur reined Llamrei to a stop, and the others reined their mounts in on either side. They had a force of a hundred men behind them.

"Merlin, can you create a cover for us?" Arthur asked.

Merlin nodded, and then closed his eyes, whispering into the air. A fog began to coat the ground, wisping down the hill before them.

"We push into the town." Arthur's words were hard. "Find O'Lynn and Morgana. And end them."

"And rescue my sister," Fionna added softly.

"So, it comes to this," Merlin said, his cambion eyes flashing.

"It has always been coming to this," Arthur said. "Ever since my half-sister set her sights on my kingdom." And with that, he kicked his heels into Llamrei's side and trotted down the hill and into the rising mist.

Galahad flashed a shared glance with Fionna before kicking his own charger forward, the clop of his horse's hooves muffled by the soft grass.

Uncertainty dogged Galahad's mind. But he shoved his misgivings aside, finding his clarity. His calm. And his blood sang a fierce battle cry to the elements as Fionna rode at his side, her white-blonde braids fluttering behind her.

For glory. For Arthur. For Caerleon.

Chapter Twenty-One

Arthur

The mist shrouded their approach. Tents eventually emerged like silent sentinels inside the curtain of thick fog. A warrior materialized before Arthur and Llamrei, and Arthur ran him through the neck with Excalibur before he could make a sound.

Galahad, Fionna, and Merlin had fanned out from him during their descent into the war camp. Though he couldn't see them in the whiteness, the hushed grunts, rustle of armor, and quiet clang of slaughter reassured Arthur that they were still close by.

He had instructed the soldiers who followed to burn what they passed. It grieved Arthur to do so, but allowing O'Lynn access to food and shelter felt like aiding his enemy. Arthur would rebuild the villages for his people and provide care within his keep's walls until they could return to their new homes.

Men's voices swam through the fog before him. He could make out the words in an Irish lilt that reminded him of Fionna's. "It isn't natural," one man said.

"Aye. Bloody faerie magic," another replied.

It was another moment before he saw them, before he saw that they were too many to take by surprise. But he would kill as many as he could before they raised the alarm.

One tall, thin man cried out as Arthur surged forward, spearing him through the chest.

Around the fire, the others scrambled for their weapons as Arthur and Llamrei leaped over the fire pit, Llamrei's sharp hooves trampling one of the men. Arthur dispatched the other two quickly, but it was too late. The cry had been heard.

Arthur felt a strange elation rise within him as he urged his horse forward, his blood crying out for battle. He was tired of O'Lynn taking from him, of Morgana taking from him. He was ready to take from someone else.

Shouts sounded to his left, where he knew Fionna was making her way through the mist as well.

Arthur focused before him, hacking and stabbing, a brutal harvest of Uí Tuírtri warriors caught unawares. It would have made Arthur's stomach curl, if not for the cruelties these men had already visited upon his people. Anglo-Saxon holy men shared of a god who insisted that a man was to turn the other cheek when insulted. Arthur snorted as he swung Excalibur, severing a man's head from his shoulders. Perhaps turning the other cheek worked in the Holy Roman Empire. But not in Gaelic lands. Here, a king stood his ground. And here in Briton, the Pendragon breathed fire and vanquished the enemies who invaded his realm.

Arthur had reached one of the little houses on the outskirts of the village, having made his way through the forest of hide tents. The sound of cracking flames and the smell of burning wood and fur followed close on their heels. They wouldn't be able to return this way. But, in her mission to retrieve her father, Fionna had identified another retreat route to the east toward Caerleon.

Arthur smiled grimly when a great wind buffeted against him, and the fog began to lift. "Morgana." He spit his half-sister's name like a curse. There would be no more easy killing from here on out.

His companions came into view as the mist began to lessen. Fionna and Zephyr, their pale forms flecked with sprays of blood; Galahad with his battle axe hewing a man nearly in two. And Merlin, shooting gouts of flame, burning the men before him where they stood. An endless sea of soldiers from Caerleon also now faced the tide of Irish clann warriors before them.

Arthur and his trusted circle halted on the outskirts of the village, though the main street was wide and open. And he could see into the village square, where a force of men were rallying. Banners were being lofted and flapped in the unnatural wind, bearing the sigil of clan Uí Tuírtri.

"To me!" Arthur called, and the others drew close around him.

"We punch through," Arthur said, "and see if we can find O'Lynn."

"I think we have found him," Fionna said, nodding toward the village square. A tall man swathed in furs was walking out of the village inn with a willowy woman in black at his side.

"Charge!" Arthur shouted, and his soldiers thundered forward, crashing into the bristling line of clannsmen before them.

Arthur fought furiously, hacking and slicing with Excalibur, but the crowd of warriors before O'Lynn and Morgana grew thicker. The clann leader was hanging back—comfortable. Letting Caerleon break itself against the rock that was a three-man-thick line of Irish warriors.

As Arthur stabbed a man who tried to slice Llamrei's side, his horse danced back, out of the way of another who took the man's place. Arthur felt his anger surge. "You hide like a child! Afraid to face me!" Arthur bellowed at O'Lynn.

"Just letting you tire yourself," O'Lynn shouted back. "I need not lift a finger. For I have Tintagel at my side!" He gestured at Morgana, and Arthur's faerie half-sister raised her clawed fingertips.

The sky around them darkened as hundreds—thousands—of crows descended upon them as if materialized from a black, gaping hole beside the suddenly shadowed sun. Sweat dripped into Arthur's eyes and he blinked back the stinging pain. Even without the momentary hazy eyesight, he struggled to take in what he was seeing. And then the swirling black vision in the sky shifted form into offensive positions. He barely had time to shout for his warriors to take cover before the birds swooped upon them in a hungry cloud, wings flapping, claws scraping, beaks pecking at exposed flesh, especially at ears and eyes.

"Merlin!" Arthur screamed, holding his sword arm up to shield his face from the attack.

A shock wave shot across the battle field, jarring Arthur to his bones. His eyes rounded at the foreign sensation, his heart in this throat. Then, crows fell from the sky, a dark rain that hammered trees, roofs, and armor alike. People from both camps lifted shields or ducked as Morgana shrieked, screaming over and over, "My crows!"

When the thumping, thundering sounds abated, Arthur swept a calculating gaze across the village to take in the damage. Smoke from the nearby fires ribboned around piles of black, feathered bodies as far as the eye could see. Easily thousands of birds littered the ground, flapping helplessly and cawing in pain beside writhing soldiers who covered their mutilated eye sockets while crying out. The sounds of torment was enough to make his ears weep.

He straightened his position atop Llamrei and grit his teeth until his jaw ached, meeting Morgana's wrathful gaze head-on. Snarling, he shouted, "Is that the best you can do, Queen of Darkness?"

Morgana narrowed her violet eyes, and then glanced to her left, beyond where he could see.

Two more fae females appeared at her side, stepping up before the inn beside her.

Arthur's blood turned cold. Morgause and Elaine. *Here.* His two eldest half-sisters. The ones who had treated him far more cruelly while growing up. The sisters who taught Morgana that he, their bastard-born brother, the product of their father's planned murder and mother's rape, deserved only eternal punishment for being an abomination in their eyes. And for bearing the title Pendragon, High King of Briton.

The onslaught was sudden and furious. A bolt of lightning crashed from a clear blue sky, striking the ground just inches from Arthur. His steed reared in fright, screaming as Arthur struggled to stay on her back.

The other sisters were muttering now while writing runes into the air. More lightning strikes hit. Some of Arthur's soldiers were not as lucky as he, and the men and horses were tossed into the sky. Claps of thunder shook his eardrums, deafening him. He swallowed his sorrow as more men he knew, men with wives and children, fell to their death atop the possessed crows. All because of him, because he was born from Uther Pendragon's line. Perhaps this was the true curse poisoning his life. He slid a glance toward Fionna, unable to bear his shame.

But that latter thought was ripped from his attention as a new fear took hold.

The ground began to rumble, and the very dirt they stood upon began to crack. A fissure appeared between Arthur and Fionna, and his eyes grew large as it snaked wider, opening into a chasm below. Men fell into the depths, screaming, and still the ground shook.

Terror clawed up from his gut as he screamed until his throat turned raw, scorched with grief. "Merlin!" Arthur looked around frantically. He caught his druid's eyes. Time seemed to slow for several beats of his heart as the man's horse danced back from a widening crack. Merlin eventually shook his head, even as he mouthed words, his hands dancing before him. Whatever spell the sisters wielded, it was too strong for Merlin to break.

They would be destroyed.

"Retreat!" Arthur cried out, and spun Llamrei, kicking her flanks hard. They leapt over a chasm, just barely clearing the wide expanse. *Fionna. Galahad.* Arthur peered over his shoulder to see Fionna and Zephyr dodging out of the way of a lightning strike. The sudden movement of the ground together with the strike sent Zephyr sideways, and the horse and rider crashed to the ground.

"Fionna!" Arthur kicked Llamrei forward, but his mare fought him, not wanting to return to the chaos of lightning strikes and cracking earth.

Zephyr scrambled to her feet, and spooked, galloped toward Galahad.

"Zephyr!" Fionna screamed.

Galahad turned, spurring his mount toward the fleeing mare.

With Fionna's attention pinned onto her horse, she didn't see the crack now slithering between her planted feet.

Arthur spurred Llamrei on, his heart about to pound out of his chest. "Fionna," he cried out at her again. "Watch out!"

She spun toward him, the horror in her eyes growing as she realized how the ground was about to give way beneath her. Arthur leaned over his saddle, stretching his arm out for her as far as he could reach. Praying it was far enough.

Fionna leapt for him as he passed. Their wrists locked. Pain groaned through him as her weight almost pulled his arm from its socket. But he had her. And the momentum of their movement helped swing her across Llamrei's rump just as the ground caved in beneath the spot where she had stood only moments earlier.

"Hold on," Arthur cried out over his shoulder.

Llamrei leapt over another fissure, and Fionna nearly slid off his horse's back. But when Llamrei's hooves connected with solid ground, Fionna stumbled to the ground. She then sprinted for Zephyr and sprang back into the saddle.

Arthur's warriors were streaming past them now. But something felt wrong. Warriors who hadn't been speared by lightning or lost to the unnatural depths of the earth were now riding for Caerleon with fresh terror gripping their sweaty dirt- and blood-smudged faces. He whipped his head back toward the war-sacked village and sucked in a ragged breath. A host of mounted Uí Tuírtri were pouring out from the west and around the village. They had taken advantage of the pitched battle, using the time to saddle their mounts and make an assault.

"Ride for the keep," Arthur shouted above the melee as he dug his heels into poor Llamrei's side once again. She surged into a gallop, flowing into the stream of riders thundering back toward the barracks within his walled fortress. He gave Llamrei her head and prayed, to whatever deity might be listening, that she would be fast enough.

Chapter Twenty-Two

Fionna

We made it into the keep a hair's breadth before the horde on our tail.

"Close the gate!" Arthur screamed, and soldiers scrambled to slam the huge oaken doors shut behind us. They heaved the cross-guard into place as a shuddering weight smashed against the outside.

I quickly surveyed the damage done to our group. We had lost perhaps a third of the warriors we had brought with us, between the fighting in the camp and the wild ride home. Dirt and sweat coated each soldier. But Arthur . . . Arthur appeared as though he dug his way free from the Underworld. "Percival," I gasped, my breast heaving from the frantic flight. But fear seized the very air from my lungs. I didn't see the copper hair of my sweet knight. "Has Sir Percival returned with his men?" I called out to the guards.

"Aye," a man answered from the courtyard. "They returned a candle mark ago."

My shoulders slumped in relief, even as another cry went up outside the gates, followed by another shuddering crash.

"They're trying to hack through the gate," Galahad said, wiping the sweat from his face. Grime smudged across his cheek and forehead. "It'll take them till Samhain at this rate."

"Get archers up on those walls," Arthur barked. "I don't want the gate compromised. Take those men down."

Soldiers scrambled to obey. I slid off Zephyr and then patted her heaving, lathered flank.

"Druid," I called out. My eyes darted around until I found Merlin amongst the tumult of men and horses in the courtyard. "We have work to do."

Merlin nodded grimly, dismounting from his own horse and motioning to me.

"What do you plan to do?" Arthur asked, stepping before me. His crown was askew, and his face was flecked with blood and dirt, his eyes red with restrained emotion. But he had never looked more handsome than he did now. A man, despite our near-defeat, in full command of the world around him. A king.

"We have one magic-wielder against three," I explained. "However strong yer walls are, they cannot hold against Morgana and her sisters, if their full magic is brought to bear. Danu told my father I have latent power within my blood. Merlin and I must find it."

Arthur nodded, looking away. As though hiding the building emotion—the fear, the grief. "This is your most precious task."

I cupped his cheek and whispered, "Arthur . . ."

He appeared as though he wanted to lean into my touch. Instead he stepped back with a sad smile and said, "See it done," before spinning on his heel and marching away.

A groom took Zephyr's reins as I stared after Arthur's retreating form. Then I hurried after Merlin as he angled his way through the thick crowd of villagers who led the injured to the Great Hall.

My body was exhausted from the fight and the ride, but my mind was alive with excitement and nerves. If I were honest with myself, there was trepidation there too. I had always been happy with Fionnabhair Allán. Being the daughter of a Dál nAraidi woman—a good wife and mother. Being a warrior, fighting with my fiann. I had been happy being me. And I had been happy in Caerleon too. With Arthur and my knights. Each man had awakened a passion and carnal femininity that had slumbered deep within me. I felt as though I needed nothing else—no power or might or divinity. I needed nothing but time on this green earth with the men I loved. But my enemies—Arthur's enemies—would take even that from me. So, I would surrender myself to the unknown. Would I be happy with the woman who emerged? If my father's tale proved true, I would be a Gwenevere. An enchantress, a goddess. But would I still be me?

"Be at ease, Fionna," Merlin said as we reached the living area of his cave. "This has been a part of you all along. If anything, you will be more you than before."

"Do yer powers extend even to reading thoughts?"

I muttered, for I knew I hadn't spoken my fears aloud.

"My powers extend to human nature. And your worry is written plain on your face."

"What do ye plan to do?" I asked. Dwelling on my misgivings wouldn't help me. Arthur needed an enchantress at his side, and so I would yield myself. For Arthur, I would yield my life, my very soul. How small a sacrifice was my identity?

"Your true essence is locked deep inside you," Merlin said, pulling bottles off his shelf and returning to his desk, where a mortar and pestle sat. "The human mind is like . . . a turtle."

"A turtle?" I scoffed.

"Floating in the water. You can see the eyes. That is the conscious mind, what we use to think and reason and process. But beneath the surface is something much larger. More powerful. I think this is where your powers lie. I will give you a potion to take you deep within yourself. I hope you can find your way to the answers."

"And if I can't?" I asked.

"Then we'll try something else," Merlin said. "Until we find what works."

Merlin poured the potion into a mug of ale, and then handed the clay cup to me. I downed the contents in one swallow, before coughing and hacking. "Awful!"

"Magic doesn't usually taste good." The druid took my arm and led me to the chairs beside his fireplace. "Sit," he said, and I dropped into a seat upon the fur cover. A fire burst to life before me in the hearth, and I jumped.

Merlin sat beside me. "You may see strange things in your mind. Visions. A guide may appear. Ask him to show you the way to the géis. Whatever happens, focus only on finding the géis. Your mind will take you there."

The room swam as a flush of heat consumed me. "I feel . . . strange," I murmured.

Merlin took the cup from me. "Close your eyes. Let the magic take you."

I did as he instructed, and another wave of heat battered against my tingling body, warming my skin, until I felt as though I were suffocating in my armor. I reached up to start unbuckling my leathers, but Merlin's hand grasp mine. "Your conscious mind will do everything it can to try and keep you from journeying deep. It's uncomfortable with the unknown. Focus inside. The feelings will pass."

I huffed in frustration but tried to do as I was told. It was dark behind my eyelids, but the darkness swam, as if alive. Moving. The darkness began to materialize—to take form. I hissed in a breath as I watched in disbelief. A forest. It was as if I were standing in a shadowy forest. On the ground before me, a form emerged, soft gray against the mossy earth. A dove.

"Are you my guide?" I asked.

The dove hopped once on the ground. I took that for a yes.

Bending at the knees, I hunched down and asked, "Can you lead me to the géis?"

The dove flitted into the air, whizzing into the forest.

"Wait!" I cried out, running after the bird.

I darted beneath branches and bounded over fallen logs, all the time wondering what in the goddess's name this place represented. And knowing that I was moving farther away from where I had started. Deeper into the unknown.

The dove flew quickly for this type of bird. Stranger still, I could move fast as well, keeping up with my winged guide. I slowed to a stop before the dove now sitting on a branch before me, expecting a need to catch my breath. But there was no breath here. My lungs didn't rise and fall with life-giving motions.

Bothered by this realization, I peered past the dove. Ahead of where we paused, a ring of trees circled inside a clearing. The landscape reminded me of the faerie ring where we had found the standing stone pointing us toward Caer Benic. But no monolith lay inside the ring. Instead, a woman stared at me. A woman trapped in a cage made of vines.

And the woman was *me*.

"Impossible," came my garbled cry. I ran forward and threw myself against the bars, wrapping my fingers around the iron. The woman within looked at me with sullen, downcast eyes, a frown dipping her mouth. But she did not speak. I pressed my face to the space between the bars, my eyes drinking in her strange form. For she *was* me. But not. This me was fae. She had delicate tapered ears and skin as white and as smooth as a first-fallen snow. I knew that men found me beautiful, but this version—she was ethereal. The animal movements of her head, the glow around the pure white hair, pulled back in elaborate braids . . . she was a dream.

"How do I free ye?" I tugged on the bars to test their strength.

"A worthy question."

I whirled, grasping for a dagger at my waist that was no longer there.

Another faerie stood before me. No, not a faerie. A goddess. She wore a dress of shimmering green and gold, the colors of spring and summer and autumn woven together in a majestic cloth finer than any mortal hand could create. Her cascading tresses were the green of the forest, interwoven with vines of ivy. Her skin was pale and glistened with dew, like a cloud. Her tilted eyes were a startling blue that raged like the sea, calm like a glassy lake, with a fluid gaze that rested on me like the gentle pool of a river.

I fell to one knee, my fingertips burying in the earth. "Goddess Danu," I said, my mind racing. I didn't know if she was a figment of my mind, but I didn't want to risk offending her on the chance she was more. Real.

"Rise my daughter," she said. Her words were the soft touch of a new lamb's wool.

I rose to shaky feet, meeting her gaze. There were so many things I wanted to say to her. To ask. Why my father. Why me. Where had she been. But . . . there was only one question that mattered right now. "Can ye . . ." I stumbled over my words. "Can ye help me break the géis?"

She glided forward, wrapping her own slender fingers around the bars and tugging. Flames alit in her hands, and I shied back. But they quickly snuffed out.

She stepped away, shaking her head. A look of pinched frustration flit across her face, an expression that appeared very out of place. "I cannot," she admitted.

"But ye placed it upon me, did ye not?" I asked. "Can ye not undo yer magic?"

"My enemies have trapped me in a remote corner of the Otherworld. It stretches me thin as the Otherworld's mist to even be here. If I were here in my full force, yes, I could undo the géis. It seems I have protected you too well. Even from myself."

"The Fomorians did this to ye, didn't they," I said. "They have returned."

She nodded. "They have. They take my court, they take my land. They will take Arthur's sovereignty and all of Briton, if you let them. They use Morgana and her sisters like pawns, playing upon their petty vengeances."

"Is there a way to break ye free?" I asked. "We need yer help defeating them."

"Perhaps when your power is fully restored, you could break my prison."

"But my power cannot be restarted until ye are free," I said slowly, now seeing the knot fate had tied us into.

"There might be another way," Danu said.

"Tell me," I asked eagerly.

"Arthur. You and he are destined for each other. He is the sovereign-blessed king of all Briton, you the goddess who will bestow the final blessing upon him."

"How?" I asked. "Tell me how and I will do it."

"Your love, and your joining. You must love Arthur, and you must marry him. And when you lay with him, perhaps there will be power enough to break even my spell."

Interlude

Morgana

The crow hopped into the herb-incensed cave. Above, crystals glittered in the flickering firelight as though twinkling stars in a midnight, moonless sky. Magic swelled in this place, filling even the crevices in the stone walls and the insect burrows in the ground. A magic the crow knew well. The familiar smoke- and flame-scrying fireplace and soothing, hypnotic tones of the ancient druid within called to the crow's own druidic and fae magic.

Not wanting to be noticed, the crow surrounded herself with the shifting shadows and whispered druid incantations. Her feathers ruffled in the swirling wind and then her lashes snapped open as she tucked black strands behind her ear and away from her face.

Morgana chanced a look around a natural wall in the cave before the narrow passage opened into Merlin's den. The druid sat beside the witch, his eyes glowing bright gold and his pupils narrowed to reptilian slits. The hearth leapt with flames that danced in the shape of fae creatures. The court of the Túatha dé Danann, perhaps? In this trance, he would unlikely sense her presence, and Morgana relaxed a notch.

Perspiration dripped down the witch's face. Her hands gripped the arms of the chair until her knuckles turned white and fingertips purple. Silver-dusted lashes rested on her flushed cheeks as she sifted through magic and subconscious thoughts to the deepest part of herself. Morgana knew the ogham runes Merlin spoke over the witch's ensorcelled form.

An invitation to Danu, the mother goddess, to find her daughter.

A plea to break a géis.

A request to open and flood the witch with her fae-born powers.

Morgana's lip curled in disgust. She had suspected Fionnabhair Allán as fae-born for years—even suspected she might be a Gwenevere—ever since she encountered the warrior in training after her first bloods. As the crow, Morgana sat above a branch and watched, curious. The witch had always contained a strange smell that was *other*. One that perfumed sweetly of earthen white magic—but not one she had encountered before. A subtle scent like heather and hawthorn and the faint fragrance of an apple blossom.

The air grew thick and Morgana narrowed her eyes just as the witch regained consciousness.

"Steady," Merlin said, placing a hand on her arm as she coughed and wiped at her eyes. "Did you find Danu?"

"Aye," the witch said, a bit breathless. "My mother couldn't unlock the géis. But she did have an idea of how I might be able to do so."

"Excellent. Tell me as we walk back to the keep and find Arthur."

The witch stood and then met Merlin's gaze. "There's more. The Fomorians have taken over Danu's court."

"Ah," the druid said. "As we suspected. Come, let us tell the king."

Morgana quickly backed out of the cave and into the night in a flight of feather-light footsteps. She needed to share this news with her sisters quickly. Before the witch regained her powers. If she was the daughter of Danu, Morgana and her sisters would need to devise a more powerful plan than the one currently in place. A far stronger magic was now needed. A far stronger Fomorian ally too.

The whispers of the desperate and dying circled Morgana in a rush of leaves and shadows and wind. Blinking her black eyes, the crow hopped onto a mossy rock and watched as the witch and druid left the cave and wandered up the path toward the keep.

Elathia had promised them aid in defeating her half-brother and securing his kingdom. But so far, the regent had done little. It was time to call in a favor. When Caerleon came for them again, they would be ready. With a weapon strong enough to defeat even a Gwenevere.

Chapter Twenty-Three

Arthur

O'Lynn's army had arrived at the keep. The maelstrom of warriors outside was deafening. Horns, shouts and war cries, horses whinnying.

Arthur took the stairs two by two, vaulting up to the top of the keep's wall where Percival, Galahad, and Lancelot grimly surveyed the scene below.

"How many?" Arthur asked, blowing out a breath.

"All of them," Lancelot replied. "Plus three dark faeries. We need Merlin up here. *Now.*"

"He's with Fionna, trying to break the géis. We must not disturb them unless it is absolutely necessary," Arthur replied.

"It's beginning to feel absolutely necessary, ye ken." Percival's normally cheerful face was grave.

"They're not showing signs of a full-on assault." Galahad scratched at the dirt-caked sweat in his beard. "It seems they plan to intimidate."

"They don't need to assault us," Lancelot said.

"They can just sit there scratching their balls and starve us out."

Arthur smiled. For once he had a counter to Lancelot's dark assessment. "They don't know we have the Cauldron of Plenty. They'll starve before we do."

"But will the curse continue to worsen?" Lancelot asked.

"One problem at a time, Lance," Arthur said. "Our focus now must be on defending the keep and watching for any tricks they might be trying to play. And we must buy Fionna and Merlin time to discover what has been hidden."

The soldiers below were falling silent, a pregnant hush falling over the landscape. The horde of warriors parted as O'Lynn walked forward with Morgana at his side.

Fionna's father Brin was slowly ascending the stairs, and then halted next to Arthur. "It's a fine fortress you have here," he said softly, his eyes fixed on the mass below.

"But?" Arthur asked, his eyes not leaving his enemies' form.

"But I know a thing or two about the calm before the storm, lad. And a great storm is about to break upon yer shores, Arthur Pendragon. I'm sorry for my part in it."

"My father set this into action long ago with his greed and treachery. No apologies necessary." Hot tears burned the back of Arthur's eyes as he grit out, "This war is now mine to finish as Uther's bastard prince."

As much as Arthur had wanted to be different, to avoid his father's bloody legacy, the battle had still found him. Here he was, unwittingly pitted against the Túatha dé Danann. The name Pendragon carried the might of a dynasty, but also all the blood that had been spilled. Yet . . . perhaps there could be another way. If Uther Pendragon stood upon this wall, he would vow to crush the army below him like an insect beneath his boot. If war was Uther's way, could not diplomacy be Arthur's? Surely there was some way to solve this through negotiations. And, if not, talking could buy Fionna and Merlin the time they needed to break the géis.

"O'Lynn," Arthur shouted, his voice carrying on the wind. "Before we suffer even more of a grievous loss of life, I would treat with you. To see if we can reach a peace between us!"

Lancelot and the other knights looked at him sharply but said nothing. In this, Arthur was king, and they obeyed.

"Peace?" O'Lynn hollered back. The scoffing tone of his voice was clear even at this distance.

But then Morgana leaned in, whispering in his ear.

What Arthur would give to be a fly buzzing about that conversation. To know what schemes she concocted, even now.

"We agree to a meeting," O'Lynn shouted. "Tomorrow at daybreak. Before yer gates."

"We each bring a delegation of four," Arthur shouted. "No more."

"Agreed," O'Lynn replied.

Arthur heaved a sigh, and then turned to Lancelot.

"You do not think there can be peace with Morgana, do you?" Lancelot was incredulous.

"Likely not. But I just bought Lady Fionna another night."

"If I may," Brin said. "Do not let yer guard down. It would be like the Uí Tuírtri to mount a sneak offensive while yer not looking."

"A wise caution, Your Majesty," Arthur said. "Lancelot, I want soldiers patrolling every crack of these walls."

Lancelot nodded. "Who will you bring?"

"Merlin and Lady Fionna." Arthur considered. He wanted Lancelot and Galahad here, commanding his troops. The soldiers were most familiar with them, and they would keep cool heads if anything went wrong. "Sir Percival, bring that adder stone of yours. You will be the fourth. We will have advanced warning, if Morgana tries anything."

"Aye," Percival said eagerly.

Arthur turned. "I'm going to see how things are going for Merlin and Fionna. Hopefully they've made some progress." He turned and hurried down the stairs, his mind racing. What could he offer Morgana and her sisters that would appease them? Presently, they wanted nothing short of his kingdom, perhaps his very life. He would not yield to their vengeful whims willingly.

"Arthur!"

Arthur recoiled as he almost smashed into Fionna. Merlin was following close behind. He let out a rueful grin. "Apologies," Arthur said. "I was not paying attention to where I was going."

"Ye have much on your mind," Fionna said. Her silver eyes were shining, and her color was high. Did they have a breakthrough? "We could hear the shouts and war cries from Merlin's cave."

"The enemies are at our gates," Arthur said. "Please tell me you have made some progress."

Fionna glanced sideways at Merlin, who stepped up beside her. "We have and we have not. Fionna did make contact with Danu. The goddess was not able to lift the géis. But, she gave us an idea for how to help Fionna break free."

"Excellent!" Arthur said. "Let's do what is necessary. What are we waiting for?"

"It is not so simple a thing," Fionna said, ducking her chin and shifting her focus to her boots.

"Perhaps I will leave you two to talk," Merlin said, and then he swooped off towards the wall.

Fionna studied the dirt beneath her, where she was toeing the ground with her boot. Her lips thinned into a straight line as an uncharacteristic spark of doubt glittered in her distracted silvered gaze. Then, in typical Fionna fashion, she lifted her head and straightened her shoulders, her eyes peering ahead as if a sentry on guard.

Arthur's heart stuttered in his chest. To see Fionna so uncertain was a strange vision indeed. He took her chin gently in his hand, tilting her face so she met his eyes. "Whatever this challenge is, we will meet it together."

She licked her lips, her eyes flicking from his.

"That's the thing, My King. Danu shared how the only way for us to break the géis is"––She sucked in a ragged breath and then the words tumbled out––"for ye and I to wed. And join together."

Arthur felt rooted to the earth as her words sank in. He and Fionna, wed? The very thought made him lightheaded with joy. He wished for nothing else in his heart of hearts––but . . . she seemed so uncertain.

"You do not seem pleased at this turn of events," Arthur said carefully. "Do you not wish to wed?"

She tore her chin from his fingers, looking away. Tears glittered in her eyes. "I wish it more than anything in this world," she admitted softly. "But I don't know if this is what ye want. I would not have you take me as a wife out of obligation, nor crown me queen consort of Caerleon if ye wish for a different political alliance."

I wish it more than anything in this world.

Her words melted into his very essence, setting his soul aflame with light and fire and desire. Fionna wanted to marry him. To have Fionna at his side, in his bed, all the days of his life––such an outcome could only be a delirious dream. "Princess Fionnabhair," he whispered, his voice cracking with emotion. "I too wish to marry you more than anything in this world."

"Truly?" She looked at him with breathless hope. "A king is to seek his future queen's hand, is he not? And ye had not asked—"

"We've been a little busy," Arthur said, his eyebrows shooting up. "And since when did Fionna Allán see fit to be bound by the constraints of Welsh societal tradition?"

A smile grew on her face, and it was as if the sun broke from behind the clouds, bathing him in its warm glow. "So . . . we're to be married?"

Arthur nodded, feeling his own grin stretch across his face until his cheeks wanted to cry out from the might of it. "We shall marry." He swooped her up into his arms and spun her around and around until he was drunk on dizziness. "We're getting married!" he shouted to the heavens and all who were listening. For in the history of mankind, he thought a man had never been happier than he in this very moment.

Chapter Twenty-Four

Fionna

The world spun beneath me as Arthur twirled me around and around, until I was dizzy with the headiness of our moment.

Arthur placed me down gently and then his lips were on mine as I staggered into his chest, anchoring myself in his strong stance, his firm foundation. His kiss set my head spinning all the more—insistent and full of promise. My toes curled at the thought of a night with Arthur—the only one of my knights I had not lain with. As though, deep down, I knew to save this special moment for last.

At the thought of my other knights, my elation dimmed.

Someone nearby cleared their throat, and I seized upon the distraction, breaking off the kiss. It was Merlin.

"Congratulations," the druid said, nodding at us. His unlined face was impassive as ever, but something about him seemed . . . pleased. "There are arrangements to be made. Shall we convene in three candle-marks time in the Great Hall?"

"Perfect," Arthur said, his arm about my shoulders. "We'll rally what we can for a ceremony. You will preside?"

Merlin inclined his head. "It would be my honor, Your Majesty."

My father, Percival, and Galahad were crossing the courtyard to join us.

"Is it true?" Brin asked. "I heard ye hollering. Is my darling daughter to be wed?"

I nodded, and my father crossed the distance between us, pulling me into his arms. "Congratulations, lass," he whispered in my ear. "May yer years be filled with happiness."

I fought the lump in my throat as I pulled back, as my father shook Arthur's hand, offering him kind words. But my eyes were locked onto Percival and Galahad, the sad smiles on their faces. Percival stepped up first, pulling me into an embrace. I breathed in the citrus scent of him, the warm aura of sunshine that washed over me. "I suppose I always knew he'd take the prize, dove," Percival said, attempting a shaky smile. "But it was fun to play. And . . . and I will still love ye until my dying breath."

Tears shimmered in my eyes, as a blizzard of emotions buffeted me. This wasn't right. To feel happy and so full of sorrow at the same time. Did marrying Arthur truly mean giving up these other extraordinary men? Resigning them to sadness and want? Galahad embraced me next, and a sob wracked my body, despite my every effort to hold in my emotions. My big knight enveloped me, as warm as a hearth fire and as strong as an oak tree. To never again see the golden stretch of Galahad's skin, tawny beneath my pale fingers . . .

"Be strong," Galahad whispered in my ear. "It is a knight's duty to sacrifice for their king. And no one deserves yer love more than Arthur."

His words emboldened me. He was right. I did love Arthur deeply, and I had never known a king or a man worthier of devotion. So why did my heart cry out for more?

"Lancelot?" I asked.

"He's watching the wall," Percival said. I looked up and spotted his dark curls against the fading dusk. He looked away as our eyes met, turning back to the army below. It would be too much to exchange these regrets with him.

I hastily wiped a threatening tear and turned with a bright smile toward Arthur. My king. My soon-to-be husband. Arthur caught the look on my face and his gaze flicked to Percival and Galahad, his own smile dimming.

"I need a dress!" I said, and hurried toward my chamber, away from the prying eyes of these men who saw and understood too much.

Caerleon's servants did an admirable job of readying the keep for a wedding, given the hostile army camping at our gate and the limited time to prepare for the festivities.

Several serving girls rallied to my aid, drawing a bath for me in record time. After scrubbing the blood and grime of war from my body, they helped me wash and then braid my hair in an intricate crown atop my head with half of my waist-length hair cascading down my back. Another found a gown, a resplendent thing in dark red trimmed in gold—the colors of my king's banner—the swooping neckline and cuffs beaded with tiny pearls. I hardly felt ready when the time came for me to walk to the Great Hall. My stomach flipped with nerves.

My father waited outside my room, clad in a fresh tunic. "I thought ye might like an escort." He offered me his arm.

"I'm so glad ye're here Da," I said, hitching my elbow through his. "If only Aideen could be here too."

"We'll get her back." Brin patted my hand.

"Aye, we will."

"Perhaps ye have one thing to thank that bastard O'Lynn for," my father continued. "I would be captured a hundred times if it meant you would end up here, where ye were meant to be. Happy."

"It would be nice for me to be happy *without* ye having to be captured and tortured . . ." I smiled.

"If wishes were horses, beggars would ride," he said.

We rounded the corner, and Arthur stood, waiting nervously by the door. He had bathed and changed too, and now looked devastatingly handsome in a tunic of dark red—a similar shade to my gown—the hems trimmed with gold. His polished oak-leaf crown sat atop his brows, one now arching as he gaze roved over my face.

"Might I have a minute with Fionna, Your Majesty?" Arthur asked, his eyes never leaving mine. "Before we go in."

"Ye're the king," Brin said, and gave me a kiss on the cheek, before slipping through the double doors.

Arthur took my hands, looking me up and down reverently. "You look as beautiful as the sunrise."

I smiled. "You'll do too."

Arthur took in a deep breath, ignoring my attempts at humor. "I have been thinking. It does not seem right for our happiness to come at the expense of my brothers'. Lancelot, Galahad, Percival . . . they love you as much as I. And I know you love them too. We are family, all of us together."

I softened, stroking his cheek, feeling the smooth skin of his fresh shave. "Never was there a more generous man than ye, Arthur Pendragon. It is one of the many reasons I love ye." An idea was churning in my mind, a dream I kept locked tight in the deepest recesses of my heart. A way that all of us might be together. If Arthur was open. And his words warmed me that he might be. But Arthur deserved a wedding. A bride. A queen. Just as I had moments with each of my knights, my king deserved a moment all to himself. "I choose all of ye, it's true. Ye each own a piece of my heart. But let us think only on the piece you hold tonight. Ye and me. I would have us focus on our joy. To celebrate our love. There will be time to discuss a different future, with all of us together, as one." I hoped.

Arthur nodded, exhaling. "I would like that very much."

"Shall we?" I held out my hand, and Arthur took it, threading his fingers through mine.

"We shall."

The servants had managed to find bouquets of wildflowers and bows of greenery to festoon around the tables nearby where Merlin stood. Candles flickered on stands behind him while unlit tapers rested in the hands of those who gathered. The room crowded with people, nobles and villagers alike, who had been ushered inside the safety of the keep's walls from O'Lynn's ravaging. In the front row stood my knights, even Lancelot. I swallowed, trying to catch his eye, but he looked straight ahead, his rugged face stoic. I tucked thoughts of them aside, as carefully as a baby bird. I had meant what I said. Arthur deserved my undivided attention at our wedding.

Merlin raised his hands above his head and said, "Let us form a circle and bless this place."

I joined hands with Percival and Arthur, who joined hands with the other knights and nobles until we formed a circle. The remaining crowd stood at our backs as we watched Merlin lift a bundle of burning sage and meadowsweet.

The druid paced the perimeter of the circle, saying, "Elements of the north, come. Elements of the east, you are welcome. Elements of the south, join us. Elements of the west, attend us now. Gods and goddesses, we invite you to witness and bless the sacred union between Arthur Pendragon, High King of Briton, to Fionnabhair Allán, the Gwenevere, daughter of Danu, and earth- and sovereignty-goddess."

Murmurs rumbled around the circle, curious eyes glancing my way. But I ignored them all.

Merlin reached for the Blessed Grail on the table behind him and then dipped his fingers into the enchanted bowl. "We cleanse this circle of any wickedness and impurity." Lifting his fingers from the water, he flicked droplets across the stone floors as he paced round and round. "May only goodness and health flow from these stones and dance in this air." When complete, he set the Grail back onto the table and then approached me and Arthur. "Come, My King and his faerie bride. Step into the circle's center and open your hearts to the Earth and all her blessings. She smiles upon your union this day." The rings around Merlin's eyes flashed gold as his pupils narrowed to slits. "Yes, she has many riches in store for you both."

Arthur led me to the center, weaving his fingers with mine. His chest rose and fell in a quick rhythm, much like my own. An energy was present, one that flowed through my veins, my muscles, tingling, dripping sweet like honey until the very sensation coated me completely.

Merlin next grabbed a candle from the stand behind him and lit Lancelot's candle, who then lit Galahad's, then Percival's and so forth until the circle illuminated with tiny, sinewy flames. The image was magic itself. The amber glow painted me and Arthur in flickering shadows and light. Dressed in the Pendragon red, we appeared as though fire-breathing dragons. Mighty. Immortal. And fierce.

With a ceremonial hemp cord, Merlin began tying a knot over my and Arthur's clasped hand, his lips moving in ancient incantations and blessings. Arthur's green eyes met mine and held me captive. He was the blazing hearth fire of home, a soothing cool breeze in summer, a sturdy oak rooted deep in the earth, and a warm rainfall in spring. But most of all, he was my king and I was his land. And, from this point forward, I possessed power over his kingship as well as the health of his people. A power he granted me willingly.

My knees threatened to buckle, my legs wobbly. Even as Arthur spoke his vows and I spoke mine. Even when Merlin removed the corded knot from our hands. And when Arthur placed a crown of golden holly leaves and berries upon my brows. Together, we ruled the seasons, all the elements, light and darkness and, through our consummation, fertility for the land and her people.

The bright, tingling power surged through me and my head grew faint at the Otherworldly feel of Arthur's mouth pressing against mine. "My Queen," he whispered across my lips, claiming the breath in my lungs and the very beat of my heart. Ribbons of smoke twirled and writhed upward from the many candles now snuffed out in people's hands.

The crowd cheered around us. Then the knights and nobles rushed toward us in a crushing embrace.

I floated on wings of ebullience through the quick, makeshift feast. Nodding when I should and answering questions as they crossed my path. But my head was full of Arthur. An energy was building within me. The same energy that entered me in the circle's center. I thought I would burst as my heart cried out to know his pulse intimately. Then he grabbed my hand, a boyish smile on those very lips I wanted to taste again, and he led me out of the Great Hall and toward the gardens.

Chapter Twenty-Five

Fionna

Waning sunlight haloed Arthur in billowing golds and corals. The evening wind toyed with his shortened strands and carried to me the verdant scents of an oak forest, freshly cut apples, and spiced wine. I wanted to bury my nose against his skin and breathe deeply.

He led me past the kitchen garden to a seam in the timbered wall nearby. From the naked eye, the hidden opening appeared as though solid beams of hewn wood. A continuing wall. But, once through the opening, a new world spread out before me, one I had never encountered in all my explorations. "Beautiful," I said under my breath.

Slowing to a stop, Arthur cupped my face, his eyes searching mine. "I love you, Fionnabhair Allán," he whispered. "With your permission, I would know you completely."

"Yes," I breathed. "Ye have my permission, Arthur Pendragon."

His eyes shuttered as he drew in a giddy breath.

"We should be alone here. Safe from both prying eyes and invading armies." He gestured to the wild garden around us, secluded by several trees and a partial timber wall jutting out from the keep, but protected by the outlaying defensive wall. Flowers in every color of the rainbow blanketed the ground and climbed trellises all around us, as though a storied faerie garden. "This was my mother's favorite spot when she wished to hide." His smile dimmed. "But I would be glad to build new memories here with you. Happy ones."

I placed my hand on his chest and he looked away, brows furrowed, though he continued to cradle my face in his hands. "I am sorry we cannot journey into the forest alone," Arthur said.

Danu had explained to me that the best chance of awakening my powers would be found if we lay together upon the earth itself. "I care not where we make love," I replied. "Only that my heart can finally know the beating rhythm of yers."

He returned his gaze to mine in a single, soft blink. "Then, My Queen," he whispered, "marry me to the land and make me your king."

We couldn't shed our clothes fast enough. Though, at the same time, we wanted to relish each new flash of skin. He untied my gown from behind until the bodice slipped down my arms and gathered at my breasts. The silk caressed my body and I shivered with delight, anticipating Arthur's touch. His lips pressed to my shoulder. Then his mouth traveled to my neck, until he nibbled on my ear lobe.

"Not even the beauty of the moon compares

to you," he whispered in my ear. His warm breath pulsed onto my skin and my eyes fluttered closed. "Nor do the stars in the night sky hold a flickering candle to the soft lines and curves of your body."

Pleasure rushed through me at his poetic words and the sultry gravel of voice.

"Your breasts," he continued, his hands cupping the soft mounds and encouraging my gown to pool at my feet. "Your skin, and goddess above, your hips . . . they hold a spell over me." He stepped away from my back and turned me gently but firmly to face him. And, when his lips brushed along mine, he whispered, "And your mouth. You taste like an orchard in bloom. I want to savor your every kiss."

My fingers trailed down the freckles of his muscled chest as his lips captured mine. His skin was deliciously warm and drew me closer until my breasts pressed into the hard, ribbed lines of his torso. I ached to be surrounded by him, to drown in the heat of his passion. His arms wrapped around my waist as his hands splayed across the toned lines of my back as our kiss deepened.

His touch humbled me——reverent and soft——as if I were the most fragile thing he had ever held. And perhaps I was, for I knew I claimed not only his heart, but his land. I owned him completely now, and there was no going back. Other marriages may handfast for a year and a day, but not ours. We were forever bound before the gods and elements.

Gently, he lowered me beneath him in the swaying wildflowers. The moss and grass cradled my trembling body. The energy wanted release. Wanted *him*.

His fingers tenderly brushed strands of flyaway hair from my face as his eyes drank me in. "I am so in love with you," he said. "I am lost in this feeling."

"Come find me, then," I said in playful reply.

A shy smile played across his lips. This boyish side of him always pulled on my heartstrings. We were a king and a queen, a ruler and a demi-goddess. But this moment, as I took in his rising blush, cherished each freckle on his face, felt the way his fingers grazed along my side, past my hip, to my thigh, we were just a boy and a girl. In the face of our enemies and tribulations, it was easy to forget that I was only twenty years old and he just two and twenty. But here, our kingdoms and duties and powers fell away until our breath formed the wind fluttering the leaves above us and our bodies became the very earth we lay upon.

He slid into me as we kissed, and I gasped as the building power swirling within me released into him. He sucked in a deep breath, his eyes closing with the feel me. All of me. The ground beneath us tremored, similar to my experience with Percival. And, for a single sand of time, I thought of this, how both Percival and Arthur were sovereign-blessed kings, and how I had joined with them both and only when the earth lay beneath my back.

Then we began to move, all else forgotten but Arthur. His strong arms embraced me as his hips ground into mine. I could feel the sculpted muscles of his chest, his stomach, the way the muscles of his back rolled beneath my fingertips. He was beautiful, a breathtaking dance of passion and love, infused with the headiest romance I have ever known. Even the way his body moved was poetry.

His lips kissed down my throat and then dragged back to mine. "I want to become the sun in your hands," he whispered. "To burn . . . to know total destruction."

My breath stirred for an intoxicating beat of my heart. And then I rolled him over until he was pressed into the moss and grass. Wildflowers swayed around my head and the wind fingered through the long tresses rippling down my back. The sun sank behind the walls and trees and brushed the sky in streaks of lavender and indigo.

Our eyes locked as my hips began to roll against his. "Burn, My King," I said, and his arms fell over his head as pleasure rippled through us both in glittering waves of bliss. Light and sensation filled my body as I watched this gorgeous, powerful man surrender to me. Bearing his neck and leaving his body vulnerable. I understood his demonstration of submission and tears pricked at my eyes. He would lay his life down before me to destroy and make whole.

"Arthur . . ." I moaned his name when the earth rose up to consume me. I was every blade of grass, the breaking dawn, the life-giving soil. Glistening dew drops rolled down my body like twinkling stars. My fingernails dug into his pectorals as he heaved for breath, his lips flushed with arousal. His fingers gripped my arse, pulling me tighter against him. Deeper. With every thrust of his hips, I died. With every roll of mine, I was reborn.

The swirling, tingling energy—I could now name the sensation. Thousands of roots curled through me and anchored me to the earth in sensual touches. Unfurling leaves of feral light shimmered along my self-control until every scintillating beam bloomed in my core. I turned to fire, ablaze with the feel of Arthur's body tangling with mine. He was an oak tree and I was his life-giving energy, our limbs the rambling roots burying deep into the soil of our future.

In this place, we were a mighty force. Armies blew away before us in a hot gust of fury. The ground healed and brightened to every vibrant shade imaginable. Our love was immovable. Our destiny unshakable.

Arthur cried out first, his body arching in muscled spasms of pleasure. I cried out next as my body became moonlight—silvered, crystallized dust and the throbbing illumination of an entire star-flecked sky. We remained still, basking in the glow of our love-making. Even as his seed dripped from my thighs and anointed the ground.

His eyes fluttered open and then he stared at me in hazy bliss. I had married my king to the land.

My hand fluttered up to feel the curve of my ear. It was human as always—no sharp faerie point. And though I had felt a taste of the earthen magic brewing inside of me when we joined, it had drained from me with our climax. I now felt the same as before. A warrior princess from across the Irish Sea who held the heart of a king and his three knights. Sated and languid with the love of a king, but not magic. Not

. . . godlike. Disappointment welled within me. Perhaps I wasn't the Gwenevere and my vision of Danu had been induced by desperation alone.

I looked around the garden and frowned. No change. Same as when I drank from the Grail at the Red Spring. Same as when I joined with Percival in the forest, even though the earth trembled beneath me.

Arthur caressed my cheek. "My wife . . ."

Tears gathered on my eyelashes and spilled down my cheeks. "It didn't work," I said through the lump growing in my throat.

"Fionna," he whispered softly. "You are all I have ever wanted. Anything else you bring to our union is a bonus. But you . . . you are more than enough. You're my every heartbeat. My very breath."

He wiped away a tear with his thumb and then gathered me to him. There, in this hidden garden, Arthur held me as I wept, our bodies entangled, my head pressed into the crook of his neck. I had once stolen his sword and risked his kingship. Now, I represented the very land he ruled. And I was still broken.

Chapter Twenty-Six

Lancelot

The stench of burning feathers carried on the wind. An insufferable scent. O'Lynn's war camp must have burned dead crows and their fallen throughout the entire night.

But the reeking haze in the air wasn't what truly bothered Lancelot.

The keep felt different this morning. Lancelot felt different. As if a weight hung around his neck, a heavy shroud cloaking his body and blocking out the air and light. Was it the enemies surrounding them, pressing at their walls with oppressive presence? Or was it the fact that Fionna was wed. She was his queen. And she was Arthur's. And queens didn't deign to fraternize with mere knights. Even if they were exiled French faerie princes.

Last night, as the delicate circlet of holly leaves was placed on her brow, Fionna had looked more beautiful than he had ever seen her. And more distant. She had tried to catch his eye a dozen times, as she stood in the circle at the ceremony, as she sipped from a golden goblet at the hasty feast. He couldn't bring himself to meet those silver pools. To see in them all that could have been. And would never be. Was it better to taste heaven's sweet essence and then have it ripped from you, or to never know? Lancelot thought he preferred the latter. It was ironic, in a way. In the end, Morgana's curse wasn't even necessary. Fate saw fit to rob Lancelot of the only woman he had ever truly loved. His Gwenevere.

He trudged outside to meet the others where they were to gather before the gates. It was time for Arthur to treat with O'Lynn and Morgana. A risk, but a risk worth taking if it bought Fionna enough time to break the géis and unlock her powers.

At the gates, she was the only one waiting. Gone was the gauzy dress of last night, the one that hugged every lithe curve. She was back in her boiled-leather armor, her swords at her hips, her hair braided in a long tail down her back. She turned as he approached, as if she felt his very presence.

"Lancelot," she murmured, her hand drifting to her heart as she gazed upon him.

"My queen," he said, bowing deeply at the waist.

"Don't do that," she crooned. The space between them felt as wide as the waters separating Britannia from the mainland.

He muttered, "It's only proper."

"Since when are *ye* concerned with propriety?" she asked. "Ye don't fawn over Arthur like *that*. Nothing has changed. I'm still me."

"Everything has changed," he replied.

His words were flint, lighting the fire in her eyes.

She stepped toward him, and he stepped back. "It changes nothing about how I feel for ye."

"I'm sure your husband would have something to say about that." Lancelot knew his words were unfair. Especially as he knew why they had wed so suddenly, with so little discussion. But he couldn't help it. Two days ago, he had been buried to the hilt in this enthralling woman, his heart soaring as though he had never flown before. And now she was wed to another.

To Arthur. His brother.

Percival and Galahad approached, and Lancelot seized upon the distraction. "You ready Percy?" he asked, but Percival ignored him, approaching Fionna and pulling her into an embrace. "Congratulations, dove," he said, and Fionna leaned into him, burying her face in his chest.

Lancelot exchanged a look with Galahad as his chest tightened with envy. How did Percival do that? Make affection look so easy. Let the twists of fate fall from his shoulders like water off a duck's back? Perhaps Percival's love for Fionna was purer than his own. A love little concerned with propriety or jealousy or competition. Unconditional. That was Percival. And one of the reasons his own heart desired this man for himself as well.

They broke off their embrace and turned, Percival still with his arm slung around Fionna's shoulder. "To answer your question, crabapple, I am indeed ready. Adder stone in hand. Well, in pocket," he finished.

"How do ye feel?" Galahad asked Fionna. His

words were careful—formal—with none of the sultry banter they'd carried in the past. Their big knight was holding himself back from their new queen as well. "Different? Powerful?" Fionna and Merlin had explained how Danu thought marrying Arthur and laying with him might be the only way to break the géis that blocked her from embodying her full Gwenevere powers.

Fionna shrugged, brushing a strand of hair back from her forehead. "The same, honestly. Like me. I'm not sure what I was expecting . . . but I don't feel anything new." Her lips tilted in a frown and she shifted on her feet, clearing her throat.

"Maybe there's a delayed reaction," Percival suggested.

"Or perhaps your magic requires a threat to activate," Galahad offered. "Your powers will appear when the time is right. Like the Grail Sword."

"Perhaps," Fionna said. "I just wish Danu could have helped me. Helped us. She got me into this, seems like she should be the one to get me out."

"Goddesses," Percival quipped. "Can't live with 'em, can't live without 'em."

"I just hope we're all living at the end of this," Galahad remarked.

Arthur and Merlin crossed the courtyard to join them. Arthur's color was high, his eyes sparkled with vigor as he met Fionna's. Lancelot supposed wedding and bedding the woman of your dreams, who also happened to be a demi-goddess in disguise, would do that to a man.

"It's time," Arthur said, pulling his gaze away

from Fionna and taking them all in. "We'll see if we can find a way through this mess. Perhaps diplomacy isn't dead."

"Be careful," Lancelot found himself saying. "Keep your eyes on her."

Arthur slid him wary look and nodded. There was no confusing who he meant.

Galahad and Lancelot stood ram-rod straight as the other four strode toward the wide oaken gates.

"Open the gates," Arthur called out, and soldiers manning the gates hopped into action, retracting the big oaken bars.

"I can't shake the feeling that this is a terrible idea," Galahad said quietly, his eyes locked onto the four figures filing through the narrowly opened doors. "Even death's ash clings to the air."

Lancelot frowned, his brows furrowing deeply. "My observation as well."

Lancelot paced stiffly through the keep. Last night he had checked on the soldiers in the barracks, secured the positions of the men along the wall. Weapons were oiled and sharpened, and bundles of arrows were stacked neatly next to jugs of oil. The Great Hall had been returned to its role as makeshift medical ward and hospital, with supplies piled and ready for any coming battle. Merlin had spent the evening making food in the Cauldron of Plenty, which, though some remarkable turn of druidic magic, had transformed to a cauldron large enough for a man to sit inside. Sacks of grain, piles of potatoes, squash, and figs, even jugs of ale all came out of this remarkable cauldron, filling their larders and stores. They were as ready as they could be for a siege or a battle.

But, still, Lancelot felt jumpy and uneasy. He had passed the unsettled feeling off as lingering effects from Fionna's wedding. But, if he were being honest with himself, that wasn't the reason. Something niggled at him, as if he had left a candle burning unsupervised in his chamber or forgotten something necessary.

His feet carried him into the hallways, through the back of the keep and toward the rear gate that led to the path down to Merlin's cave. Though they normally kept the gate open, the secret door in the keep's wall was invisible from the outside when the doors were closed, vanishing into just another stretch of formidable stone and timber. It was the only other way into the keep beside the front gate. And, unless a person knew it was there, they would never find the opening.

A lightning bolt of realization struck him. "Idiot!" he shouted at himself, so loud he startled a passing serving woman. In all his concern over rescuing Fionna and Percival from their own fool rescue plan, followed by Fionna's Gwenevere powers, and the wedding, he had completely forgotten that Morgana apprenticed to Merlin. She knew about this secret door. She knew exactly where to find it too.

Lancelot broke into a run, his boots flying on the stone floors. They needed to reinforce the door. They needed to station men at the entrance in case O'Lynn attempted an assault. O'Lynn and Morgana would, without question, take advantage of a distraction created by peace negotiations to break in the back door.

He burst out of the main keep, barreling across the narrow courtyard to the back wall. He took the stairs two at a time, shouldering past surprised servants. Morning fog still clung to the ground outside the keep, not an uncommon sight in this marine climate. He hung over the edge of the wall, squinting into the mist. Then at the figures he saw moving there. A silent host, bristling with weapons. Readying to invade the keep.

Chapter Twenty-Seven

Percival

Percival gripped the adder stone tightly in his pocket, its jagged edge cutting into his palm. He didn't know what they would find when they stepped outside the gates, but he suspected it would only be trouble.

No one waited for them on the stone path outside the main gates as Percival, Arthur, Fionna, and Merlin walked slowly to the agreed upon spot to meet O'Lynn. In the distance, three horses approached.

Percival tried to keep his gaze fixed ahead on the horses trotting toward them, but he found his eyes gravitating toward Fionna. Her shoulders were tight; the muscles in her fine jaw were working furiously. She seemed like a notched bowstring waiting to be released.

It hadn't been fair to Fionna—the wedding night she had enjoyed. A ceremony hurried through with enemies at the door. She deserved joy and she deserved a celebration unlike Caerleon had ever seen. She deserved a languished morning naked in the sheets. He swallowed at the memory of her lean body beneath his, the silk of her skin. She deserved the very world.

He wasn't sure why Fionna's marriage to Arthur hadn't hit him like it had his sword brothers. Perhaps because he had known it was inevitable. This was the finale they had been dancing toward this entire time, was it not? Her marriage didn't have to change things. The wedding hadn't changed Fionna's heart, he was certain of that. Nor his. In his and Fionna's Gaelic worlds, lovers outside of marriage were a normal affair and permitted before their laws. And intimacy between warriors was also common, even between noble-titled warriors such as princes and queens. Especially as, unlike Wales and Briton, women were equal among the men and permitted as fellow warriors. So, Percival would keep pushing his luck until his king told him to back off.

The horses were growing nearer, and Percival could make out the riders. Two he recognized, two he did not.

"O'Lynn," Fionna spat.

"Morgana," Merlin said, the gold rings in his eyes flashing with magic.

A dark warrior with a shaved head and a long, black beard rode the last horse. Behind him was a beautiful young woman near his own age, with curls the color of chestnut.

Fionna hissed in a breath next to him, her eyes fixed onto the young woman. "Aideen," she breathed.

Percival and Arthur both looked at her sharply before looking back with a more appraising eye. So, this was Fionna's sister—O'Lynn's new, unwilling bride.

The group reined in their horses about fifty yards from where Percival, Arthur, Fionna, and Merlin stood.

Morgana slid gracefully from her black mare. Her dress was of the deepest blue and showed far more of her pale bosom then Percival imagined was proper. Atop her dark locks sat a sort of crown fashioned of antlers. It reminded Percival of Fionna's stag helm from the day she had earned her place as their fifth knight.

This crown made him uneasy, though. The black-painted bones whispered of dark magic and even darker nights.

The bald warrior before Aideen helped her from the horse and onto the dirt road. It was then that Percival noticed a thin collar around her neck, threaded with a chain the warrior held firmly in his meaty fist.

Fionna must have seen it too, because her swords rang in the crisp morning air as she pulled them from their scabbards. "I'll run the bastard through," she grit between clenched teeth.

Arthur held Excalibur before her, blocking her from O'Lynn's party. "Easy Fionna," Arthur said. It was the voice of a king speaking to his knight, not a husband to his new bride. "He brought Aideen to provoke you. Do not play into his hands."

Fionna mumbled a curse but gave a sharp nod.

Arthur dropped Excalibur, but Percival noticed Fionna did not re-sheathe her swords.

The last to dismount and swagger up to them

was Donal O'Lynn himself. The tall broad man was burly, with dark hair and a thick beard. He wore a gold torque about his neck. His boiled leather armor resembled Fionna's, the only thing that set him apart was the emerald green cape that was draped about his shoulders . . . that and the cocky-arse smile on his face.

Percival had never even met the man and he already wanted to slice him through. He couldn't imagine what restraint Fionna must be exercising.

"Arthur Pendragon," the man drawled in his Irish brogue.

"Donal O'Lynn," Arthur replied.

"Aren't ye going to welcome us to Caerleon, one king to another?"

"You have no need of a welcome. I've already seen how you've made yourself quite at home."

A smile spread across O'Lynn's face before he released a low laugh. "Such a fine land," he said. "Shame it's cursed."

Arthur pursed his lips. "Yes well, you need not concern yourself with that small detail. We have a remedy well in hand."

"Does not appear you do, *brother*," Morgana said. Her voice slithered like cold fingers up Percival's spine.

"We are here to discuss the terms of a possible peace between our people," Arthur said, his tone as hard as granite. "You have brought a hostile army to my shores. You have burned and ravaged my villages. But . . . the inevitable clash between our warriors would result in a great loss of life. I am willing to grant you this one chance to reach an accord between us. What is it that you want?"

"Straight to the point," O'Lynn said. "There are a few things I want, lad. That fancy sword of yers . . ."

Arthur's lips tightened into a straight line.

"All yer lands, the keys to this fine keep of yers . . . and that witch at yer side." He nodded toward Fionna.

"This is a peace negotiation," Fionna spat. "And yer request for me is an insult." Her face was furious, her silver eyes flashing between O'Lynn and where Aideen stood demurely with that horrible collar around her neck.

O'Lynn's thumbs were hooked in his belt loops, as if he were having the time of his life.

Arthur held up a hand and Fionna fell silent. "I'm afraid the possession of my wife is not part of our negotiations."

Morgana's eyes widened, and Percival thought he saw something there—something like fear. But the emotion was gone as quickly as it appeared.

O'Lynn's smile slipped but he recovered quickly. "Seems we've both tasted the nectar of the Allán women. Though, I admit, I found the vintage a bit sour."

"Captivity can do that to a woman," Fionna gritted out. "Perhaps if ye could find one ye didn't have to chain—"

But Arthur looked at her, and she fell silent, her fuming rage palpable. "Let me tell you what my terms will be," Arthur said. His composure hadn't slipped a hair's breadth the entire time. Percival had to admit, he was impressed. Arthur continued. "You turn over Aideen to us, and then you leave these shores, never to return. You take no more aggressive action toward Clann Allán and you never conspire with my half-sister or her two sisters again. Those are my terms. What say you?"

O'Lynn smiled deepened as his eyes glittered wickedly. "Appears we will be unable to reach an accord, Pendragon."

The gate creaked open behind them and Percival dared a glance over his shoulder.

Lancelot slipped through the doors, hurrying toward them.

"What is this?" O'Lynn said.

"Peace," Arthur said, holding up a hand. "There must be a matter of some importance. He means you no harm."

"I'll be the judge that. The agreement was four, Pendragon, and here I see five."

Lancelot whispered in Arthur's ear even as O'Lynn bellowed at him.

Percival watched as Arthur's face darkened, turning stormy. He whipped his head back to the party before them. "My second tells me that there are Uí Tuírtri warriors surrounding our keep even now. You have broken the terms of this engagement." Arthur pulled Excalibur from its sheath. And the sound vibrated through Percival's very chest.

Following suit, Percival pulled out his blade, not sure what would happen next. Would Arthur engage? Or retreat to the keep?

But something very unexpected happened,

something that robbed all thoughts of battle from his mind. Darkness fell over their party as thick as pitch. Cries of alarm arose from both Arthur and Lancelot.

But with the adder stone in Percival's hand, he peered through a strange bubble of daylight. Morgana's hands were up, the darkness oozing from her like squid ink.

O'Lynn hurried to his horse. He was fleeing.

Relief washed over Percival. They would not come to blows. Not yet anyway.

Then, in the bubble of light, he caught sight of something that chilled the blood raging through his veins.

Fionna—blind as a bat, bathed in unnatural darkness—sprinted across the distance between them and O'Lynn. Toward her sister.

"Fionna!" Percival couldn't help the cry that escaped from his mouth. For the warrior who held Aideen's chain had pulled a knife from his belt, a blade as long as his forearm, and swung the knife wildly before him. And Fionna was running straight toward the warrior.

Fionna connected with her sister. Their hands grasped at each other, the women crashing together with the force of a lifetime of sisterhood ripped apart.

Percival sprinted toward Fionna even as the warrior who held Aideen's chain stabbed blindly. But it was too late.

The warrior brought his wicked dagger down— into Fiona's back.

She stiffened in surprise, her mouth opening in a silent scream, her body going rigid in Aideen's arms.

Percival was crossing the distance, but his legs were too slow.

The warrior pulled the knife out and stabbed again. And again.

Aideen screamed her sister's name. Tears coursed down her face.

Percival rammed the man through to the hilt with his sword in the strange darkness, a roar of fury bellowing from him.

"Percival?" Fionna said as she staggered backward into his arms.

"Fionna!" Aideen cried out, but O'Lynn moved his horse between them, and it was all Percival could do to get a grip under Fionna's back and knees and haul her up into his arms.

He turned and lunged toward the keep, Fionna's blood slick on his fingers. Her eyelids fluttered.

It all happened in a few split heartbeats of time—the few measures it took Merlin to counteract Morgana's strange darkness.

Daylight flared once again and Percival blinked at the brightness, almost running into Arthur. His king's eyes went wide at the sight of Fionna in Percival's arms. Fionna bleeding. And dying.

Chapter Twenty-Eight

Galahad

Galahad jogged back from the barracks, breathless from rallying the soldiers to defend the keep. Longbow archers were arrayed along the wall above the secret western gate while men boarded up the doors, barricading the narrow corridor with furniture, stray stones, anything they could find.

Galahad had an uneasy feeling in his chest—a tightness. As if in a moment, everything could change. He was eager to return to the courtyard and make sure their king was all right. And their queen. He shoved aside all the emotions that word bubbled to the surface. Fionna was their queen. Arthur's wife. And that was that. A man didn't lie with another man's wife. Certainly not his king's. This was strict code within the Norse village where he'd been raised, and one he took seriously.

The gates were creaking open now and the figures retreating through sent a lance of fear straight to his heart. In Percival's arms was Fionna. Bleeding and unconscious.

"Fetch the chirurgeon, and her father!" Galahad bellowed at a servant, who startled like a skittish deer before running back toward the keep.

"What happened?" Galahad asked as he met them.

Arthur's face was haggard, as if his king had aged a lifetime, while Lancelot's face was more furious than he had ever seen. Even Merlin wore an expression of shock and doubt, more emotion than Galahad had ever witnessed from the stoic druid. Percival appeared as though the only one determined, his arms firmly fixed beneath the body of their fifth knight and queen.

"She went for Aideen," Percival said, his voice breaking. "And was stabbed."

"Her sister was there?" Galahad asked, mouth falling open. What kind of man would flaunt a prisoner at a peace meeting?

"Later," Arthur snarled. "Let's get her inside."

"The Great Hall," Galahad said. "It's been set up as a medical ward." He received his first real look at Fionna as he hurried beside them, and his mouth went dry. Her face was as pale as death, except for the crimson flecks that dotted her lips. Her wound must be grievous indeed. Was she even still breathing?

"Merlin?" Arthur asked as they raced through the halls, as fast as they could go without Percival jostling Fionna too much. "Can you sustain her with your magic?"

"I am trying," Merlin said. The lines furrowing about his mouth and brow deepened. "She is weakening. Perhaps with the herbs in my cave—"

"The cave is cut off," Galahad said. "There's no way."

Merlin grimaced. "I will do what I can."

"Do everything, man," Arthur snapped. "If you have to lend her your own life essence, you do it."

"Of course, my king."

"Set her down here," Galahad said, knocking a bowl and a pile of linens off a table to clear a space.

Percival set her down gently, and when he stepped back, wiping his hair back from his forehead, Galahad saw that his hands—his leathers—were drenched in blood. "My gods," Galahad whispered. Swallowing back his fear, he placed a trembling finger to her wrist, hoping to still feel a pulse.

"She was stabbed in the back," Percival managed as he hiccupped back a sob. His crimson hand hovered before his mouth, his eyes not leaving her. "Three wounds."

Galahad leaned an ear down over her mouth, trying to listen over the thunder of his heart. To feel some faint whisper of breath. Some sign of life. Something more than the silence he was feeling in her wrist. The absence of movement where a pulse should be. From his vantage with his head crooked, Merlin was in his line of sight. The druid met his eyes and pursed his lips into a thin line. And infinitesimal nod. No. No. Merlin was confirming what the signs were telling Galahad, the ones his mind was refusing to accept.

Galahad slowly straightened, placing Fionna's arm back down at her side, curling his fingers around hers. When he spoke, the words were a rasping whisper. "I'm . . . I'm sorry, Arthur. She——" He sucked in a sharp breath. "She's gone."

Fionnabhair Allán was dead.

Silence settled upon them, thick and deafening. Percival's bloody hand still fluttered before his mouth, while Lancelot looked as white as Fionna, as if he himself had been struck by a mortal blow. Arthur's eyes were wide and wild, and he only shook his head, over and over, his breath coming in tight and quick.

The light that was their Fionna had dimmed and snuffed out.

Galahad looked at her, part of him needing to double check. Wanting to be wrong. Fionna was tough as nails, unyielding as the winter wind. It would take something far more than a blade to wound her. To rip her from this world.

A keening note ripped from Arthur's lips and he fell upon her body, grasping her limp hand in his own, pressing his forehead to her breast. "My queen. My love," he mumbled, and then the sobs came, wracking his body, tearing open the wound Galahad was so valiantly trying to hold together—with little more than determination and duty. For this was Arthur's time to mourn. She was his wife. But Arthur's grief sang to a note in Galahad's own soul that he couldn't fight. Tears began to fall, hot and salty, gathering in his beard.

Percival rubbed at his face, her blood streaking down his eyes and cheeks. He muttered, "I didn't reach her in time. Oh gods——" His body began to shake as his own tears streamed through Fionna's blood. "I couldn't save her," he sputtered through his grief. "I couldn't save her. I'll . . . I'll never forgive myself." Lancelot turned Percival away from the awful sight and then the two men clung to each other. Percival buried his head into Lancelot's shoulders, their dark knight becoming a solid rock against the tide of sorrow. But an ember of volatile grief flickered in Lancelot's steeled eyes and, when the vengeance emerged, Galahad knew that O'Lynn would never know what dark, violent power of wrath sliced him and Morgana through.

Arthur gripped Fionna's body to his, her head lolling off his arm. Every part of Arthur shook as he openly wept, apologizing over and over again to her corpse. Silver eyes stared absently at Galahad.

Galahad turned, a shudder of sorrow clawing down his spine. He was unable to bear the sight of Fionna's perfectly still body any longer. Hushed stillness where vibrancy and life had been only moments before. Her body looked frail and small without the vitality of Fionna's essence. His king's keening sobs pierced the remainder of Galahad's resolve. He wiped tears from his cheek with the back of his hand, knowing it was useless, for more quickly followed. His eyes darted from object to object, anything to distract him from his reality. Anything to dull the pain. Skipping past Merlin, Galahad's gaze fell upon the Cauldron of Plenty, sitting quietly in the corner of the Great Hall, forgotten by all including the shocked servants who stood about, their eyes wide with the sight of their king's wild grief.

The Cauldron of Plenty. Hadn't Merlin and

Vivien shared how the Cauldron was rumored to be so powerful that it could even raise the dead?

A spark flared within the cold corners of Galahad's heartbreak.

He strode over to Merlin and seized the druid's arm, spinning him around and pointing at the Cauldron with a desperate finger. "Could it work?" He gripped Merlin's muscular bicep tighter, clinging to this last vestige of hope. For a different future.

Merlin's eyes rounded. "By the gods, it just might."

Galahad staggered back, wiping away his tears. Purpose and hope surged through him bright as a sunrise.

"Arthur," Merlin barked. "The Cauldron. The relic resurrects. Bring her here."

Arthur lifted his head, his eyes clouded and hazy. "She is gone," Arthur whispered, then spat, "Do not toy with me, druid."

Merlin clapped his hands, and it seemed the very thing to break Arthur free of his fog. "We have a chance to save her! Bring her body here!"

Blinking back his tears, Arthur scooped up Fionna and strode across the room.

"What magic is this?" Lancelot asked as he and Percival pulled apart.

"The Cauldron of Plenty is a powerful relic of the gods," Galahad said. "It's rumored to be able to resurrect the dead, remember?"

Percival's eyes lit up. "Och, what are we waiting for?! Do it!"

"We are doing it," Merlin snapped. He was helping Arthur lower Fionna's body into the cauldron. She disappeared into the black bowl as their hands released her body. Galahad and the others crowded closer. Fionna's body was curled into the fetal position on the bottom of the cauldron.

"You four," Merlin said. "Arrange yourselves around the cauldron." He stepped back and allowed each of them to form a circle around the relic. "Lancelot and Percival, you switch." Merlin said.

"What are you doing?" Galahad asked.

"Something I thought when we were first searching for a fifth knight, but the idea has only just crystallized in my mind. There is preternatural strength in your connection. The five elements. Fire," he pointed to Lancelot. "Earth," to Arthur, "Air," to Percival, "and water" to Galahad. "Fionna is the aether, the fifth element that binds you. I will draw on your essence while working the cauldron. It will strengthen the spell, and hopefully pull her soul back into her body."

"What must we do?" Lancelot asked.

"Just be willing," Merlin said. He pushed up his sleeves and closed his eyes. He then began chanting in a voice that raised the fine hairs on the back of Galahad's neck. Magic made him uneasy, but for Fionna, he would endure anything. A wind rose, even in the closed room, fluttering the tendrils of Galahad's hair. Merlin's words seemed to course through him, mingling with his blood until they were galloping through his veins, filling him with a tingling feeling unlike any sensation he had ever known.

The timbre of Merlin's voice rose, and the interior of the cauldron started to glow with lavender light. Galahad was shocked to see that the eyes of his fellow knights started to glow as well, as if their life force was bolstering the magic of the cauldron. Arthur's eyes glowed the vibrant green of grass in the summer sun; Lancelot's as red as the embers of a hearth fire. Percival's brown eyes now glowed silver, like Fionna's sometimes seemed too. The wind picked up and Merlin was shouting now, his arms raised.

Galahad held up his hand before his face and his palm reflected a blue glow, no doubt from his own eyes. He set aside his shock and focused on the cauldron, willing his energy, his life, his love, into that dark space. Into Fionna. Take all of me, Galahad thought. Take whatever you need, Fionna. I am yours. I would give my life a thousand times over, if it meant you could live.

A great bolt of lightning snaked from the ceiling into the cauldron's bowl, and Galahad threw up his hands against the brightness of the image. A crack of thunder followed, as deafening as the fall of a great oak.

Then silence.

Galahad slowly lowered his hands, straightening.

Merlin's shoulders sagged, but he was nodding. Footsteps raced behind them and Arthur turned. From the corner of Galahad's eye, he could see Brin Allán slow before them, his face bloodless, his shoulders shaking.

Ignoring everyone around him, Galahad peeked over the edge of the cauldron. Into the black space.

Breathless with anticipation. With fear and hope.

And he started like a hare before a wolf as a pale hand reached out from the darkness and clapped onto the rim of the cauldron.

Chapter Twenty-Nine

Arthur

Arthur dared not hope. True, Merlin had said that the Cauldron of Plenty had the power to resurrect the dead. But the lands of Briton were littered with objects with supposed supernatural powers. These claims were not always true. Yet as Merlin spoke in words of power, Arthur could not deny that he felt magic pulsing through him—emanating from him—and mingling with power from the others. And then, as quickly as the magic had begun, the whirlwind ended, leaving only Arthur and the ragged edges of his heart. Fionna was dead. His love. *His wife.* Why did the fates see fit to torment him so? To find love only to have it ripped from him—

A hand emerged from the recesses of the cauldron, gripping the lip. His hope flared to life like a shooting star blazing across the moonless night sky.

The others had jumped back at the unexpected movement.

Percival had his hand to his chest. "Merlin's balls,"

he practically yelped.

From the corner of his vision, Arthur could see his druid look sideways at the knight. But Arthur's gaze was fixed only on the cauldron. On the figure emerging from the mist within.

"Fionna?" Galahad murmured softly, stepping forward.

Then it was Arthur's turn to press a hand to his chest, as if he could keep his beating heart from galloping away. For the figure was Fionna. But also . . . not. Beside him, Brin whispered his daughter's name with reverence.

As she climbed to her feet, Arthur recognized the familiar. Fionna still wore her boiled armor stained with her lifeblood. Her silver-white hair was braided as it had been. But . . . a bright white light emanated from her once-silver eyes, and her skin glowed like milk in the moonlight. Her ears were also tapered to delicate points.

"Galahad?" Fionna asked, turning to him, blinking the light away. The glow died, leaving only her feather-soft lashes and her quicksilver eyes.

"Fionna!" Galahad closed the distance between them, wrapping her in his arms.

Percival whooped with joy, jumping a foot in the air. He dashed forward, embracing Fionna too, even while Galahad's arms remained around her, his golden locks splayed across her shoulder.

Across from him, Lancelot was shaking his head in disbelief, leaning forward, his hands on his knees.

Brin crossed the distance and joined the celebration of limbs and laughter, taking his daughter's face in his hands before openly weeping at the sight of her.

Arthur observed it all through his tears, even as a sweet rush of relief stirred him with force enough to weaken his knees. Fionna was alive. Fionna was . . . fae.

Brin, Galahad, and Percival broke off their embrace, stepping back while wiping tears from their eyes. Lancelot straightened and nodded as their eyes met.

Then Fionna turned to him. Arthur's stomach flipped. Gods, he was nervous! Fionna had always been beautiful, even unnaturally so. But now . . . She was radiant. Ethereal. Otherworldly. She was the moon. She was the snow in winter. The spread wings of a hundred swans in flight. An earth goddess. A Gwenevere. Who was he to deign to love her? Let alone be wed to her. Lay with her—

"Is my husband just going to stand there like a daft imbecile?" Fionna put her hands on her hips. "Or are ye going to embrace me?"

A startled bark of laughter escaped him, even as his cheeks reddened.

"It isn't every day I come back from the dead," she continued, stepping out of the cauldron and toward him. "I would think some congratulations are in order."

Yes, she was the first Gwenevere in a thousand years. A white enchantress of tremendous power. But she was also Fionna. His wife. And you didn't keep Fionna waiting. Arthur stepped forward, taking her face gently in his hands. Her skin was as soft as goose down and he could swear it glittered faintly beneath his dirty fingers.

She met his eyes and smiled. "Now kiss me, ye idiot."

Arthur smiled too, and drew her mouth to his, tasting the first thaw of spring, the wild whortleberries in summer. She tasted like eternity. And possibility. And also, distinctly, like his Fionna.

"Is it just me or does fae Fionna seem feistier than human Fionna?" Percival mused to himself as Arthur broke off the kiss.

"Not sure that's possible," Galahad replied. "You can only contain so much feisty in one body."

"One human body, aye," Percival countered. "But her body is fae now. The normal rules don't apply."

"You two are idiots," Lancelot said, but his words were light.

Fionna tucked herself under Arthur's arm, acknowledging each of them in turn. "Thank ye. And Merlin." She turned to the druid. "Thank ye most of all. For bringing me back from the darkness."

"I owe ye all a life debt, twice over now," Brin said.

"Da . . ."

"Brin," Arthur began, "Your Majesty, there is no debt to be paid."

"But—"

Arthur placed a hand on the older man's shoulder. "Peace. Let us talk no more of death and debts."

Fionna smiled at her father. "For our connection runs far deeper than death. As my foot touched the

Underworld, I still felt a tether to yer heart," she said first to Galahad, "And yers," to Percival, "and yers," to Lancelot." Her eyes softened and rested on Arthur, and she whispered, "And yers, My King."

Merlin inclined his head. His hands were tucked in his robes. "Indeed, it was your connection to each knight that saved you. I was just the conduit for the magic to work."

Fionna's eyes went thoughtful at that, and she exchanged a look with Arthur.

"So, is it safe to assume that the géis is broken?" Lancelot asked. "You look different. Do you feel different? Powerful?"

"I do feel different," Fionna said. "I can sense things. Like . . . I'm connected to it all. I can feel the sickness in the land. And as for power . . ." she closed her eyes. "There is something there. A well. I am not sure how to access it though." She furrowed her brow, and a gust of cold wind curled past, making Arthur shiver.

"Is that . . ." Galahad pointed to something in the air between them.

"A snowflake," Lancelot said, incredulous, stepping closer.

"Where?" Fionna asked, opening her eyes. The snowflake vanished as the room re-warmed.

"Morgana and her sisters will tremble before the might of your snowflake." Percival nodded with mock seriousness.

Fionna reached out and cuffed him gently. "Just wait until the snowflake brings friends."

Lancelot gaped at Fionna, a strange look for his

friend. "I can't believe it," he eventually pushed out in a breathy whisper.

"What?" Arthur asked.

"Morgana's curse. She said that I would love a Gwenevere as pure as the driven snow. I always thought it meant Fionna's fair coloring. But what if it was more? Fae don't have the ability to lie, but they speak in riddles and poetry. Perhaps Morgana foresaw how this Gwenevere's magic would have the ability to affect the weather. To bring snowfall, even in the heat of summer."

"Wait, so Fionna can't lie?" Percival grinned. "Whose manhood is lar––"

"She's only half fae," Galahad said, taking his turn to cuff Percival.

"Merlin," Lancelot turned to the druid. "Do you think you could teach Fionna how to wield her magic, so she could bring blizzard-like conditions?"

"Possibly," Merlin answered. "We'll need some time, however."

"How much time?" Arthur asked. "Because Morgana and O'Lynn won't give us much."

"Magic usually cannot be learned in an afternoon. But since it is in Fionna's very essence, I suspect she will be a quick study," Merlin said.

An idea was coming to life in Arthur's mind. "What's the status of O'Lynn's armies?" He asked.

Lancelot replied. "A soldier came and told me that the men behind the keep's wall had retreated. They were hoping for a stealth attack, not a drawn-out engagement. When O'Lynn learned we knew of his treachery, he must have pulled them back."

"But the reprieve will be short," Arthur said. "Tomorrow, at the latest, they will engage. They won't sit around too much longer."

"Aye, yer king speaks truth," Brin added.

"It's a big army to feed," Galahad said. "And with the sickness in the land, they won't be able to rely on foraging."

"Finally, something works to our advantage," Arthur murmured. "If Fionna can summon a blizzard, I want to bring the battle to them. Do you think you can manage it?"

Fionna nodded, a grim smile on her face. "To trounce Morgana and O'Lynn? I'll be ready."

Arthur took her hand, threading his fingers though hers and squeezing. "Good. I grow tired of Morgana's games. I grow tired of O'Lynn's soldiers darkening my doorstep. Ready the soldiers for battle. We attack tonight."

Chapter Thirty

Fionna

I was inundated with sensation. Merlin and I couldn't risk being caught unawares in his cave, so we ducked into a back corner of the library, where my knights had received strict orders to leave us alone.

But even here, in this hushed dusty place, I was overwhelmed. With my new fae senses, I felt like I was coming up from a lifetime underwater. Every fiber of Merlin's robes, every whorl of his tattoos, I could see them more clearly than I knew was possible. The smell of crisp, aging pages and old leather threatened to submerge me. So potent were the scents in the air that I could taste each one on my tongue. My ears perked at the sounds of a moth's wings brushing against a leather spine one row over. My ears—I couldn't help but feel them again, the delicate tapered points. Was this the true me? It didn't feel like me. It felt like stepping into someone else's body. I hoped this sensory saturation would settle in time.

But nothing was more foreign than the feel of magic. My skin felt alive with it—everywhere, tingling all around me. In the Great Hall, I hadn't understood how Arthur and each of the knights felt so different, so strange to me. Yet, familiar . . . like an old lullaby you had forgotten until you heard the familiar, comforting melody on someone else's lips. Now, I think, I was beginning to understand.

"Your Majesty. Did you hear me?" Merlin snapped his fingers in front of me, and I jerked to attention. "Magic is a lot to take in," he continued, his tone softening. "If these studies are too much, tell Arthur. You should not be expected to have mastered all the lessons in a few hours."

I squared my shoulders. "They're depending on me. Caerleon is. If I don't master my magic, people will die. There's no real choice."

"Then pay attention." The words were harsh, but his face held kindness. Understanding.

"Start again." I sighed, focusing on him. My sight zoomed in until I could see every pore. I shook my head, struggling to adjust.

"You know of the five elements," Merlin began again. "They are the basic building blocks of all life. They are also the fundamental essence of magic. To manipulate matter, you must understand its component parts."

I nodded sagely. I think I was following.

"Druids use aids to access these parts, to mold them as we will. Spells, herbs, other ingredients that will aid our manipulation. You, however, have those elements within you. You need no help to utilize them."

"Like the snowflake in the Great Hall," I said.

"Exactly. Anything you might want to change or create is all just a matter of fitting the elements together in different combinations and patterns. Most fae have an affinity to one or more of the elements. You, Fionna, are almost all aether."

"Great," I said, pausing to take in his words. "What does that mean?"

"Aether is space. The space between elements, where the spark of life itself begins and lives."

I pursed my lips together. "I don't know how that translates to magic."

Merlin considered, leaning back. "Imagine that performing a spell is like . . . planting a garden. You need the seed, the air for the sprout to breath, water, and the warmth of the sun. But you also need a place to plant it. Fertile soil. That is aether. That is *you*, Fionna."

That did make some sense. Though, the concept brought me no closer to doing actual magic.

"Let us try. You seem like the type where action may be preferable to theory," Merlin said. "Close your eyes."

I did as instructed and, almost immediately, a new sensation filled me. A light tug on my awareness.

"You must first find where within you your magic resides," Merlin said.

I knew that's what this feeling was. The moment I yielded to the tug, it was like I was pulled sideways within my own essence, into a place of infinite darkness. But it was not a fearful darkness. It was just . . .

empty. Waiting.

"This inner place may feel like—"

"I'm there," I said, cutting Merlin off.

A pause. "Very well. Now you must locate the other elements. Bring them into this space, and then use your will to mold them into what you wish them to be."

"And that will . . . make things happen? Magic?"

"Indeed. This is the law of correspondences. One of the immutable laws of the universe. As within, so without."

I was already reaching out, feeling for the elements. This was harder, I didn't know them like I knew aether. Like I knew myself.

But then, my consciousness brushed against something familiar, and realization flared within me. This feeling—this essence—it was one I knew. It felt like . . . Arthur. Like hearth and home, the smell of fresh churned soil, and fresh-baked bread. Earth.

I reached for the other elements eagerly, already knowing what I would find. I was familiar with them, the feel and taste and touch of them were written on my heart, on my very soul. I found air next, the feel of Zephyr galloping beneath me, the wind whipping my hair about my face. Trees fluttering in the breeze, bearing the scent of berries and green grass and the sound of laughter. Percival.

Then water. The strength and stamina that was Galahad, a raging river carving its way through the rocks and soil until after a patient millennia, all had yielded to the current's curving path. It was the strange feel of buoyancy as I floated on my back in a lake, face upturned to the heavens, supported by everything and nothing all at once.

Lastly there was fire. The heat and smell of a bonfire raging beneath the wide-open sky, the warmth of the embers shining in Lancelot's eyes. The feel of the sun as it filtered through a green forest, dappling my face with its sweet kisses. *Fire*, I thought. *I would know you anywhere.*

Tears trickled down my face as I pulled the elements to me, molding them in this space. Each unique—each essential for life. Every bit of flora and fauna that graced the earth, every man, woman, and child. Without all four, the world would fall to dust.

And, so would I.

I opened my eyes and found that my tears were joined by a warm deluge. Rain poured from the air above us, dripping down me and Merlin in rivulets. A surprised laugh escaped me as I put my hands up, blinking against the droplets.

"I think Arthur might appreciate it if you did not drown his entire library." A hint of a smile flitted across Merlin's lips.

Chagrined, I retreated into the space within myself, pulling the elements apart, wishing them well on their journeys back to their source.

When I opened my eyes again, the rain had stopped.

Merlin wiped his face, flicking the water to the ground. "Well. I think it's safe to say you have the source of your magic."

I surged to my feet, my heart soaring within me. "Aye. Aye, I have."

Chapter Thirty-One

Percival

Arthur had bid his knights to meet in his study when their tasks were complete. So, Percival found his feet bearing him that direction, though his mind was elsewhere. With Fionna. The morning's events seemed a strange dream. She had died. And come to life as a shining goddess, her appearance reflecting the wonder that Percival already knew was within.

It had taken all of them to bring her back. Merlin had set them around the Cauldron, and Percival had felt the magic tug on him, pull from him. He had known all along—the curse over the land, the blessed five, the Grail—from the very beginning they were tied and tangled together in a web of magic and emotion that could never be unknotted.

Percival stopped outside the door to Arthur's study, rallying his courage. He needed to tell his king. Fionna belonged to all of them, and herself. Percival wanted to marry her too. If she would have him.

His heart stuttered nervously as he stepped into the study. Lancelot, Galahad, and Arthur were gathered around Arthur's desk and standing over what looked like a crude map.

Their dark knight was leaning over the table and pointing at the paper in a way that displayed the formed muscles of his legs and finely-shaped arse. Percival jerked his eyes upward as he realized where they lingered, his face heating. A man could objectively admire the fine form of another man, no? *Never mind*, his mind whispered. His admiration for Lancelot was anything but objective.

"Ah, Percival," Arthur said. "The armory has provided the extra arrows we need?"

Percival nodded. "The bower discovered a few extra bundles of arrows inside a dusty chest in the corner of the armory. He placed them beside the cauldron for Merlin when he finishes with Fionna."

"Excellent," Arthur said. "I think we're all set here too." He put his hands on his hips. "How do we think our Fionna is doing?"

"Yer Fionna is faring well," Fionna said, striding into the room, her eyes shining like incandescent pearls.

Percival took a step back, despite himself. Fionna had always exuded force and confidence, but now . . . her very presence made him want to fall to a knee before her. She was *majestic*.

"You have accessed your magic?" Arthur asked.

She smiled. "Merlin is a wonderful teacher. And I am an apt pupil, if I do say so myself."

"And a humble one at that," Lancelot quipped.

"The battle plans are set," Galahad said. "If you're ready, we can attack at nightfall."

"I'm . . . almost ready," she said. "There is something I must attend to before we ride for battle. My King, may I speak with ye privately for a moment?"

Arthur nodded, and the two crossed the room to a corner, whispering in hushed tones.

Percival swaggered to the table and examined the map, wishing with every fiber of his being that he could look over his shoulder and lip-read what was going on in that corner. For he had something he needed to say too. But he wasn't sure if now was the right time.

Lancelot had no such compunctions. He was watching Arthur and Fionna with hawk eyes.

"And the three of us on the outside," Galahad rumbled softly. "How it ever shall be."

Percival looked up at that, unaccustomed to such moroseness from Galahad. He supposed losing the woman you love could do that to a man. In a way, she had died twice to them.

"It should not be so," Percival said. "I have not given up hope."

Lancelot reached out to cuff him, and Percival grabbed his wrist before he made contact, stopping his hand mid-air. Their eyes locked and Lancelot slowly raised an eyebrow. "Look who's all grown up," he murmured.

"I am," Percival said, perhaps a bit forcefully. "And I plan on asking for Fionna's hand. The worst he can say is no."

"The worst he can do is execute you or throw

you out on your ear." Lancelot eyes darkened, and a muscle pulsed along his jaw. Then he dropped his voice for Percival alone. "And I . . . I can't lose—"

"This is Arthur we're talking about," Galahad said quietly, interrupting. "He would never."

A throat cleared and the three of them snapped to attention. Fionna stood before them, Arthur a few paces behind.

"It's not every day a woman dies and comes back to life," she began. "And it makes a person realize a thing or two about what's important. When I felt the knife pierce my back, my mind was filled with the woeful thought of leaving Arthur. But more than that. I was filled with sorrow over the thought of leaving each of ye."

"And we ye, dove," Percival whispered.

She took in a long, shaky breath, and then lifted her chin. "The fact is, I love ye. Each of ye. And I think, despite the necklace's charms, that ye each love me. Truly."

"Ye know I do," Percival said.

"There's no other," Galahad agreed, resignation written across his handsome face.

Lancelot nodded slowly. "As much as I've tried to fight it, my heart is yours."

"When I tried to access my magic, I realized something. We are tied together, us five. By honor, and duty, and respect. By love. But by more than that. There is magic deep in each of us, in each of ye. It sings in yer blood, in yer very soul. I knew the magic, because I know each of ye intimately. The gods, or fate, or chance . . . something brought us five together. And fused us together with unbreakable bonds. Bonds of love. I may be the Gwenevere, but my power is tied inextricably to each of ye."

"What are you saying, Fionna?" Lancelot asked. His face was hard. "You're married to our king and now our queen."

"Aye." She turned and reached a hand back to Arthur. He grasped hers and squeezed. "Arthur is my husband." She twisted back and met each of our eyes. "But in Ireland, a woman may take more than one husband." She dropped Arthur's hand and approached Galahad until she stood before his immense bulk. "Sir Galjorheledanik of Swansea——"

"You finally learned to pronounce my Norse name," Galahad said, a smile crossing his face.

She laughed. "I did. Galahad, I claim ye. I would have ye as my husband, if ye would pledge yerself to me."

Percival hissed in a breath. Truly? Was this truly happening?

Galahad looked at Arthur with cautious expectancy. "This isn't Ireland."

Arthur merely nodded his assent.

With a huzzah, Galahad pulled Fionna into a bear hug, spinning her around before claiming her mouth with a kiss. Then the big man began laughing and, Percival swore, tears formed in Galahad's eyes.

Percival watched with breathless excitement. For he was next.

"Sir Percival of Caer Benic, His Majesty, the Fisher King," she said, as Galahad put her down on somewhat shaky legs. Looking at her in that moment,

Percival thought his heart might swell to bursting. "I claim ye, pigeon. Would—"

"Aye lass, I willingly join yer harem of husbands. Now kiss me already," Percival said, grinning as he dipped her back. In the background he could hear the other knights' laughter, but Fionna filled his awareness. Her lips and tongue now buzzed with power and magic, hitting him in a heady wave. He lifted her back up, breaking their kiss, and then he blew out an excited breath. Joining with the Gwenevere would be an . . . invigorating experience.

Then it hit him. She called him "pigeon." He slid her a sly smile and she winked.

Fionna turned to Lancelot next. His jaw was set, his fists clenched at his side. As if he couldn't dare believe such good fortune would come his way. "Sir Lancelot du Lac, Prince of two worlds," Fionna murmured, reaching a hand up to caress his chiseled cheek. "I claim ye. Will ye marry me, and let me show ye how much I want ye all the days of yer life?"

"My King?" Lancelot raised his eyes to look at Arthur across the room. "Are you sure this is what you desire? Our brotherhood means too much—"

"Peace," Arthur said, stepping forward to put a hand on Lancelot's shoulder, closing the circle beside Fionna. "I was thinking of this harem of husbands, as Percival put it, far before Fionna brought the idea to me. It has been my honor to share my kingship and my hearth with such fine brothers as you all. I can think of no one else whom I would want as *family*."

Fionna turned back to Lancelot, who was blinking back emotion. Then, in one powerful move, he seized Fionna by the arse and lifted her up astride his waist, spinning slowly while their lips met. As they joined in a kiss, an energy filled the air, lighting the circle with power that heated Percival's blood. Fionna broke off the kiss and, with her legs still wrapped around Lancelot, leaned back to kiss Arthur, claiming their king with her lips.

Galahad reached out with a reverent hand to brush a stray braid from her arched throat, and Fionna responded by pulling back from Arthur. Their Gwenevere's eyes were alight with desire and love and magic, and she leaned forward to kiss Galahad once more.

As she did, Percival met Lancelot's eye and saw such a grin of genuine happiness there that it nearly took his breath. He wrapped one arm around Lancelot's shoulder, pulling him close. "Joy suits ye, brother," Percival murmured, and Lancelot turned his head until their faces nearly touched. Something passed between them, different from Fionna's magic. A tingling, a knowing that Percival recognized, a current of magic. The same one he experienced the first time he first glimpsed Lancelot riding through the forest. A recognition of kinship. And love.

"I learn from the best," Lancelot murmured softly, and then leaned in for a kiss.

Chapter Thirty-Two

Lancelot

Soldiers filled the dark courtyard. Rows and rows of armed warriors waited silently for the gates to open, for their king's command. Lancelot shifted, scrunching his toes in his boots to keep them warm. Though it was nearing midsummer, his breath fogged the air, the chill cutting through his leathers to rest deep in his core. Where their enemy slept, in the quiet camp beyond, a steady snow began to fall.

Fionna had taken to magic like she had to everything—effortlessly. She stood atop the keep's wall like a white sentinel, her eyes closed, her form barely visible in the low light. It was a full moon tonight, but the heavy clouds Fionna had summoned blotted out all but the faintest glow of Cerridwen's light.

"A good night for a dark deed," Lancelot said under his breath.

Arthur, standing at his side, glanced his way. "I fear our course lacks honor. Attacking under cover of dark. Is this the coward's way?"

"Our enemy has no honor," Lancelot said. "O'Lynn wouldn't hesitate for a second to take Caerleon by stealth or trickery. And don't get me started on Morgana. Remember the Castle of Maidens?"

Arthur's hand floated to his side where he had been wounded by the faerie spear. "How could I forget."

"This is the best way. And will result in the least loss of life, on both sides. You know that."

"I do," Arthur sighed. "It's only that sometimes I wonder if chivalry is dying."

"Let's stay alive to save it then," Lancelot said, clapping Arthur on the shoulder. "And secure Fionna a wedding gift in the process."

"Eh?" Arthur raised an eyebrow.

"Her sister's freedom."

Arthur's eyes narrowed and his jaw set. "I think it's time to be on the move. Fionna's magic has chilled the summer's dawn for an hour now. The snow will muffle our movements and reduce visibility. Let's just hope the Uí Tuírtri don't know we're coming until we're already upon them."

Their king gave the signal and the gate squeaked ominously as the oaken doors opened. Fionna left her post and descended the stairs, making her way to where a groom held Zephyr's reins.

The sight of her set Lancelot's heart on fire like a young lad. Part of him still couldn't believe that Fionna was going to be his wife. He kept expecting to wake up from a dream. But here she was.

Joy. Bliss.

He tried to channel Percival's endless optimism,

but all he could think of was that now that she had bound herself to him, he had something to lose. And there were about two thousand things that stood between all their happiness—two thousand Uí Tuírtri blades.

"Ye look like ye ate something sour," Fionna remarked, leading Zephyr to stand beside Cheval.

"Just promise me you'll be careful," Lancelot said, trying to memorize every feature of her transformed, elfin face.

"Ye forget, Lance. I'm immortal now." She swung into the saddle as the last word left her mouth.

"Only half immortal," Lancelot muttered.

"I'll be careful," she said. "Promise."

"Good." He mounted his own horse and then leaned in close. "Because I want to take that new faerie body of yours for a ride it won't ever forget."

He was rewarded with the sight of Fionna blushing up to her hairline as he kicked Cheval into a trot.

The farther they rode from the keep, the thicker the snow fell. The plan was simple. Sneak in while clearing a silent path through the clannsmen in their way. Find O'Lynn and kill him, before demanding the rest of the clann surrender. Cut off the snake's head and the body will die.

Lancelot shivered and pulled his cloak tighter about him as a gust of freezing wind, swirling with fat snowflakes, hit him. The gust's icy fingers trailed down the collar of his armor. He tried to think of the wind as Fionna. Fionna caressing his skin, warming him, her soft touch drifting down his chest, down farther to the line of dark hair beneath his navel . .

. His cock stirred painfully against his armor and he tried, unsuccessfully, to adjust himself. Never mind. Bad idea. The snow was just snow.

The creak of leather and the soft snorts of horses were stolen away by the storm. Lancelot and his soldiers were nearly upon the first sentries when men emerged from the snow. But Percival and Galahad's arrows were quicker than the men's cries, taking the soldiers in the throat before they could raise the alarm.

Tents appeared in the distance, and the soldiers fanned out to sneak inside and dispatch the inhabitants. Brutal work, to kill a man in his bed. And as Arthur said, lacking in honor. But Caerleon's warriors needed to ensure their avenue of retreat wasn't cut off, if the alarm was roused. The cruelty would save more lives in the long run.

A cookfire appeared out of the snowstorm, and two dark forms huddled close. Lancelot wasted no time in spearing the nearest man through.

He gurgled a cry, and the other man shouted before Lancelot spurred Cheval forward and stabbed him through.

The world around them silenced in a deafening hush. Lancelot's breath was loud in his ears.

The dark forms of soldiers nearby froze where they stood. All tilted ears to the wind, waiting to hear if another had picked up the cry. But there was no sound.

Lancelot blew out a soft, shaky breath, adjusting his grip on his sword.

Close. Too close.

They had only entered the main ring of village buildings.

He nudged Cheval with his heels, motioning forward with his hand.

Then the snow began to lessen.

And, as they made their way closer, the snow stopped. The air hung heavy against him, like an inhaled breath. All around, the warriors of Caerleon halted too, suddenly exposed in the night air.

Lancelot turned to Fionna, who he could now make out a dozen yards away. He motioned to the sky in an inquiring way.

She shook her head, her jaw set. She hadn't stopped the storm. Which meant that someone else had.

An arrow zinged through the air, catching a soldier next to him in the shoulder. The man toppled backwards off his horse.

"Charge!" Lancelot cried out, slapping Cheval's rump with the flat of his blade. The stallion leaped beneath him, as another arrow whizzed by his head. The arrow's shaft and fletching were so close, he could feel the arrow's movement in the air.

Uí Tuírtri warriors poured out of buildings with guttural cries of rage. The men and women were unarmored, without the normal bristling assortment of weapons each warrior held. Caerleon had taken them by surprise. Still, the warriors were fierce.

A woman ran screaming at him with an axe held high above her. Lancelot swung his sword, slicing her across the chest. Cheval barreled into another warrior before him, and Lancelot felt the man go down beneath his horse's hooves.

The village center loomed before them as more warriors poured out of houses and buildings, blocking their path.

"To me!" Lancelot shouted above the melee, spurring Cheval forward, toward the enemy. Galahad and Percival, together with a dozen of their best soldiers, funneled into the wide main street, forming a cavalry charge into the thick of invading warriors.

A calming battle focus settled over Lancelot, and his vision narrowed. In this heightened state, he easily parried two fast blows from a warrior with bared teeth, dispatching the man with a powerful blow.

Lancelot's task was clear. Punch a hole through these men, allowing Arthur and Fionna to ride in their wake into the center of town. To attend to their mission.

To find and to kill O'Lynn.

Chapter Thirty-Three

Arthur

The fighting was thick. Little by little Arthur's warriors gained ground, hacking and slicing their way through men and women and beasts.

Excalibur's hilt was slick in Arthur's hand from the snow and sweat and blood. But as many soldiers as they felled, it seemed as though more took their place.

This was the part of their plan that had been a risk—a terrible, terrible risk. Two thousand Uí Tuírtri warriors slept in this camp. Caerleon had invaded O'Lynn's war camp with less than a thousand-armed men. If the entire force was roused from sleep and then surrounded them . . . Caerleon would be destroyed. Their plan depended on finding and killing O'Lynn quickly. Then demoralizing the rest of his men. But the time ticked by, time filled with clashing blades and ringing metal and screams of dying men. Time they could ill afford.

Fear began to bubble up in Arthur. "Fionna!" he

shouted, taking advantage of a moment within the onslaught to find his fae warrior. "We must move forward! To the inn!"

She nodded before twisting her body out of the way of a dagger thrown at her by a snarling woman. Fionna spurred Zephyr and charged the woman, reaching down and disabling her with a skillful blow of her blade. She tried to close her eyes to focus on her magic. But another warrior came at her and she was forced to rein Zephyr back, dancing out of the way of his blow. She needed time and space to perform whatever magic she attempted.

Arthur roared his fury and dug his heels into Llamrei's side. Together, her hooves and his blade cut a path forward, until they flanked Fionna just yards from the steps of the inn.

"There are too many," Arthur yelled over the maelstrom of weapons and warriors. "We must find O'Lynn."

"He must be in there." Fionna gestured toward the inn with her head and then swung off Zephyr.

Arthur slid off Llamrei's back and then caught her hand. "And if he isn't?"

"He is," she said, her breast heaving. A glow wreathed around her in the darkness, as if she were a celestial body reflecting the light of the moon. "Cover me." She closed her eyes and, within a couple thunderous heartbeats, the ground beneath their feet began to shift. Boulders jutted up from the ground in a semi-circle, forming a defensive perimeter.

Llamrei reared, screaming, her eyes wild, and Arthur had to leap up to catch her reins.

Enemy warriors shouted in fear, scrambling out of the way, their eyes growing owlish with fear of Fionna's powerful magic.

Her eyelashes fluttered open when she finished. The land around the inn was now protected by craggy rocks as tall as a man's chest. Warriors would be able to crawl over them, but the stones would slow them down.

Fionna swiveled toward him, her jaw set. "O'Lynn."

"O'Lynn!" Arthur's eyes widened as the front door of the inn exploded outward, kicked by a powerful blow. O'Lynn emerged from the opening. The man wore full Dál nAraidi armor, the leather oiled and gleaming, and a dark helm atop his head. One hand gripped a huge battle axe, his eyes glowing like malevolent embers from inside his headgear.

"Speak of the wretched man and he appears," Fionna spat.

"That's not a very nice thing to say about yer kin. We're family now, Fionnabhair." O'Lynn reached inside the door and jerked something toward him. A chain.

A cry went out as a woman stumbled into him, falling to her knees on the splintered remains of the inn's door. Aideen. O'Lynn shoved a fist into her hair and then jerked her back to her feet. Aideen yelped in pain and Fionna stepped forward, hissing.

Fury rose within Arthur. He could taste Fionna's matching anger on the air—like the energy before a storm. Fionna was about to do something stupid, or reckless, or both. Though, he couldn't blame her. If his mother or Fionna were paraded before him in a similar fashion, he might behave the same despite his training as a warrior. Still . . .

"Hold Fionna," Arthur said quietly as O'Lynn pulled Aideen back against his body, laying the blade of the huge axe against her exposed throat. The young woman's eyes brimmed with tears as they widened, as if silently pleading.

"I'm afraid ye've made a miscalculation, Pendragon," O'Lynn gloated. "For yer force is surrounded, and if ye don't surrender, I'll spill the blood of this woman before ye without a second thought. How'd ye like to see yer sister die, Fionna?"

Arthur feared Fionna's rage would boil over into a tempest unlike any they had ever seen, so he hurried on. "You won't do that, O'Lynn."

"Why not?" he sneered.

"Because then you would lose your only bargaining chip, leaving you defenseless."

"I'm hardly defenseless, ye pompous Welsh bastard! I was slitting heads with this axe when yer mother was still wiping yer arse!"

"Yet we found you inside that inn, rather than on the battlefield with your men."

O'Lynn's eyes glittered dangerously.

Arthur continued. "Let's end this without further bloodshed. Single combat. For the future of Caerleon."

The axe blade lowered slightly, and Aideen took in a shuddering breath. "Aye. Single combat. Ye and me."

"No," Fionna said. "Ye and me."

Part of Arthur railed against it, but he knew that he could not deprive Fionna of her vengeance. She was as good as, or a better fighter, than he.

"Ye would have yer bitch fight for ye? The gelding of Caerleon, eh?" O'Lynn scoffed.

"Fionna is many things," Arthur said, his voice ringing clear and true. "She is my wife. She is a warrior. A princess of Tara, heir to Clann Allán, queen of Caerleon and overqueen of Gwent. She is the most powerful sorceress in a millennia. The fae-born daughter of the goddess Danu. But of all things, she is a free woman, beholden to no man, not even a king. She makes her own choices. And it will give me great pleasure to watch her spear you through like a mewling pig."

O'Lynn growled at that while tossing Aideen hard to the inn's threshold. Then he opened his arms before him and held his great axe out as he took a step forward. "Daughter of Danu or no, I'll enjoy killing ye more than ye can know," he spat at Fionna.

"The feeling is mutual," Fionna replied, also stepping forward, her twin swords bared.

Arthur held his breath—unable to move in the pregnant moment before the two warriors charged each other. Before the clash began.

But he could never have predicted what happened next. Aideen Allán, rising like a vengeful wraith with a wicked blade in one hand. Where she had been hiding it, Arthur didn't know. But he recognized the skill she wielded as she leaped onto O'Lynn's back, her arms clinging to his neck. As she drove the dagger deep into his exposed windpipe—all the way to the hilt.

O'Lynn froze, seemingly unable to comprehend what was happening. Aideen pulled the dagger out and drove the blade in again, this time angling the point up, into the man's chin.

Arthur closed his eyes against the violence of it, the lethal precision of those blows.

Fionna had no such compunctions. A gasp of delight escaped from her and she ran forward, scrambling over the boulder separating them from O'Lynn and Aideen.

Aideen then crumbled to the ground and Fionna grabbed her hand, pulling her out of the way of O'Lynn's blade.

The man dropped to his knees. With a *thunk*, his axe fell to the ground as his hands flew to his throat. As if he could hold in his lifeblood with only his fingertips.

Fionna darted forward and seized his helmet, wrenching it off his head before retreating to where her sister stood. Face bared, O'Lynn's wound was even more horrendous, his face draining of blood. Always his eyes remained on the two women who stood before him, brimming with hate.

"A wedding gift," Aideen said. Her shoulders were squared, her back straight. "Courtesy of Clann Allán."

O'Lynn fell face first to the ground—dead.

Aideen's hand flew to her mouth as she let out a sob. Matching tears coursed down Fionna's cheeks as she pulled her sister into a tight embrace, murmuring into her hair, rocking her gently.

Arthur turned to where the battle still raged outside the ring of protective boulders. It was time to end this war. He summited a boulder and faced the soldiers.

"Men of Clann Uí Tuírtri!" he bellowed. "Your chieftain is dead! Lay down your weapons and you will be permitted to leave these shores and return to your homes! Keep fighting and Caerleon will show no mercy! Every last warrior will be slaughtered!"

Arthur would never execute men who had surrendered, but he thought O'Lynn's warriors could use the added incentive.

In the distance, Arthur watched as a man raised his hands in the middle of a fight with Galahad, dropping his sword. The muffled sound of the weapon hitting the dirt was repeated all around the village and camp as enemy fighters began to drop their weapons.

Relief flooded Arthur. By the gods, they had done it. They had won.

The earth beneath their feet rumbled once again and he lost his balance. As he hit the ground, the boulders around them slowly began to sink into the earth. Arthur whipped his head Fionna's direction with a raised eyebrow. But her face was stricken.

"It's not me," she said.

The sea of fighters parted as a woman in a black dress and flapping violet cloak strode toward them. Morgana. Her pale purple eyes were baleful as she spoke, her voice echoing over the hushed silence. "I'm sorry brother, but we're not done here. Not even close."

Chapter Thirty-Four

Fionna

The air crackled between us. I sensed more than saw the moment before Morgana struck. The bolt of lightning shot from her hand, streaking toward me like a viper.

I dodged out of the way, rolling to my feet while summoning the elements to me. I welcomed each one into the void within me. The sky above Morgana darkened right before ripping open. Then a hailstorm erupted, dumping sheets of solid ice upon the Queen of Darkness. The hail was so thick, I couldn't see if the ice stones had smothered her or not.

Until another bolt of lightning struck my side out of nowhere. I fell to my hip, hitting the ground hard. My teeth clamped together as pain exploded through me. I struggled to my feet, ignoring how my very skin felt raw, ignoring the throbbing that I hoped didn't signal a serious wound. But I had no time to consider. My eyes focused on where Morgana's crow form flapped into the air.

I blew a jet of air at her, tumbling the crow out

of the sky.

She turned back into a female, mere heartbeats before her fae form collided with compacted grass and dirt. Afraid to lose my momentary advantage, I summoned earth and water to me, liquefying the ground beneath her into a pool of quicksand. Morgana shrieked as she began sinking into the muck, her knees, then her thighs, as the mud lapped at her fine gown.

Panic flashed in her eyes while she struggled to free herself, her hands now mired in the sludge. I prepared and released my own lightning strike, but my bolt missed her as an invisible force jerked her up, pulling her body out of the quicksand. Morgana's eyes widened—it wasn't her doing this.

I whipped my head to peer over my shoulder as I spun on my heels, and my eyes narrowed when two more faeries approached from an alley between the houses. A brunette in a scarlet dress and her fair sister in gold. Elaine and Morgause.

Morgana pulled swirls of magic to her, spinning her dress into a new form, ridding herself of the heavy, sticky mud.

I shot a gout of flame at her during her wardrobe change. But Elaine deflected my attack with green fire of her own. The combined flames, an eerie blend of red and green, crashed against a nearby building and whooshed up the thatch roof.

I sent water at the blaze while pulling the air from around the building. The situation would only get worse if the village started to burn too.

"Fionna!" Arthur shouted. He and my knights

were pressed against the inn, watching the magical combat with fear tightening their faces into frowns and scowls.

A chill scraped down my spine in a violent strike as the air around me shifted to a rapidly plunging cold. A bitter cold that threatened to freeze the blood in my veins. My breath puffed from me in quick foggy bursts as I struggled to summon fire to warm myself. Limbs stiff, I returned focus toward the alley and grit my chattering teeth. It appeared the sisters had taken advantage of my distraction.

I was one, and they were three. I needed to do something quickly to end this fight before they wore me down. Or before I made a mistake. My magic was new to me while they had cast spells since childhood. I might be more powerful, but they were more skilled.

I summoned the wind to me, spinning the air into a cyclone the size of which frightened even me. My braids whipped at my face, stinging me as they thrashed like serpents. I tossed the storm at the sisters and they scattered, sprinting for the cover of a nearby building. I wanted the cyclone to chase after them. But I hesitated to destroy the building. The structure could contain innocents who were also sheltering from the madness on the battlefield. So, I let the storm dissipate.

In my peripheral vision, I glimpsed my knights again. Arthur pointed behind me. Then I saw my name on his lips. But I couldn't hear his voice over the rumble that shook beneath me, as if the ground itself began to rebel. The sisters were working a spell.

And it was a powerful one.

I fell to the earth and sharp pebbles scraped my palms. I tried to pull apart whatever spell they were weaving, but the magic wouldn't yield to me. Sweat beaded my brow. Something was brewing. Something strong.

Morgana and her sisters huddled together, chanting in unison. Energy surrounded them. Then the landscape rended before me—a thunderous rip in the earth—releasing a white-hot jet of flame that surged hungrily for the sky.

I dove out of the way, covering my head as a shower of embers rained upon me.

"Gwenevere," I heard Morgana shout. "Let's see how your magic fares against the power of Domnu's children!"

My heart stuttered in my chest.

Domnu . . . the sire of the Fomorians. The ancient enemy of Danu, my goddess—my mother. A gripping urge to run from this place seized me, but I held firm. I was the only one who could stand between whatever came out of that chasm and my knights. The rest of Caerleon. I would lay down my life for the ones I loved . . . no matter what happened here. Even if this fight demanded all of me.

Still, my resolve was tested when a giant rock and amber hand, streaked with flaming embers, crashed against the lip of the chasm. My pulse skidded to a stop. A horrific, fearsome beast was clawing topside from below. The hand alone was as tall as I was.

I scrambled back as the other hand appeared. Then the face—if I could call the gruesome monstrosity atop its shoulders a face. The creature had vaguely humanoid features—two eyes that reflected the chaos of Dubnos, the great abyss, above an opening that could perhaps be described as a mouth, one filled with blue and white licking flames.

My eyes flicked to the dark faerie sisters as my mind worked for a solution, for a way to end this beast. The Morrígan were intent, their eyes wide, their figures stiff. As if summoning this monster wasted every bit of their energy. Apparently, they were willing to destroy Caerleon rather than allow Arthur to continue sitting on the throne.

The fire beast pulled itself from the chasm and stood. And when it roared, I thought my eardrums might blow. Screams sounded behind me as soldiers from both camps blended together in a unified mass of terrified, fleeing humanity.

The beast took a step and flattened a nearby wagon. The ground shook as it moved. The creature fixed its fathomless eyes in the distance, drawn to the movement of the fleeing people.

"Fomorian!" I shouted while waving my arms, foolishly drawing its attention back to me. I knew not how to defeat this thing. Water perhaps? Ice? I summoned a rain cloud, as big and black and as heavy as I could create. I opened the deluge above the beast and it roared in pain as steam rose from its glowing magma-formed body. Boiling water rolled down its crags and crevices to the soil in near-vaporous rivulets.

Yet, the creature didn't stop.

I struggled to turn the water to ice, perhaps to

freeze the fire beast within a glacial cocoon. But the beast was too strong. It writhed and broke apart the ice as soon I could crystalize the water. The Fomorian was just too hot.

The monster took two steps toward me and kicked out with its flaming foot.

I threw myself back, falling onto my arse and scrambling back out of its way. My hands scrabbled in the clover and weeds poking through cracks in the cobbles of the village square.

A jolt of understanding crashed into me. This creature was unnatural. It crawled out from the earth's deep, and back to the earth it needed to return.

My knights were moving behind the roiling heat of the beast, trying to sneak around the square toward Morgana and her sisters. Perhaps my knights could get to the dark enchantresses and incapacitate them, as the sisters were still intent upon the creature.

I needed to slay this monster from the abyss. No more thoughts or second guesses. Instinct took over and I reached down, past bedrock, to the earth's deep, feeling within the bubbling rivers of fire for the dormant life that lay there. Danu's power—the power of green things. Trees and grass and the wild creatures of the earth. I reached within and I summoned the powers of my goddess.

I invited the roots from the sacred trees—oak and ash and yew. My magic cried out for them to come to me. And come they did, exploding out of the ground like powerful warrior druids crackling with nature's endlessly looping energy. The gnarled roots wrapped around the flame monster like coiled tendrils of rope. Treed tentacles lashed at where the beast stood, and then sank trunked fingers back into the soil and began to grow, even as the beast thrashed violently, striking at the rambling limbs to free itself.

The vines and roots grew larger, until the creature's legs looked like two thick tree trunks wrapped in ivy. Up and up the tree grew, forming all around the fire creature. Bark and wood grew faster, hardening around the beast. The monster's arms were now stiff, and its torso was quickly enveloped until only its head remained free. White and blue fire blazed from its grotesque mouth as the beast roared in a promise of vengeance.

But Danu's power was stronger. My power.

What was meant as a scream of hatred became a hissing death rattle. The unnatural fire snuffed out, cooling the remnant traces of reds and oranges to grays and blues. Ribbons of smoke curled from the monster's mouth and danced upward toward the sky. The tree trunks continued to grow despite the creature's violent transfiguration from life to death to rebirth. Limbs, branches, and flower buds exploded outward and around the beast's rocky surface. And then leaves—forming a broad green canopy over the beast.

I felt the tree settle as the leaves shivered out into existence, before growing still with contentment.

I slumped onto my elbows and gazed up in awe at the sight before me. A massive oak tree stood in the middle of the town square, its limbs stretching wide, shielding the buildings from the light of the stars. With intricately knotted roots, the tree looked as if it had lived there for a thousand years—at least. But rendered in the gnarled bark, one could almost make out a face, and the twisted, frozen scream of a Fomorian fire beast.

Chapter Thirty-Five

Galahad

Galahad seized a faerie from behind, laying his blade across her pale throat. The blonde faerie—Elaine he thought she was—stiffened beneath him. Next to her, Lancelot seized Morgana as Percival rested his blade on Morgause's fine collarbone. The sisters had been so intent upon fighting Fionna's efforts with the fire beast, that the knights had no trouble sneaking up on them.

A screech erupted from Morgana as she glared at Lancelot with baleful eyes. But even she must see that the battle was lost. O'Lynn was dead. The Uí Tuírtri were scattered. And the faerie sisters' magic had been routed by Danu's and Fionna's power. The Gwenevere.

Fionna pushed to a stand, staggering toward them. She looked dead on her feet, even her ethereal faerie countenance drawn and exhausted.

"You have trapped our magic!" Morgana screamed at Fionna as their queen approached. "Give it back!"

Fionna shook her head wearily, but she managed to straighten her spine, throwing her shoulders back as she faced the sisters of Tintagel. "Ye have done nothing but harry my king and this land. Why should I return yer power?"

"Because we are part of the balance," Elaine, the faerie Galahad held, growled. "I admit my sisters and I got carried away these past months in our anger at the Little Dragon King—"

"You have been angry with me since my birth, of which I had no control over," Arthur gritted between clenched teeth. "The punishment must stop. Let us be better than Uther Pendragon."

Elaine considered his words. "Yes, brother. Let us be better than that vile man." She flicked a look at Morgause, then said, "We will swear to never do harm to you or any you love, if the White Enchantress will merely give us our power back."

Morgause nodded in agreement. "Without our magic, we will die. To secure its return, we will gladly make you such a promise."

"Even you?" Lancelot asked Morgana.

She bared her canines at Lancelot with a snarling glare but finally relented and gave a curt nod.

Arthur approached, his hand resting on Excalibur. "You will each swear." Arthur put an arm around Fionna's waist and she sagged against him gratefully. Gods, she might collapse any moment. "Each of you swear on your sisters' lives that you will never again interfere or harm or seek to harm myself, my knights, my wife, or the kingdom of Caerleon and its people. If you do, Fionna will return your magic to you." He looked at her with a raised eyebrow, and

Fionna murmured her agreement.

Galahad had no idea how Fionna had trapped the faeries' magic, or even if she could release it. But he supposed that was why he was here, holding a simple sword while Fionna performed great works of magic.

Each of the sisters said a vow on the lives of the others and, when they finished, Fionna closed her eyes. The trunk of the great tree Fionna had created shivered and moved, and a small hole appeared. One that looked as though an owl might nest there. Then, out of the hole flowed a stream of shimmering light that fell upon each of the sisters.

Galahad held himself still against the burning impulse to release the magical creature beneath him. But as the returned power settled upon her, he felt his limbs go limp. She stepped out of his hold as Morgana turned into a crow and flapped out of Lancelot's arms and flew away.

Relief washed over Galahad as strength flooded back into his arms.

Morgause and Elaine stepped together, turning to face them. "We apologize, brother," Elaine said. "For all that has been done to you and your land. Let this be the turning point in relations between us."

Arthur nodded. "No more animosity. After all, we are family."

"Indeed," Morgause said, and a misty portal opened behind them. They stepped through and were gone.

Fionna swayed against Arthur. Her eyes slid closed right before she fell toward the ground. Arthur caught her deftly, swinging her up into his arms.

Galahad wiped his sword, returning the blade to its sheath. His hair was a tangled mess around his face, sweat and dirt coating him from head to toe. Yet, he felt better than he had felt in ages. He had just watched Fionna battle a demon monster from Hel, turning it into the most beautiful oak tree that he had ever seen. But that was their fifth knight.

Her eyes fluttered as they walked toward their horses. "Is she all right?" Arthur asked him.

Galahad lifted her wrist, feeling for her pulse. "I believe so. Her strength is likely depleted from the battle."

"I can't imagine how much energy it takes turn a fire monster into a tree," Percival added.

"We won't hear the end of this," Lancelot quipped. "Every time we do something she doesn't like or if we don't appreciate her, she'll say . . . 'remember that time when I defeated three powerful sorceresses, and you all sat around with your thumbs up your arses?'"

Arthur chuckled. "I for one would be happy to take such abuse."

Lancelot smiled, and it was clear that he would too.

"Let's get back to Caerleon," Arthur said.

Lancelot strode away to find a commander to relay instructions to. The wounded would be brought home, while the remaining soldiers were to oversee the orderly return of the Irish warriors to their boats. From the Uí Tuírtri's shocked and weary faces, Galahad didn't think they would be putting up much more of a fight. But it was always best to be careful with such things.

Arthur tapped Llamrei's leg, and then mounted. Galahad and Percival helped to secure Fionna in the saddle before him. Her head lolled down, her braids hanging white against Llamrei's black coat.

"I can't believe the battle with my sisters is finally over," Arthur said as they made their way out of city and back to toward the keep.

"Looks like it isnae completely over, ye ken," Percival said. He pointed to a patch of brown grass where the curse still showed.

Arthur frowned. "I should have insisted Morgana and her sisters remove the curse over the land."

Galahad knew that he should be concerned, but with everything that just happened—that they had just survived—he felt deep within that the land would heal in time. "I'm sure if we make a special request to Elaine and Morgause, we will be able to get the curse lifted."

Arthur considered Galahad's suggestion, then said, "I think they will be far more inclined to work with us."

"Or perhaps Fionna, with her newfound powers, will be able to break the final part of the curse," Galahad replied. "Once she has time to consult with Danu."

"Curses and goddesses. Can we talk about what's really important?" Percival asked.

"What?" Lancelot asked, as he trotted up to join them.

"The wedding! Arthur's already married to Fionna, but I'm not."

They all laughed at their younger knight. Typical Percival.

"So eager?" Lancelot asked.

"Och, do ye blame me?" Percival asked. "She was beautiful and fierce and intimidating *before* she was fae, before she was a Gwenevere. But now . . ." His eyes fell upon Fionna's sleeping form. "I cannae believe I would be lucky enough to be with her. I want to lock her down before she changes her mind."

"You think her feelings are so changeable?" Lancelot said. "You find yourself so unworthy of love?"

"All I know is that if there's one thing men do best, it's screw up their relationships with women," Percival said quietly, then blew out a long, slow breath. "I would rather marry the lass before that happens."

Galahad laughed. "I must admit, I wouldn't mind holding the wedding sooner rather than later." He raised an eyebrow at Arthur.

"It's only fair," Arthur agreed. "We can make all the arrangements, so when she regains her strength, we will be ready."

As the keep appeared over the horizon, the large, wooden gates standing tall before the rising sun, Galahad felt his spirit soar up to meet the dawn. He was to be married. And he couldn't wait.

Chapter Thirty-Six

Arthur had decided the ceremony should take place in the library. This was a small affair, just for them. Servants had adorned the shelves and tables with boughs of greenery threaded with tiny white flowers. Arthur and Merlin stood before the leaded glass window, waiting for the others to arrive.

This time, instead of the groom, Arthur would serve as a witness. To watch joyfully as Merlin, his oldest friend, joined in matrimony the woman he loved with the three men he loved like brothers. Brin and Aideen Allán would also bear witness. Together with the gods.

After the battle against Morgana and her sisters, Fionna had slept for a day and a night. Her sister Aideen had barely left her side. When Fionna awoke, after eating enough for three people, she had expressed her eagerness to hold the ceremony. To make their bonds of love more permanent. And then, once wed, and with the help of Merlin, she wanted to break Danu free and reclaim the Otherworld from the Fomorians. Life was certainly an adventure with Fionna.

Arthur's throat grew tight as his sword brothers entered the library.

Galahad—broad and strong as the oak Fionna had raised in the village. His honey-blond hair was washed and brushed, dusting the shoulders of the green linen tunic he wore.

Percival—his eyes bright, his grin wider than Arthur had ever seen it, wearing a tunic of rust with bronze accents.

And then there was Lancelot, with his signature black curls and blue tunic. But he had changed too—he wore a look of ease and happiness that made Arthur want to weep with joy.

Arthur smiled at Merlin as each of the men took their places. The druid softly smiled in reply, the gold ring around his eyes flashing. Arthur knew that his old friend understood what this ceremony meant to him. To have found a family to love, who loved him in return.

Galahad watched with bated breath as Fionna appeared in the hallway. She glided through the doors like the goddess she was, her father on one arm, her sister on the other.

She was everything to him. And she had honored Galahad by choosing him—an honor more powerful than he had ever imagined possible. He was the oldest son of a Norse blacksmith, and he was about to marry the daughter of a goddess and a king. But more than that. He was marrying Fionna. The woman he loved.

A smile spread across her face as she moved toward them. Her dress was the glittering silver of a moonlit reflection dusting a lake. In her hands, she held a bouquet of heather, hawthorn, and other greenery. At her brow was a circlet of holly leaves, similar in style to Arthur's oak leaf crown.

This woman set his blood racing in a way he had never known. He wanted every moment with her, again and again. To taste her skin, to feel her silken touch, to hear her laugh. To see her perhaps, one day, swell with child. Every moment with Fionna would be a treasure. And he could think of no one better to share it with than these men whom he had come to respect and to love in kind.

It was all Percival could do to keep himself from jumping up and down. He had never been so excited as he was when Fionna reached their cluster in the library's front. She embraced her father, then her sister, squeezing them each tightly. He knew how much their nearness meant to her, to have her family safe at last. And here to witness her vows.

Fionna took her place across from Merlin. They were a circle. Percival stood across from Arthur, Lancelot across from Galahad. Percival winked at Fionna, and she winked back.

"I admit," Merlin said, clearing his throat, "since living at Tintagel in Cornwall and now Wales with Uther's line, I have not presided over a wedding as found in the other Gaelic lands. But," Merlin paused a heartbeat then continued, "I can think of nothing more fitting than a number such as this. Five is the sacred number of elements on this earth. Each of you brings something unique and powerful. When joined together, the elements create all manner of wonders. I see this in you five. In a way," Merlin said with a humored smile, "we owe Morgana a debt of gratitude, for bringing Fionna into our lives."

Lancelot snorted at that.

But it wasn't untrue. Percival thought on all that had happened in the past months since Fionna had arrived so suddenly, besting every knight in the kingdom at the tourney. The Grail Quest. Seizing his Fisher King heritage. Defeating Morgana and drinking the blood of the land. Lancelot's kisses and touch. . . . Throwing off his vow of chastity—finally! Life would always be interesting with her.

He longed to see what adventures unfolded next. And he longed to share them with her. His eyes flicked to Lancelot. And his brothers.

Lancelot couldn't take his eyes off Fionna. Nor could he believe that in the next few moments she would be his. Truly his. He kept expecting another catastrophe to arrive. The roof to cave in, a stray spell to explode. But there was nothing but the perfect sweet smile on her face. The fresh herbal smell of the flowers in her hands and strung around the library. The brightness of Percival at his side, Galahad's steady presence, Arthur's beaming smile.

Growing up on the Isle of Man, he swore that he would never marry a faerie. Lay with them, dally with them—sure. Use them as they used him. But never marry one. He had declared this vow again after the foolishness of Morgana.

But here, today, he knew deep in his heart and soul that marrying the Gwenevere was the right decision. He had come home in Caerleon. He had come home in Arthur, and he had come home in Fionna. Here was a family who inspired him, who challenged him, who filled him with passion. He glanced sideways at Percival and then Fionna. A family who accepted him for who he was. He was meant to be here. And as Merlin began to speak, asking each of them for their vows, Lancelot couldn't say the words fast enough to bind his life to these warriors at his side. This king, these knights, this goddess. They were who he wanted in his life. Forever and always.

I struggled with the tears threatening to fall as each warrior in the circle said our promises to each other. I wanted to give each of my men a moment . . . to show my knights how much they each meant to me. They were my friends, my compatriots, my trusted allies, my equals. They were the sun and the moon and the stars above. Each man held a piece of my soul and my heart and, together, they lit me afire—a burning inferno that would never be quenched.

After I had slept, eaten my fill, and bathed . . . I ached to celebrate our triumphs. We had seized upon the slimmest of chances and made it ours. Through our ingenuity and our hope and our trust in one another, we were victorious.

I wanted nothing so much as my wedding night with these beautiful men, and my eternity after. I wanted no more worry over curses. I wanted no more talk of politics or faeries or goddesses. I only wanted skin and lips and the coiling desire within me sated by the men I loved.

As I spoke my vows and sighed into each kiss, my body, mind, and soul trilled with the possibility of what the future would hold for me.

Chapter Thirty-Seven

The horses' hooves clopped softly through the swaying grass and over the moss-blanketed earth. The warm night wrapped around me as we journeyed toward the forest across the Usk River that held a pond Arthur oft visited. The same pool in which the Lady of the Lake had appeared—offering Arthur Excalibur and a new destiny.

A cool breeze fluttered wisps of my hair across my eyes. I tucked them behind my ears and back beneath my hooded cloak. We were sneaking away from the keep and didn't want to draw any attention. Only Merlin and a few of Arthur's most trusted officers knew of our whereabouts this night.

Our honeymoon night.

I followed behind Arthur and Llamrei as his black mare plunged into the river. Water lapped at the toe of my boots in inky waves. Behind me, Galahad, Lancelot, and Percival splashed into the same shallow section of river atop their chargers. The energy between us swirled in comfortable silence, our hearts full of the promise of passion to come. The love we would share. A new consummation for each of us, since I had transformed into my fae form and become the Gwenevere. I was not only Arthur's faerie bride, but my fellow knights' as well.

Zephyr nickered as we crossed the line between light and shadows and entered the forest. A few heartbeats later, the trees opened to reveal a circled patch of stars. Beneath the indigo sky, a small pond shimmered in dusted moonlight. A silver-misted waterfall hushed the leaves' lullaby in the breeze as a creek spilled over an outcropping of large rocks covered in ferns and moss. But, as enchanting as this place was, the curse visibly lingered. Black fingers of death had left their marks on tree trunks. Brown, brittle ferns dotted between healthy, new growth. I dismounted and considered the swirls of yellow moss cutting through the green.

Merlin speculated that, similar to the Blessed Grail, my magic would fully heal Caerleon and Briton as I joined with each man. Marrying the sovereign-blessed king—Arthur—to the land once more as his Gwenevere wouldn't be enough, as Galahad, Lancelot, and Percival still carried a piece of Arthur's sovereignty from being knighted with Excalibur. It was strangely fitting. Our magic and love were interlocked in an endlessly looping knot. In this Otherworldly place, we would know if our joining healed the land—this time truly.

We busied with unpacking our bedrolls and supplies for the night. Percival scoured the underbrush for kindling and logs to burn and then began a fire.

Lancelot placed jugs of wine and pewter chalices near a basket of cheeses, pear tarts, and other delicious samplings from the keep's kitchens. Arthur removed Llamrei's saddle as I unbuckled Zephyr's.

Galahad passed by me after gathering all our saddles and tack to lay across a log within a stone's throw from our camp.

I began untying my cloak when a pair of arms wrapped around my waist. Galahad nuzzled my neck with bearded kisses before spinning me around to face him. "Join me for a dip?"

"Is the water safe?" I asked.

"Aye, lass," Percival said nearby. "We tested the pond earlier today."

Lancelot sidled up beside me with a chalice of honeyed wine. "The waters here are protected by The Lady of the Lake. But we weren't sure if the curse had also destroyed Vivien's magic."

Zephyr moved behind me and I turned to find Arthur leading the horses to a copse where they could graze. Our eyes touched as he lifted a soft smile before returning to his task. I enjoyed a long sip of mead and then re-focused on my knights. And frowned.

Galahad's glorious mane of hair was up in a messy knot, his typical style for weaponry practice or battle. Handing my now empty chalice back to Lancelot, I stood on tip-toes, reached above Galahad, and pulled the leather strip. Wavy strands fell around his face and shoulders in a rippling cascade of gold. I sighed in contentment at the sight. My fingers tangled in his silky hair as I tugged him closer, closer,

closer still. Our bodies collided in a sensual dance of lips, arms, fingers, and hips. His kisses tasted better than bridal mead. Lifting his tunic up and over his head, my mouth explored the expanse of his muscled chest. Tasting the ambrosial saltiness of his skin while drowning myself in his honeyed scent of sweet hay, leather, and sex. And I wanted more.

Lancelot pressed to my back as he gathered my waist-length, un-braided hair and draped all my tresses—glowing white under the moonlight—over my shoulder. His quickened breath pulsed hot on my neck as he finished untying my cloak, and my lids fluttered closed. The wool fell to the forest floor around my booted feet. Then his hands cradled my throat as he tipped my head back to nibble my earlobe and kiss my neck before his fingertips brushed down my chest to palm my breasts.

I heard a soft splash and opened my eyes. Percival waded into the dark waters, and I bit down on a forming smile. Moonlight touched the play of muscle and sinew on his back. And gods, his tight arse. I want to feel his soft flesh in my hands as he thrust into me. Memories of our time together came rushing back and I grew impatient with each remembered touch.

Percival peered over his shoulder and winked at me before diving in, resurfacing in the middle of the pond with a shake of his head. Droplets sprinkled the water surface around his glistening body as he grinned.

"Come in, dove," he shouted. "I'm waiting for ye."

Galahad rolled his eyes with a quiet laugh. "The lad has the patience of a frolicking goat."

"Do you blame him?" Lancelot asked as his hands traveled farther down to the laces of my riding breeches. "Fionna, naked . . . and wet."

"Mmmm," Galahad murmured in agreement.

Both men made quick work of undressing me until I stood before them bare, heat coiling between my thighs in anticipation. Especially as Galahad slowly pulled off his breeches, providing me a feast of muscle and skin and sultry, knowing smiles. As Galahad undressed, Lancelot kissed my shoulder, the shell of my ear—even the sensitive point—while his calloused fingers played against my nipples. I knew his eyes were upon Galahad and enjoying the show as well. How could he not? Galahad was the most godlike man I had ever seen. And he was mine.

Lancelot gently pushed me toward Galahad once the giant of a man stood before me naked. Then I heard my dark knight begin to undress.

I placed my hands onto Galahad's ribbed torso right as he scooped me up, one arm beneath my knees, the other beneath my arms. My plan to melt into his warmth quickly dissolved, however, when he ran for the pond. I shrieked, to my horror, and screamed again when he splashed in and tossed me toward the center of the pond. Galahad's roar of laughter followed me through the air, the rumbling vibrations even traveling through the water to mock me when I submerged into the obsidian depths.

I gasped for breath when I surfaced, a growl low in my throat. That man would pay. The infernal knight was still laughing. So much so, he didn't notice me. My lips curled in vengeance before I dipped back into the water to swim toward where he stood. In a few strokes, I had reached him and pinched his calf—hard—until my nails dug into his skin. Caught off guard, he lifted his foot and I could hear him boom a swear word, providing me an opportunity to yank his other leg out from underneath him. The great knight fell into the shallow depths with a giant splash. Before he could surface, I pounced on him, our limbs tangling in a wrestling match. I could hear the garbled sounds of Arthur, Lancelot, and Percival cheering for me.

Both Galahad and I shot up into the air, laughter streaming from us in rivulets. But I refused to give him quarter and shoved him back hard with a foot to his stomach. He fell again, to the boisterous humor of everyone, especially Arthur. Sprawled out in the pond, his knees and shoulders poking out as though in a bath, Galahad arched an eyebrow at me.

"Surrender," I mock-demanded.

"A draw." The man grinned at me in challenge. "You can't best me, Fionna."

"Keep up these sweet nothings and I'll make ye wait until morning," I cooed, my hands firmly planted on my exposed hips. The men laughed again.

"Make him kneel before you and beg," Lancelot called out. "No mercy!"

Arthur gifted me another soft smile as he and Lancelot waded into the water—in a location safe from Galahad and my antics.

"You can't resist me," Galahad said, ignoring

the others, while swimming toward where I stood. "You've never able to resist me." Droplets raced down his body as he slowly rose from the water, and goddess help me. I couldn't help the stab of jealousy I felt toward each rolling drop of water for knowing every divine part of him so intimately.

"I think she's resisting ye, ye big oaf," Percival called out from near the waterfall. Galahad's playful glare shot daggers over my shoulder at the younger man.

Taking Percival's lead, I pushed back into the water. My eyes remained fixed on Galahad while I treaded away from him, the we're-not-finished smirk on his face matching mine. Percival came up from behind and tugged me through the waterfall as our limbs tangled together. The alcove was small. Just big enough for two, maybe three, bodies. Maidenhair ferns sprouted from crevices in the rocks and mist shrouded our forms.

"Ye are so beautiful," Percival said. "Especially when ye take down Norse giants."

A smile twitched my lips as I wrapped my legs around his waist and wiggled over his hardened cock. "Oh aye? Ye find that sexy do ye?"

"Och, to fall to a goddess in battle . . ." He whispered, affected by my touch, his eyes blinking closed for a slow heartbeat of time.

I brushed a wet strand of copper hair off his cheek. "Be my first tonight, husband," I whispered back.

A triumphant grin brightened his face. "Slay me, then, fair goddess-wife. But gentler than ye handled Galahad. I'm already weak for ye."

Laughter bubbled from my chest. "Ye fool man."

Percival found Fionna's mouth with his. That first taste of her lips nearly slayed him. Her laughter had filled his heart to brimming until he overflowed with wondrous sensations. They remained locked in a slow, passionate kiss as they gradually floated back toward shore. Her legs were still wrapped around his waist and hovered just above his growing cock. From the corner of his eye, he could see the other men watch them.

Cupping her arse, Percival emerged from the water and carried her toward where the fire now blazed in a hypnotic rhythm. Gently, he lay her on the spongy moss by his bedroll, remembering that she needed to remain connected to the earth to marry them each to the land. Light flickered across her damp skin and reflected in her silver eyes.

"I love ye, Percy," she whispered while studying his face.

He brushed her cheek with the back of his fingers. "Ye own my heart, dove." Then Percival slid into her waiting body in one smooth motion. A ragged breath left her mouth as he whispered across her swollen lips, "I am yers, always."

"Make me coo, pigeon," she teased, and he released a low chuckle.

Stealing a kiss first, Percival pushed up on his arms and then rolled his hips. He wanted his pelvis to dance across hers and grind to the rhythm of their drumming pulse. A satisfied moan filled his ears, rewarding his efforts. Encouraged, he increased his tempo while dipping down to take her breast into his mouth. Feeling her soft flesh and the hardened tip of her nipple bounce against his tongue elicited a moan of his own. How could one woman hold so many delights?

Percival pulled away from her breasts and drew in an excited breath as *he* lowered before Fionna's tumbling swirl of long, white hair. His prince. Firelight caressed the handsome planes of Lancelot's face, turning his dampened black locks to dark bronze. Shadows outlined his muscled body and tattoos, and Percival was riveted. Ice-blue eyes, framed by long, black lashes, fastened to the sway of Percival's hips as he arced into each thrust. Licking his lips, Lancelot lifted his gaze to Percival's. Lust and longing and heat softened every beloved feature on the man's face as he stroked up and down the length of his thick shaft. Percival bit his bottom lip as he slowed and emphasized his grinding motions for Lancelot's viewing pleasure.

Fionna reached out and gripped Percival's arse as she turned her head toward Lancelot and flicked her tongue across the crown of his glorious cock. With a deep moan, Lancelot leaned into her touch until her parted lips slid down his shaft. Then Lancelot began rolling his hips, his cock moving in and out of her mouth as his heavy-lidded gaze locked onto Percival's. Like a moth to flame, Percival stretched toward Lancelot until their mouths crashed in a burst of passion—his own length buried deep into Fionna's core, Lancelot's between her soft, warm lips.

A flurry of pleasure overcame Percival in a blizzard of wild sensations. Lancelot bit down on Percival's lower lip and every muscle in Percival's body stiffened as a heady rush cut through his, Fionna's, and Lancelot sensual haze. His head grew light. His legs began to shake.

Fionna's nails dug into his arse and dragged him harder against her.

Percival cried out as his body pulsed in hot, breathless waves into Fionna. And he swore he could feel the earth move beneath them as she cried out in release with him.

Lancelot pulled out of Fionna's mouth before he peaked. Percival still filled her, his head thrown back in a groan as his body shook. Around them, an invisible but palpable energy flit from rock to tree to the wild grass, graceful and whisper-soft like butterfly wings. The velvety moss beneath their bodies deepened in color and thickened as Lancelot stretched out beside Fionna, until his skin pressed to hers.

She was ethereal under moonlight, silver dusting the hard lines and soft curves of her toned body. Lancelot knotted his fingers into her hair as he captured her wicked mouth with his. Gods, that mouth had the power to destroy him. Those plump, berry-red lips too. Her tongue teased his in a playful flick. And, for a quavering heartbeat, he could taste himself. Hungry for more, he deepened his kiss until their tongues twined in a seductive cadence of give and take.

Percival rolled off Fionna to his back and lay beside her, one arm behind his head, his muscled chest rising and falling in deep, sated breaths. Lancelot pushed to a seat and pulled Fionna up with him. An impish smile flashed across her face as she straddled his hips, lowering—achingly slow—onto the heat of his throbbing cock.

"Do ye want pretty words?" she whispered to him.

His answering reply was sliding her up the long length of his shaft and pushing her back down until he was buried to the hilt.

With a moan, she wrapped her legs around his waist. "I want yer passion," she whispered into the crook of his shoulder as she kissed his tattoos. And then her hips began to writhe. A hard, up and down motion that sent his head spinning until he was dizzy.

"And I want yer pain."

Then, to his surprise, she bit him, where she had been feathering soft kisses a moment before. The points of her short canines broke his skin and sank into him as she lapped at the wound. Fire rolled across his shoulder and curled into his chest. Her tongue then flicked at the bite to soothe the wound.

She had bloody claimed him as her mate!

In the way of the fae!

"Oh gods," Percival whispered at their side. He had nearly forgotten about the young man in his delirium.

Overwhelmed with emotion, Lancelot tangled his fingers back into her hair and yanked her lips to his in a bruising kiss. They collided in a heat so intense, he felt the steeled remnants of every bit of grief melting away. She was an inferno of passion and pleasure and he wanted to burn to ash with every searing touch of her body.

"Tell me ye want me," she whispered into their kiss.

He smiled. "I want you."

"Tell me again."

"I want you all my days," he replied in a heady whisper.

Fionna grabbed his shoulders and shoved him down toward the moss. But, before his head touched the forest floor, he rolled her onto her back. Then he pushed into her in a single, quick thrust. And again. Each pump of his hips as hard and fast as his pounding pulse. She traced her fingers along the swirls and knots inked onto his chest and shoulders.

"I want yer strength, Prince Lancelot du Lac. My husband." Her eyes flicked to his.

His breath caught as he blinked back the hot tears gathering behind his eyelids. "I want your strength,

Fionnabhair Allán. My Gwenevere." He lowered and softly tasted her lips and whispered, "My faerie wife."

In a rush of breath, his heart emptied into the moon-touched magic of their kiss as the heat of his body emptied into hers. The ground beneath her gently quaked and Lancelot orgasmed again, moaning her name to the night sky and the stars above.

In the wake of release, lichens bloomed on the trunks of neighboring trees and across stones. Spectral ribbons of mist slithered across the pond and rolled onto the banks, where reeds and water irises sprouted and then speared up into the blue, shimmering air.

Galahad bided his time by staring into the fire and drinking mead. Lancelot and Percival had been caressing the tantalizing curves of Fionna's naked form following their intimacies—one man before her, the other behind. Galahad wanted her to rest before enjoying him next, especially after their bout earlier this evening in the pond. A corner of his mouth quirked up. Gods, he loved it when she stormed in fury at him.

"Thinking of my victory over ye?"

She now stood before him. A soft glow illuminated the pale skin of her luscious body in the firelight.

He grinned, slow and lazy. "I demand a re-match,

Lady."

"Do ye, now?"

Galahad fell back onto his bedroll as Arthur snorted nearby. Their king had also imbibed in a few chalices of honeyed wine. "Are you afraid you'll lose?" Galahad teased.

Fionna knelt between his legs with a mischievous glint in her eyes. And then she began kissing his calf, behind his knees, and up his thighs. At his groin, she lifted her head and met his shuttered gaze. "I hear fear in yer voice, fair Knight."

He boomed with laughter at her attempts of intimidation. As his humor faded into the dark air, she licked up the hard length of his cock, and his quieting laugh quickly dissolved into an appreciative moan.

"Ye want more?" she asked.

"What's your price?"

"Beg me." Her eyes were bright with mirth.

Lancelot grunted with approval on the other side of the fire circle.

Galahad pushed up onto his elbows and arched an eyebrow her direction. "I might need another sample of your ardor first."

"Like this?" She swirled her tongue across the crown of his cock and all the breath in his lungs expelled on the airy wings of pleasure.

He whispered, "Yes, My Queen," as his back pressed into his bedroll once more.

"Now beg me, warrior." Her warm breath caressed his shaft and he shivered.

"Own my body," he half-whispered. "Make me yours. Please."

Satisfied with his desperate entreaty, her mouth slid down his throbbing length. Heat curled in his belly as her tongue carved her name along the sensitive underside. He heaved for much needed breath and then clutched fistfuls of her hair, guiding her head up and down, up and down. Slowly, he thrust into her mouth, his hips wanting to increase in speed. But she pulled away from his aching body before he could, and the fires of Hel danced in her eyes.

"What is your plea?" she purred.

"Gods, woman," Galahad groaned. "You're cruel."

"I can be crueler." Fionna leaned back and tilted her head. Long, white strands of hair fell over her shoulders and draped across her pert breasts. She then cupped his balls and gently tugged as she massaged each one between her fingers. "Tell me, warrior. What do you desire?"

"Destroy me," he growled. "No mercy, My Queen."

Biting her lower lip, she crawled up his body until she reached the patch of hair just below his navel. Then she flicked out her tongue and licked the rippling muscles across his abs, up his ribbed torso, to his pectorals where the tip of her wicked tongue and the sharp edges of her teeth tortured his hardened nipples. His hips bucked with need. His hands clawing for her waist. Amused, she lowered her lips to his with a little laugh as her wet sex rubbed along his cock. Their mouths crashed together in a single sword strike. The spark of her metal against his ignited their bodies into motion.

Forget being dominated. His entire being strained against the urge to fight back, to disregard the unspoken rules of this battle. Until he did. Flipping Fionna onto her stomach, Galahad lifted her hips and sank his cock into her—deep, hard. A low growl rumbled from his chest as his pelvis grinded into her arse, his fingers gripping her soft flesh. She moaned—loud. Then again, louder this time before crying out. Her body spasmed and tightened around his cock. Gods, the scent of her arousal, the way her breasts bounced. It was enough to drive a man to madness.

Gently, he wrapped an arm around her waist and pulled her against him, sliding his hand between her legs to massage her swollen nub. Her head fell back onto his shoulder and he claimed her parted lips as he rocked into their joined bodies. Blood hammered the anvils in his ears. Sweat dripped down his face. His muscles flexed and stiffened as pleasure flooded his veins.

"Fionna . . ." he breathed, her name a prayer on his lips. "Oh gods."

She fell back onto her hands as his seed dripped down her thighs and onto the moss and leaf-littered forest floor, even though he remained buried deep. Brittle ferns brightened to vibrant greens and wildflowers bloomed all around their camp in a rainbow of colors as a rush of energy flooded his body, making the hairs on his arms rise.

Bending over her arched spine, he caressed the silky skin of her sides and stomach as he kissed her back, whispering, "I love you, wife." Then he collapsed onto his bedroll.

She curled up against him and rested her head on his chest. "I love you, husband." Kissing the salt from his skin, she then murmured, "I won this bout."

Galahad burst into laughter, unable to contain himself.

Arthur sighed in contentment as he swept a gaze across the fire circle. Galahad snored atop his bedroll, Fionna in his arms. Arthur chuckled to himself. He swore the large Norseman fell asleep within seconds of finishing.

On the other side of the flickering flames, Lancelot had pinned Percival's hands above his head and passionately kissed the younger knight as their bodies rubbed together in slow, erotic strokes. Their soft moans filled the night air and Arthur smiled. This wasn't the first time he had seen male warriors make love. It was a common affair among Celtic soldiers. His heart soared for his foster brother. Percival would be good for Lancelot, in more ways than one.

Arthur was about to curl up in his furs for the night when he noticed Fionna stirring. She sat up and stretched her arms, first taking in Lancelot and Percival, then him. Their eyes connected, and she smiled. A heartbeat later, she lowered next to him and pulled his fur blankets up and over both of their bodies until only their faces were exposed to the night.

"How do you fare, My Queen?" Arthur softly asked.

"I have never known such happiness until this day," she whispered back.

"Nor I." Arthur kissed her forehead. "Rest, Fionna."

"Not yet." She leaned up on her elbow. "I have not joined with ye."

The corners of his mouth tipped up as he caressed the curve of her cheek with his knuckles. "I would not ask intimacies from you after you have given yourself to the others."

"But the curse—"

"Can wait until morning or later tomorrow, even. Taking advantage of your body when you must be spent doesn't sit well with me."

"And if I want ye?" She brushed a finger along his bottom lip in feather-light touches.

He swallowed. "Fionna . . ."

"Arthur Pendragon," she whispered as her fingertips left his mouth to rest over his heart, "ye are the most beautiful man I have ever known."

Moved, he leaned in and kissed her lips, a sweet, chaste embrace. "Fionnabhair Allán. My wife. My Queen. My Gwenevere." His hand wandered up her face and he traced along her ear to the point. "I am so very much in love with you."

"Allow me to show ye the depth of my love?" she asked.

He studied the silver pool of her eyes before

granting his consent in a single, breathy word. "Yes." Then he added, "But only if you promise me this is truly what you want right now."

Fionna kissed his throat and then buried her face into his neck, whispering, "Ye are always what I want, Arthur."

A blush warmed his face at her confession.

"And," she whispered into his chest as she kissed his skin, "I adore your freckles."

"Ugh," he said with a shy laugh. "Those infernal things."

"Beautiful, My King. Ye are beautiful, inside and out."

She positioned the furs over her back as her waterfall of hair curtained around their faces. Then she pressed her mouth to his, sliding onto his hardened cock. They remained in this place for several heartbeats—their lips dancing to a melody only their hearts knew while their bodies sighed with bliss at being one. Slowly, she began to move, and he shuddered with pleasure at the feel of her hips rocking back and forth across his.

Arthur cradled her curving hips and deepened their kiss. Her skin was unbelievably soft for a warrior. He drank in the feel of her body coupling with his, her heather scent, and the love that passed between them swelling in his heart. For him, there was no woman who could compare. No love as bright and pure.

He peered up at the star-flecked sky as her mouth roamed the expanse of his muscled chest. To think, their story could have ended far differently. Many outcomes and many possibilities. But, in the end, she chose him. She chose all of them—Lancelot, Percival, Galahad. His Gwenevere, created just for them and they for her.

My head grew faint at the enormity of Arthur's love for me, shown in his gentle touches, the reverent brush of his lips across mine, and the way he sighed—not only in pleasure, but in contentment. I made this man happy, a king who had known only heartache and injustice.

His body was perfection. Freckles spilled across his skin as though stars in the night sky. The sound of his breathy moans aroused me further. His warm lips captured mine in a languid kiss, as slow and sensual as the undulating rhythm of our hips.

As I pulled away, he surprised me with a delicate flower he had plucked from beside where we lay, tucking the violet behind my ear. My heart fluttered wildly as I realized—it was Arthur who had placed the bouquet of wildflowers upon my bedroll during our trip to Chester. Flowers I had kept in my saddle bag and then later pressed into a book as a keepsake.

Beneath the fur blankets, his hands traveled up the length of my back and sank into my hair, tugging my lips back to his. The building heat between my thighs trembled into a long, thundering spasm.

"I love ye," I whispered, kissing his jaw, his cheek, his flushed lips. "I love ye so much."

Gently, he rolled away from the fire and toward the moss, until my back pressed into the earth and the moon bathed me in silver, the fur blankets all forgotten. Wildflowers covered our bodies from sight and framed my king against a backdrop of midnight blues. His body slid in and out of mine, his breath warming my bare skin.

"My fierce Fionna . . ." he whispered. "My love." And then his face tensed as his muscles stiffened, a powerful moan escaping his parted lips.

The ground beneath me quaked, as though the earth and stones and water cried out in reply. Trees swayed a lover's dance as the black fingers of death disappeared to reveal strong, healthy bark. More wildflowers and ferns sprang up from the ground, and Arthur and I quickly returned to his bedroll in laughter. I squealed as he covered our heads with the fur blankets, our happy smiles turning into happy kisses, his body gathering mine close to his. Pulling the blankets off our faces, I laughed again, soaking in the sight of our land, whole and hale.

Beside us, Galahad continued to snore, his arms and legs spread out languidly. Lancelot and Percival returned our grins as we took in our surroundings. The land was healed. Truly healed.

Mere months ago, I was a warrior princess tasked with travelling across the Irish Sea to steal a faerie sword from a king. That king now claimed me as his queen, as did these knights who fought beside me proudly. Men who helped me unearth the secrets of my life—of me.

I snuggled into the crook of Arthur's arm and shoulder as he tucked his other hand behind his head. His heart raced beneath me, and I couldn't help the grin that stretched wide across my face. I stared out into the forest, lost to reverie, as his breaths evened and as he fell into a deep, restful sleep. From the sounds of our camp, Lancelot and Percival slumbered too. A yawn escaped my mouth and I buried deeper into Arthur's warmth. But, before my eyes fluttered closed, lulled by the bliss of making love to my knights, my king, I watched as a lily grew along the forest's edge. A white lily that glowed in the shadows beneath the goddess moon.

The End

Historical Notes

Greetings, readers! This is your *Knights of Caerleon* lore keeper, Jesikah Sundin. This final book was an interesting tale to undertake as it was more about our twist on Celtic mythology and less about historical notations. But, as we've discussed in the previous *Historical Notes*, Arthurian Lore is a blend of Roman/Celtic history and Celtic mythology that is assimilated by and regurgitated into something new with each generation. Think of it like perpetually making new meals out of leftovers. That is the collection of Arthurian Cycle stories. Speaking of, if you've missed the *Historical Notes* for the first two books, you can read up on all the juicy details here:

1) <u>Who Was Arthur Pendragon?</u>

2) <u>Who is the Real Gwenevere in Arthurian Lore?</u>

And now onto the fun and somewhat controversial origins of Lancelot, Galahad, Percival, Morgana, and Donal O'Lynn. I'm leaving Merlin out of this line-up as his history is just waaaaay too long and complicated and dates to when the Milesians came to Ireland (later known as the Túatha dé Danann).

LANCELOT

Arthur Pendragon had existed for centuries before "the greatest swordsmen in the world" arrived on the scene and stole the entire show. And, yes, this is what Lancelot was known as, because obviously only *the best knights* come from France *sticks French tongue out at the rest of the uncivilized world* We can thank the French poet Chrétien de Troyes for this hunky knight, who created Lancelot in *Le Chevalier de la Charrette*, a collection of poems between 1180 – 1240 A.D., which was finished by Godefroy de Lagny after Troyes died. The sole purpose of Lancelot was at the behest of the Countess Marie de Champagne, daughter of Louis VII of France and Eleanor of Aquitaine, to illustrate the pros and cons of "courtly love." Lancelot's famous adulterous affair with Queen Guinevere being the ultimate offense and why kingdoms *obviously* fall *French evil eye to young noblewomen checking out all the hot knights* *J'accuse!* In the French courts, Lancelot took center stage and forced Arthur to become a side-character. As in our story, Lancelot is the natural born son of King Ban of Benoic (Benwick) but raised by Vivien, Lady of the Lake, hence his romantic name: Lancelot du Lac.

GALAHAD

The bastard-born son of Lancelot du Lac and Elaine of Corbenic (Caer Benic . . . yeah, Percival's origins. There's a reason for this. I'll explain in a bit). As with many medieval stories (especially French ones), the woman tricks the man to sleep with them *side-eyes trickster Eve archetypes* and then arrives sometime later with the news, "Surprise! You have a son and he's destined for great things." *side-eyes Christ archetypes, to redeem the fall of man because of Eve archetypes* And poor Lancelot is no stranger to the trickery of fair maids, as many a young Frenchmen experienced back then. Apparently. And, thus, "Galahad the Chaste" was born. Yeah, "The Chaste." His holy virgin status allowed him to finish the Grail Quest, where his father had failed because Lancelot shagged the queen. Plus, the stories of "Sir Percival"—who had no relation to their beloved Lancelot, whatsoever—was boring the French courts, and so they wanted a new Grail hero.

Claire and I decided to make Galahad a Welsh-born Norseman from the Danish seaport village of Swansea, as you know. And definitely not chaste! But we did give a nod to his origins in book 2 when Lancelot says that if he ever has a son, he'll name him Galahad in his sword-brother's honor.

PERCIVAL

AKA "the original Galahad" that entertained the courtly-love thirsty French of the 12th and 13th centuries before Galahad was born. The earliest "Percival" mention is also by Chrétien de Troyes in his unfinished *Percival, the Story of the Grail* (around 1190 A.D.). Known as "Percival the Chaste," son of Elaine of Corbenic (Caer Benic) and sometimes the oldest son of King Pellinore, he eventually finds the Holy Grail and becomes the Fisher King. Some stories have him dying a virgin after claiming the Grail, sadly. Poor, pigeon . . . Eventually, Percival was kicked to the curb for "Galahad the Chaste," son of Lancelot du Lac. But scholars believe Troyes was inspired by Peredur of sub-Roman Celtic Mythology. Peredur is also found in Arthurian "histories" by 11th century Welsh author, Geoffrey of Monmouth and, later, in the old orated Welsh tales that were written down in the *Mabinogion*, including the famous "Peredur the Son of Efrawc," which we leaned on heavily for Grail Quest adventures in *The Third Curse*.

AND since our series revolves around so much Grail lore, we decided to go with the original Grail Quest characters: Arthur, Lancelot, Percival, and Galahad . . . but refashioned by our clever fairy tale re-telling brains, if I do say so myself *high-fives Claire*

MORGAN LA FEY

Her origins are as misty as the Otherworld, especially as her name is linked to the Celtic Morrígu (aka The Morrígan), the goddess of war and death, and one of the three sisters in the triple goddess head, The Morrígana. In Irish mythology, she would shape-shift into a crow, shriek over the battle field, and collect the heads of fallen soldiers as trophies. Um . . . that's some creepy shit. The Celts were dark, though. And not afraid to die, or apparently have their heads collected by a shape-shifting sídhe. But, I digress . . . The name Morgan (male) / Morgain (female) means "water nymph" in Breton (Celtic Cornish / Welsh)—which makes sense, since most

Celtic deities were water born. But Morgan being a strictly male Celtic name was lost in translation with the French and, thus, they crowned The Morrígan, Morgan la Fey. Despite her circling carrion crow form, she wasn't a feared goddess. Rather, The Morrígan was also revered as the patron goddess of art and beauty, because that totally makes sense given her decorating tastes.

Interestingly enough, in most Arthurian tales, she's not evil. That's more of a neo-pagan / modern fairy tale view of her. In the original Arthurian Cycle stories, she had two older sisters (Morgause and Elaine *points to The Morrígana explanation*), and she loved her half-brother and even brought Arthur to Avalon for healing when he was mortally wounded in the Battle of Camlann. Still, Claire and I went with the more modern take on Morgana. Because evil is fun. And she was such a fun, sexy villainess to write.

DONAL O'LYNN

Clann O'Lynn are a real, historic clan from Ulster, y'all. And, they are possible descendants of Colla Uias, the famed 4th century High King of Ireland. The Irish Gaelic version of their name is Ó Fhloinn (which I think is pretty) and they were part of the Tuírtri area of Northern Ireland (now incorporated into Antrim), and originally hailed from Lough Insholin in Londonderry, which means "Lake of the O'Lynn Island." Savvy? Cool. So, eventually they conquered and inhabited most of County Antrim sometime in the 12th century—even Fionna's area in the Glens of Antrim. And they ruled this region until the 15th century when the MacDonnells swept in. See what I did there? Donal O'Lynn . . . MacDonnells defeated the O'Lynn . . . he was his own worst enemy. #HistoryGeekGirlHumor. Now, I'll be honest . . . the 12th century is a hazy date. O'Lynn was a prominent clan in the area and their expansion/settlement into Antrim might be earlier, like when we set our story: the mid-1000's. If you're an O'Lynn of Antrim, let me know! And, we hope you didn't mind us making a fictional descendant a villain. Your ancestry tied so well into our *Ulster Cycle*-inspired Fionnabhair. Bad guys are cool, right?

THE FOUR ANCIENT ARTIFACTS OF IRELAND

Also called "The Four Magical Treasures of the Túatha dé Danann." The more you dive into Celtic and Irish mythology, the more items in British Isles fairy tales and folklore begin to make sense. Especially in Arthurian Legend tales. Here's a quick overview without getting too detailed with the mythological stories behind each artifact (and I'm presenting them out of order, sorry Irish scholars):

THE SWORD OF LIGHT "Shining Sword" (Sword of King Nuada of the Túatha dé Danann) was a weapon that symbolized and "illuminated" truth, justice, law, and punishment to Ireland's enemies during conflict.

Arthurian Treasure: Excalibur

LIA FÁIL "Stone of Destiny," also known as the Stone of Scone and the "Talking Stone," was originally on the Hill of Tara and where the ancient Kings of Ireland were coronated. But only after the stone roared, which it would only do if the rightful king stood upon it. The Lia Fáil was eventually brought over to England by Edward the 1st in 1297 and is now the Coronation Stone in Westminster Abbey.

Arthurian Treasure: The Stone, as in The Sword in The Stone.

SWORD OF LUGH "Invincible Spear" or the "Spear of Victory" belonged to the Celtic sun god, Lugh of the Long Arms. The longer the spear was held, the hotter it would become. And, its perfect targeting powers also thirsted for blood. So much so, it wept blood. This spear is later used in Grail stories and connected to the spear that pierced the side of Jesus of Nazareth during his crucifixion (the son of god vs the sun god).

Arthurian Treasure: The spear that wept blood during the Grail Maiden's odd and fantastical Grail procession, and the spear that maimed the Fisher King.

THE CAULDRON OF THE DAGDA is a magical vessel that could heal through food and drink to whomever deserved such blessings. And raise the dead too, just for kicks and giggles. The food and drink never ended, either . . . as the cauldron was bottomless. Hence the saying, "bottomless pit" to describe those who are always hungry and pack in their meals.

Arthurian Treasure: The Holy Grail. A grail (graal / sangrael) a small, common household bowl (aka cauldron), which later became synonymous with the bowl used by Jesus during the Last Supper (Cup of Christ) and the vessel Joseph of Arimathea used to catch the blood that spilled from Christ's pierced side. If you drank from the Grail, you would be healed of all your ailments and injuries and, perhaps, even gain immortality (think communal wine and bread).

And, for fun (yeah, this is fun to me), I want to address a few misconceptions about hygiene in the Middle Ages as well as homosexuality within Celtic cultures, especially among warriors. As a refresher: Celtic culture in this context are the people of Ireland, Scotland, and Briton (Cornwall, Wales, and parts of western Scotland). The Norse are the Vikings, from the Nordic/Scandinavian lands as well as those who settled in the British Isles.

DID PEOPLE BATHE REGULARLY IN THE MEDIEVAL ERA?

Yes! Big, emphatic YES. In fact, in Celtic, Norse, and Mediterranean cultures, good hygiene was part of daily life. The movies consistently paint dirty, grimy peasants with blackening teeth and shiny-faced nobles with perfect smiles (remnants of Victorian classist culture). According to the <u>Medievalist</u>, there are extensive medical texts waxing poetic the benefits of bathing—for the common and noble man alike. They even understood that washing your hands and face before meals was essential for better health. By the medieval era, bathing culture across the Isles was a thing, hence all the funny tapestries and art depicting people in tubs.

And this well-known poem, dating back to the 1300's:

Hey! rub-a-dub, ho! rub-a-dub, three maids in a tub,
And who do you think were there?
The butcher, the baker, the candlestick-maker,
And all of them gone to the fair.

"Three men in a tub" who "were out to sea" was a change made in the late-1700's to be "safe for children." Which begs the question: what was this poem really about? You're gonna love this. *clears throat* Men of industry who were going to the village fair to see a peep show of naked, young maidens bathing each other in a tub. Sexy times!

DID CELTIC CULTURES ACCEPT HOMOSEXUALITY?

They didn't even bat an eye at two men as lovers, or two women for that matter. Sexuality wasn't a complex issue to the Celts. Partly because marriage in Celtic cultures was for childbearing only. Brehon Law (ancient Irish law that existed through the 17th century and that bled into other Gaelic lands) permitted married couples to have lovers outside of their handfasting vows. And why this allowance? The Celts saw marriage as a necessity for politics and clan building, but lovers were for the soul. And so, many had lovers, including same-sex partners. But homosexuality was observed most among the warriors. It was so common, <u>Warrior Lovers</u> became a well-noted thing, even causing the <u>non-homophobic Greeks to raise an eyebrow</u>. This changed in the late-Middle Ages with Christianization, however. Now, open sexuality was ONLY among the Celts. The Norse didn't practice homosexuality as a culture. Like today, the Nordic land's equivalent to "gay" was an insult to a man's masculinity.

WAS MEDICAL KNOWLEDGE ONLY RESTRICTED TO HERBAL LORE?

Uh, no. Some of the best artifacts from the Middle Ages are all the fantastic medical texts. So. Many. Medical. Texts. Their illustrations are wonderfully entertaining too. Medieval people practiced all manner of surgeries, even cesarean births. And the believed cures for various ailments or concerns (like wrinkling skin) are sometimes hysterical. They even washed their hands before medical procedures. Modern scientists are now looking back at the texts and folklore from the Middle Ages as they're finding interesting leads to medical discoveries, such as the "healing soil" in Ireland once used by druids, which was recently documented as effective treatment for four of the six world's superbugs.

Whew! We did it. We covered all the major Celtic culture and Arthurian Lore tie-ins.

But as this is fiction, and fantasy fiction no less, there are some historical inaccuracies. *J'accuse!* Heh. The biggest one? At no time, that we know of, did a war camp from Clan O'Lynn travel to southern Wales. We bent history for our plot. Sorry-not-sorry. As mentioned above, Galahad was the son of Lancelot du Lac and Percival was "The Chaste" before Lancelot and his son stole the Grail Quest show. The small, nameless villages mentioned outside of Caerleon are from the fictional realm inside my and Claire's heads. The village Inn is also a fast-forward into history, as medieval inns didn't appear until the 14th century. The UK does not have chipmunks (I feel sorry for you, UK friends. They're sooooo cute!). Still, we used this nickname for Galahad because it just felt perfect. If you can suspend belief for faerie magic, then pretending adorable, chubby-cheeked chipmunks roam the UK shouldn't be too hard a task. And I'm sure there are other historical inaccuracies too, though I tried to keep proper details intact for the most part.

All errors that may exist while trying to represent Celtic and Welsh culture, mythology, geography, and Arthurian Legend elements are entirely mine. I am a storyteller, weaving together information that builds and forms worlds in our imaginations. In the famous words of Nennius, a 9th century Celtic monk, "I have made a heap of all that I could find."

Your *Knights of Caerleon* lore keeper,

Jesikah Sundin

More Books

Claire Luana & Jesikah Sundin

THE KNIGHTS OF CAERLEON
The Fifth Knight, book 1
The Third Curse, book 2
The First Gwenevere, book 3

Claire Luana

MOONBURNER CYCLE
Moonburner, book 1
Sunburner, book 2
Starburner, book 3
Burning Fate, prequel

THE CONFECTIONER'S GUILD
The Confectioner's Guild, book 1
The Confectioner's Truth, book 2
The Confectioner's Coup, book 3
The Confectioner's Exile, prequel

Jesikah Sundin

THE BIODOME CHRONICLES
Legacy, book 1
Elements, book 2
Transitions: Novella Collection, book 2.5
Gamemaster, book 3

CLAIRE LUANA grew up reading everything she could get her hands on and writing every chance she could. Eventually, adulthood won out, and she turned her writing talents to more scholarly pursuits, going to work as a commercial litigation attorney.

While continuing to practice law, Claire decided to return to her roots and try her hand once again at creative writing. She has written and published the Moonburner Cycle and the forthcoming Confectioner Chronicles, a trilogy about magical food. She is currently working on the Knights of Caerleon trilogy, an Arthurian Legend fantasy romance series, which she is co-writing with Jesikah Sundin. She lives in Seattle, Washington with her husband and two dogs. In her (little) remaining spare time, she loves to hike, travel, binge-watch CW shows, and of course, fall into a good book.

www.claireluana.com

JESIKAH SUNDIN is a multi-award winning Ecopunk SciFi and Forest Fantasy writer mom of three nerdlets and devoted wife to a gamer geek. In addition to her family, she shares her home in Monroe, Washington with a red-footed tortoise and a collection of seatbelt purses. She is addicted to coffee, laughing, and Dr. Martens shoes ... Oh! And the forest is her happy place.

www.jesikahsundin.com
www.jesikahsundin.com/moontreebooks

www.ingramcontent.com/pod-product-compliance
Lightning Source LLC
Chambersburg PA
CBHW070752190726
48292CB00002B/514